For

+ Ruth Campbell —
with the best of
good wishes

Temple Bailey.

August
1927.

WALLFLOWERS

WALLFLOWERS
By TEMPLE BAILEY

THE PENN PUBLISHING
COMPANY · PHILADELPHIA
1927

CONTENTS

CONTENTS

WALLFLOWERS

CHAPTER I

THE FIVE SENSES

RUFUS FISKE had always loved the view from that corner. He remembered a bleak March day when he had come with his parents to Roosevelt's inauguration. He and his mother had walked from their hotel to St. John's church for an early service, and afterward had stood looking out across Lafayette Square to the squat White House, simple yet heart-thrilling with its bright flag flying.

" A thing to remember, Rufus."

" It is more wonderful than palaces, isn't it, mother? "

The flag was flying now for another president, and the Square was gay with June bloom and beauty. But St. John's had been spoiled by a new coat of paint and a sky-scraping building back of it. There were hundreds of motor cars in place of the high-stepping horses and leisurely carriages.

Washington had been to the boy a place of enchantment. The man had returned to find much of the glamour gone, a thing to be blamed not, perhaps, on the city, but on himself. The lad who had come to Roosevelt's inauguration had lost many of his illusions.

He sauntered on, seeing on each side of him the shops which had replaced the fine old residences. At

7

one of the shops he stopped and stood looking in. There was a wide window, with a display which caught the eye. A frail beaker of green glass, like water at great depths, was backed by a length of silver-embroidered satin which trailed from a chair with carved knees and claw-and-ball feet. The window was set into what had been, apparently, the brick front of a house with an English basement. One went in by a door on the ground floor and turned to the right.

Rufus, entering, was met by a young woman in horn spectacles.

He asked: " May I see Mr. Maulsby? I have an appointment with him."

She seemed flurried. " Mr. Maulsby will see you in a moment. We've just had an accident."

" No one badly hurt, I hope? "

" Oh," she clasped her hands together in a gesture of great distress. " Worse than that. It was one of a set of Chelsea figures. Mr. Maulsby's almost out of his head."

A nervous voice sounded from the other room. " I could forgive you, if you seemed to care."

Another voice, impudently: " I don't want your forgiveness. I want my check."

There appeared then in an archway a man and a boy, their flushed faces and heated air proclaiming their agitation.

" I beg your pardon," the man said as he saw Fiske, " I didn't know there was a customer."

" I am not a customer," Rufus told him. " I talked with you over the telephone about some ivories you might want to buy."

"I remember. I'll be with you in a second." He turned to the boy. "Go over to the Stocks Building, and Miss Deakin will give you your check. I'd rather pay you than argue about it. But nothing can ever pay for what you've done."

The boy flung himself out of the front door, and Maulsby, with a murmured apology to Fiske, picked up the receiver of the telephone and got a number. "He's a cold-blooded little beast, Miss Deakin. You might have thought he had broken a china cup, instead of a priceless piece. And will you put an advertisement in the paper? I've got to have some one here at once. I can't be tied to the shop."

He rang off and came forward. "Sorry," he said to Rufus. "Will you follow me out to the garden? It is cooler there, and we can talk."

He led the way through the rooms. Lighted by low lamps they glimmered and glowed — old silver, satin-wood, tapestries, prints and portraits. Beyond the rooms was a garden — a green, quiet space which might have been a thousand miles away from the city. The brick walls which enclosed it were hung with ancient ivy, and some old rose bushes were blooming. A group of pointed cedars made a background for a stone bench and threw their black shadows across the smooth sward. The garden chairs of Chinese cane had linen cushions. The whole effect was cool and charming.

Maulsby had a keen face and a nervous manner which matched his voice. He wore glasses on a black ribbon and swung them as he talked. His gray hair was thick and fine and stood up on his head.

"It is too bad you were let in for such a scene," he

said, as he sat down, " but I find it very hard to get any one who fits into this sort of thing. That boy, when I took him, had had some experience in shops like mine, but he is utterly without love for the work. He handled registered Worcester as if it were earthenware."

As he voiced his grievances, Maulsby smoked nervously, one cigarette after another. At last he came to the matter in hand. " Did you bring the ivories? "

" Yes." Rufus opened a leather case and set forth on the marble bench five small figures, magnolia-tinted, touched with magic. They represented, he explained, the five senses.

The older man, bending over them, was at once aware of their perfection. Charming nymphs, exquisitely carved, one with a shell to her ear, another dangling a bunch of grapes above her lips, a third sniffing a rose, a fourth surveying herself in a mirror, and the loveliest of all fingering the soft fur of the leopard's skin thrown about her thighs, they were treasures to make any collector avid for possession.

" Seventeenth century? "

Rufus nodded.

" What do you know of their history? "

" Not much. But you can see that they're authentic."

" Where'd you pick them up? "

There was a moment's hesitation, then young Fiske said succinctly, " Heirlooms."

Maulsby dangled his glasses. " You've got something. I can't be fooled in such matters."

" I'm not trying to fool you."

" What's your price? "

" Two thousand."

" Too much."

Rufus smiled. " You know it isn't. You're saying that automatically."

Their eyes met. " They're worth it," Maulsby agreed, " but I don't believe you're going to get it."

" I must get it. I've got to have the money."

Maulsby's keen glance weighed him. Fiske did not look like a man in need. He was exceedingly well-dressed. His manners were those of a gentleman. And he was good-looking. Tall and thin, but with the grace of youth in his strong body.

" I'm going to get my price," he repeated with a smile, " and I think you are going to give it to me. I hate to seem mercenary, but my wares are worth it."

" There's no hurry, is there? "

" Yes. I've got to have it off my mind. And Griselda's." Little sparks of amusement shone in Rufus' eyes.

" Griselda? Your wife? "

" My cat . . . ! "

Maulsby stared at him. " Your cat? "

" Yes. I live in what is called an ' efficiency apartment.' A few weeks ago I was foolish enough to take unto myself a Persian pussy who was being ill-treated by her owners. The court which is bounded by our apartment house is Griselda's only place for exercise and refreshment. And it is really no place for a lady of her rank and attainments. Besides, she is always being chased by dogs. So I'll get her out into the country, where her mind will be at ease."

He laughed and Maulsby said, " You're not serious, of course."

" I think I am. But, there's more than Griselda's comfort in it. I feel penned-up in an apartment — I've always known wide spaces . . ." His voice trailed off into silence.

He went on presently. " I'm writing a book. I tried to rent a cottage, but there seems to be none available. So I'll buy and sell when I'm tired of it. Your two thousand will help finance it, and I'll make a payment on a car. The rest is on the knees of the gods."

" You seem very sure of my — two thousand."

" Why not? You know a good thing when you see it, don't you? "

It was a challenge, and Maulsby met it with, " Give me until tomorrow morning."

" Why put it off? "

" Great guns — I can't make up my mind in a minute."

" If you don't want them, I can try Tidman."

" Tidman is purely commercial. I should hate to see them wasted."

Rufus reached for the little figures and put them in their case. " I'll come in early and have it off my mind."

" Good."

They rose and went into the shop together. Just inside the door a customer claimed Maulsby, so Rufus wandered through the rooms alone, stopping now and then to bend above some object of breathless beauty, to study a trademark, to start the chime of a bit of choice glass with a fillip of his finger.

He came presently to a small alcove where were hung a half-dozen framed prints. Only one light was on, and illumined the top picture so that it stood out from among the others, its color clear and bright.

Rufus had often seen the picture. He had, indeed, seen the original when he had visited the famous gallery in which it hung. He remembered that in the gallery there had been several others by Vigée LeBrun, and he had gone back again and again to look upon the sparkling countenance of The Boy in Red — the parted lips, the eyes with the merry, sidelong glance, the quick turn of the head, caught by the painter and immortalized. There was something in it that had always held him. Some vivid, arresting quality. Youth, he felt, should be like that, with laughter on its lips, light in its eyes.

His own youth had not been like that. As he stood looking up at the print, he thought of the boy who had been himself, a bit hardened, disillusioned, fighting blindly against forces which threatened to overwhelm him. When the boy who had been himself had laughed, it had not been with the sparkling gaiety of the Boy in Red, but with a touch of cynicism, because of his lack of faith in the things a boy should believe.

With the memory of the things which had hardened him darkening the sunlight, Rufus walked the streets for an hour before going home; so that when at last he reached his apartment, his watch showed a late dinner hour. As his exchequer was low, he decided to dine with Griselda. Bread and milk would do for both of them, and tomorrow, with Maulsby's check in his pocket, he would feast like a king in a

delectable inn some miles out in Maryland, and Griselda should have a pot of cream to console her.

He found the white cat waiting for him on the little
balcony which overlooked the court. As he entered
the rooms, the air felt close and hot. He turned on
the electric fan, took off his coat, and set forth his
simple fare on the blotter of his big table. Griselda
had her saucer on the floor beside him. So they dined,
each with apparent zest. If Rufus thought of the time
when he had had silver candle-sticks in front of him and
a butler at his back, he gave no sign. The war had
taught him many things. And not the least of his
lessons had been to learn that accessories do not make
an appetite.

When the meal was over, Rufus smoked a cigarette,
sitting in the long window which opened out of the
balcony. The white cat stretched herself on his knee.
He could feel the steady throb of her contented song.

All about him were other balconies. Most of them
were empty at this hour, when everybody went to ride
or to the moving picture palaces, or at least to show
themselves in the reception rooms downstairs. The
few people who remained were mothers putting young
children to bed, busy wives washing up late dishes, or
tired men content to get the air at the back of the
house and listen to the jazz dinner-music broadcast
over the radio.

Across the court, and on the floor just above him,
Fiske saw a woman come out and stand with her hand
on the railing of her balcony, looking up at the square
of the sky which the court bounded and which was
reddened now by the sunset. She was not a young

with two tiny beds in it. My own bed shuts up on the back of the living-room door in the day-time and is pulled down at night. When it is down, it literally fills the room. Sandra calls the nightly transformation ' shifting the scenery.' The whole thing seems to me rather like living in a tenement. No privacy. Apparently it has the stamp of approval for people of modest income, but it is incredible that any one can stand the close contacts for any length of time. No wonder divorces are rampant in this generation!

" My dear, you mustn't think I am unhappy. I thank the good Lord every day for the comfort of my Government job and my regular pay day. I'll try to make the best of things until the girls are married, and then I'll come back, and if Windytop hasn't fallen down in the meantime, you and I will live there together, and let the rain drip and the shutters slam, and adore it!

" Write as often as you can. It is like a breath of fresh air from my Virginia hills to hear from you.

I am ever your own,

MADGE."

Having finished her letter, Mrs. Claybourne put a stamp on it and tucked it in her bag ready to mail in the morning. After that she took a bath, put her hair up on pins, drew down the bed from the back of the door, made herself comfortable on her pillows, and with a reading lamp adjusted, gave herself up to the enjoyment of a book which one of the girls had brought from the library.

But her mind was not on her book. It was on her

daughters, gay at their party. She could see them surrounded by partners, Sandra's eyes shining. Theodora's cheeks burning. Once upon a time she had been
like that. How long ago it seemed! She had worn a
rhinestone pin high in her hair, copper-colored like
Sandra's. And her first ballgown had had a bustle!
She smiled to herself at the vision she had conjured up.
And how she had waltzed with Bob Claybourne! And
now all that was gone, and some day her girls, those
lovely young creatures with shining eyes and burning
cheeks, would be dull and gray like herself, and glad
of the comfort of an evening alone in a let-down bed!

Oh, well, she mustn't indulge herself in self-pity like
the heroine of a Freudian novel. The end was not yet.
There might be years ahead for all of them at Windytop. And if not . . . perhaps the good Lord would
make Heaven something like their old home . . . with
Bob coming in with the roses he had gathered.

She fell asleep over her book and dreamed, not of
Heaven and her husband, but of her darling daughters
dancing with winged feet! Partners fighting for their
favors! The world theirs for the asking!

It was late when she waked. She picked up her book
and began to read, but she found her dreams interpos-
ing between the pages. She had a feeling that at the
very moment her lovely daughters were in the midst of
triumphs. She could hardly wait for their coming.
They would have so much to tell her.

CHAPTER III

DANCING FEET

D ANCING feet!
   " Sandra, stop laughing.   There isn't anything funny about it."

"There is!   Oh, we thought we knew how to dance,
Doady! "

"Nobody will ask us again.   I had to stop three
times.   If I hadn't had a polite partner! "

"Mine wasn't polite."

"Well, mine was.   I stepped all over his feet, and he
said: ' A bit hot, don't you think?   Shall we sit it out? ' "

"Doady, he deserved a crown!   Mine said, ' Gosh,
is that how they do it down your way? '   And I said,
' What way? '   And he said, ' Aren't you from Virginia
or something? ' "

Sandra's eyes had gay lights in them, but Theodora
saw no humor in the situation.   "What must they
think of us? "

"I don't care what they think."

"You do."

"I don't."

"Oh, well . . . we're wallflowers. . . . Not a soul
has come near us for hours . . .! "

"It hasn't been ten minutes."

Some one was approaching.   Stephanie!   All in yellow!   Like a daffodil in the spring!

" My dears?   Sitting off here alone? "

Alone?   Well, why not?   It's your fault.   To get us here . . . and then play sheep and goats with your guests!   And Sandra and I are the goats!   All this not on Theodora's lips, but beating in her brain.

It was Sandra who answered Stephanie.   " We're not so far off, really.   It's a mental rather than a physical distance."

Stephanie stared, " My dear? "

" I mean," Sandra was blunt, " we've never danced the Charleston, and all the men are fighting shy of us. We each had a partner.   Theodora's was polite, but mine wasn't.   And it was all the same in the end . . . neither of them came back."

Stephanie bridged the dreadfulness of the moment with, " I'm sure it isn't as bad as it sounds."

" It's worse," Sandra's smile softened the words. " You see we've always been fairly popular down home, and our pride is hurt."

Sandra's smile was magnetic, and Stephanie found herself smiling back.   The child's frock was frumpy and old-fashioned, yet in spite of it she had an air of distinction.   The other sister was better looking and better dressed.   But both of them lacked the things that belonged to Stephanie's crowd.   She hadn't dreamed they would be like this!   A pair of white elephants.

Thinking quickly, she asked, " Have you met Gale Markham? "

They had not.

" Oh, well," eagerly, " he doesn't dance.   And it is such a gorgeous night.   He'd be keen to rush you around the Speedway in his roadster and get you back in time for supper. Would you like it? "

" Adore it," Sandra said.

Stephanie rushed off, and Sandra, looking after her, said: " She's turned the pumpkins into a fairy coach."

Theodora blazed: " I wish you wouldn't talk like a book. It's terribly middle-class."

Theodora didn't want a fairy coach. She wanted a partner. She wanted to stay in the snug little ball-room of the apartment hotel where Stephanie made her home. It was a charming place with its spring flowers, its silken hangings, its great round lights like gold balloons. She didn't want to be bundled out into the night with a man who couldn't dance.

She voiced her exasperation: " She's probably telling him we can't dance. He'll know we're wallflowers. He'll know we couldn't get any partners."

Sandra was serene. A moonlight night — and all the glory of the out-of-doors! " I don't care what he knows about us, Doady, if only he can drive a car."

The place to which the sisters had retreated was be-tween one of the big windows. There was a gilt-legged bench done up in gold brocade. Theodora sat on the bench, and Sandra stood beside her, so that it was Sandra whom Gale Markham saw first as he approached with Stephanie. He was not aware that she made more than a slight impression on his mind, yet years after, when he thought of her, it was as she had ap-peared to him then, a slender, smiling child clothed in a pink frock as became her youth.

As for himself, he was stockily built and walked with the swing of a sailor. He had a thick-curled

thatch of sandy hair and the clearest blue eyes that
Theodora had ever seen. It was his eyes that Theodora noticed, and it was typical of the two sisters that
Sandra should observe the sailor-like swing and wonder about it, without thinking of his eyes. Gale Markham was not handsome, he was not graceful, and he
lacked the air of sartorial perfection which marked the
two young men who had danced with the sisters and
deserted them.

Theodora, weighing him critically, decided that he
was one of the goats. His dress-clothes were shabby,
and when they went out to his car they found it a
rackety roadster.

The girls and Gale were crowded into the rather
narrow seat. Theodora resented the whole thing. *It
is utterly provincial . . . we might be two farmer's
daughters riding on the driver's seat.*

She made a stab at the proprieties. " Down our way
this would be an adventure. Without a chaperon."

" They're extinct, aren't they? Since the war? And
I'm old enough to make it proper. Stephanie knows
that, or she wouldn't have trusted me with such a pair
of — pretty things."

The way he said it was delightful. Flinging it off.
Pretty things! Theodora found herself smiling, unexpectedly.

The rackety little car went sailing down Sixteenth
Street, with the great houses ghostly under the moon.
A twist and a turn around a circle or two, then the
Avenue, the White House and the fragrance of blos-
soming plants, other white buildings as they reached
the Mall, the towering shaft of the light-tipped Monu-

ment, the Speedway, the river, silver masses of marble, the Lincoln Memorial — beauty, breezes, the Virginia hills beyond.

" I kiss my hands to them," Sandra said when she saw the hills. " They are bone of my bone, flesh of my flesh."

There she was again, Theodora reflected, talking like a book. And people didn't do it. The light touch was the thing. Stephanie would never have quoted the Bible, nor would those two young men who had tried to dance with them.

Out of her thoughts she found herself asking, " Mr. Markham, why don't you dance? "

" A stiff bone or two in my foot. The war, you know."

" Oh, are you as old as that? "

" As what? "

" The war."

" I had four years of it. I'm thirty."

They had not guessed it. He did not look it, with his boy's face and the youthful swing of his figure.

" We are eighteen," Sandra vouchsafed.

" Twins? "

" Yes."

" You're not in the least alike."

" I'm darker than Doady, and smaller."

" When we get back to the light, I'll have another squint at the two of you. Stephanie says your mother knew her mother. How do you like Washington? "

Theodora let Sandra answer him. As for herself she was still flaming at having been bundled from the ballroom. *It is just because we haven't the right clothes.*

*Or the new dancing steps. If I had on a dress like
Stephanie's. And gold slippers . . . and the newest
hair cut . . . with a little duck's tail on each cheek
. . . well, the world would look . . . ? "*

Sandra's voice imposed itself on her twin's tense
train of thought. "Windytop is in a backwater.
That's why we came to Washington. We wanted to
sail the high seas."

She laughed, and Gale Markham laughed with
her. Sandra resumed: " Our voyage ended — in a mill
pond. Nothing has happened. Our sails flap in a
calm."

" And you wish you had stayed at Windytop? "

" Oh, we couldn't. We had to have an income. And
everything at Windytop leaks and rattles. There are
bats and rats and things so we can't rent it. But there
are pines and oaks and roses in the garden, and if the
house falls down, well, there are still the pines and
roses."

" It sounds attractive."

" Mother says she's going back when Doady and I
are married. You see there's no such word as matrimonial failure in Mother's lexicon! No woman in the
Dabney family ever passed her twentieth year without
having a husband. So mother counts on that. And in
the interim Doady is to get something to do, and I am
to keep house for the two of 'em."

Markham chuckled, " ' In the interim ' is priceless."

Sandra went on recklessly: " Mother's dreams lead
straight to wedding cakes. She isn't in the least a
matchmaker, but she can't see any other future for a
woman."

" Can you? "

" For myself, yes. But not for Doady."

Theodora, in an agony of self-consciousness, interrupted flamingly, " Don't be silly, Sandra."

" I'm not. It's the truth, Doady. You always need some one to jack you up. And I don't. Mother says I am the cat that walks by itself. I like people, but I can get along without them."

Gale Markham drove slowly. He was enjoying himself hugely. It was delightful. To listen to the confidences of this naïve child, and now and then to that other voice which came so engagingly out of the dark.

He was sorry when it was time to turn back. " They'll be having supper before we know it."

Theodora hoped that when they reached the ballroom, Stephanie would introduce them to some one besides Gale. She liked him, but she didn't want to be set apart. Gale was shabby, his car was shabby, and she and Sandra were shabby. She wanted something shining and snug to offset the effect of isolation.

Stephanie saw them as they entered, and at once came forward. " Where's Gale? "

" He had to find a parking space for his car."

" Have a good time? "

" Marvellous."

" We're just going in to supper."

She moved with them toward the dining-room which was on the same floor.

On the way she annexed two young men, presented them, then left Sandra and Theodora at the mercy, as it were, of their imperturbable escorts, who did the proper things like automatons, without an apparent

spark of interest. Having rushed away as soon as they
got the girls seated, they came back with plates on
which were dabs of salad, infinitesimal sandwiches,
flanked by infinitesimal cakes. Then, their duty done,
they talked conscientiously while they, too, ate and
drank. They had an air of wanting to get away, but
not knowing how to do it. Theodora told herself bit-
terly that it was worse than being alone. She had an
hysterical feeling that if she could say " scat " it would
relieve the tension and send the bored young men flying.

And even as she thought it, Sandra's plate was being
handed to the young man who had brought it. He
grabbed it as if it were a life-preserver, flapped his
wings and flew away, and it was plain as the nose on
your face that he would never come back.

But Sandra was not stranded for more than a second.
Gale Markham swung up to her and said:

"Look here, can't I take the two of you home?
Stephanie tells me you came in her car. I'd like it no
end if you'd give me the pleasure."

Theodora, with one ear cocked to hear what Gale
was saying, wished he hadn't asked them. She didn't
want to ride again in the rackety roadster. She wanted
to lean back luxuriously in Stephanie's limousine with
the uniformed chauffeur. It had given her a great
sense of affluence and of importance as she rolled along
the golden-lighted streets.

Sandra was, however, accepting eagerly. " We'd
love it."

Sandra, too, had liked the limousine. But she
wanted to go home with Gale. She felt as if she had

known him for a long time, and was absolutely at ease with him.

The bored young man at Theodora's side said, with an accession of interest, "Are you friends of Gale Markham?"

"Never met him before tonight."

"Must like you a lot or he wouldn't ask you to ride in his car."

Theodora's brain rapped explosively. *Well, who wants to ride in his — rattletrap . . . !*

He went on, "Stephanie Moore is mad about him."

Theodora stared. "Stephanie? Why?"

"War record. Wonderful. Decorations all over him. And he's one of the Georgetown Markhams."

Theodora's subconscious registered: *Well, what if he is? I never heard of them . . . and we're Claybournes of Virginia . . . !*

But — Stephanie! She found herself leaning forward, speaking to Gale with warmth in her voice.

"Do you really mean we are to ride home with you?"

Gale turned his smiling eyes on her. "If you will . . ."

"We'd love it . . ." she was repeating parrot-like Sandra's phrase. She couldn't think of anything else. *Deceitful, that was the way it sounded. . . . But it wasn't. She really liked him. Only it had been hateful to be classed with the goats.*

Sandra was saying to Gale. "Do you know what you looked like to me when I saw you coming?"

"No."

"Like a ship to a castaway."

He laughed. " Great stuff. Ships. Don't you think? "

" I've never seen the ocean, but I love it just the same."

" By jinks . . . think of never seeing it! I've had years on it. Annapolis first. Then submarines."

She caught her breath. " Really? "

" Yes. Some people didn't like it. But I did. Darned interesting."

" I should think so."

" Can't get my mind on anything else. Have a berth in the Navy Department, but I hate desks. If I had my way I'd charter a tramp steamer and sail round the world."

" Why don't you? "

" Anchored. Mother and kid brother to take care of." He ran his fingers through his curled thatch. " Look here, have you been down to the water front? Not much, of course — but the boats come up from the Bay — oyster boats and all that. I can't keep away from it. I'd like to take you and your sister some-time."

" How splendid! "

" We'll have lunch . . . there's a restaurant . . . over a commission house beyond the market. It is on the second floor, and there's a porch which looks across the river. Best seafood in town. Plain, but spick and span. We'll eat there and go down to the War College."

Theodora, with her ear still cocked, was registering commendation on Sandra's acceptance. Lunch with Gale Markham of the Georgetown Markhams, who-ever they might be!

Dancing had begun. Theodora's young man deserted her. " Sorry," he murmured, and flapped his wings and flew away!

Gale had the two of them on his hands and was quite content. He demanded of Sandra presently.

" How did you get your name? "

" From Alexandra of England. Mother is a hero-worshipper. She has always thought of Alexandra as the perfect lady, and of Theodore Roosevelt as the perfect gentleman. So she named us after them. Doady is Theodora."

Gale made a little gesture of salute. " Theodore Roosevelt is the captain of my soul."

Sandra was illumined. " Oh, I am so glad. I have his picture, autographed. He knew my father."

Theodora breaking in, informed them: " All the people have gone back to the ballroom. Sandra, I think we'd better not stay."

The sound of music came to them, the whine of the saxophone, the dull boom of the drums.

Sandra agreed. " Only we oughtn't to drag Mr. Markham away so soon."

Stephanie appeared in the arched entrance to the dining-room. Her quick eye appraised the situation. Gale making a martyr of himself for the white elephants!

" Everybody's dancing," she said. " Why can't we find a quiet corner and talk." She had an air, Theodora thought, of throwing a life-line.

Gale said easily, " I am going to take these pretty things home."

" Krebs will do it," Stephanie said. " When they

are ready, I'll have him called."

" They prefer my roadster to your limousine," Gale was smiling.

" But — you'll come back? " there was about Stephanie a slight effect of breathlessness.

" It will be late enough for me to turn in. And I'm a bit of a figurehead at a dance, Stephanie."

"Nonsense! I'm not going to let any of you go as early as this. I haven't had a moment to talk to these — pretty things," Stephanie used Gale's phrase with charming effect, her hands thrown out in a little gesture of invitation. " Oh, come on, all of you. Nobody's in the reception-room; we'll go there."

In the reception-room was a sofa of green brocade. Stephanie sat on it, making a picture of herself, more than ever like a daffodil in the spring. Theodora decided that Stephanie was fully aware of the effectiveness of the green background. *" She does things like that deliberately . . . to make herself attractive. And why shouldn't she? I shall . . . some day . . ."*

Other people drifting in joined Stephanie's group. There were at least a dozen of them. Yet in spite of the fact that Stephanie sat on the green sofa, enthroned, as it were, it was Gale who was the center of things. Thinking it over afterward, Theodora told herself that it was another of Stephanie's deliberate effects to thrust Gale into the limelight. She had effaced herself that he might shine. Yet she had shone, too, in a sort of reflected light, like the moon and the sun. There seemed to be a trick about it, to efface oneself yet not be overlooked. Theodora wondered if ever, in the years to come, she would be able thus adroitly to play up to a man's popularity and lose nothing in the process.

Sandra, having a less analytical mind, was not aware of Stephanie's subtleties. She was aware only that Gale Markham was the most interesting man she had ever met. And she thought Stephanie beautiful, sitting on the green sofa in her daffodil dress. She thought it would be wonderful to look like that — delicately-fashioned, exquisite in every detail.

Before he left, Stephanie got Gale alone for a few moments. "I hope you haven't been bored to tears."

"Bored?"

"With my white elephants?"

"Is that what you call them?"

She nodded. "I shouldn't have asked them. They are out of place, poor things."

"My dear child, don't pity them. They're getting more out of life than you and I. I wish you could have heard them a while ago. Out in the moonlight. They are simply eating up life. They don't know it, but they are."

She gave a little shrug. "They struck me as a bit *gauche*."

He shook his head. "They're not that. I fancy there's as good blood in them as in you or me."

"Oh, of course — but they've been poor so long."

He gave a shout of amusement. "If I am poor long enough, shall I be — *gauche?*"

The blood went up in her face. "Gale!"

He was repentant. "I shouldn't have said that. But you mustn't be so high-hat."

"I'm not."

"You are, my dear. But I'll forgive you — because you're too charming for any man to hold a grudge against."

" Do you really think that? "

" Of course. And now, I must be going."

She touched his coat sleeve with the tip of her pointed finger. " Shall we take a walk on Sunday morning? "

" Same time? "

" Yes."

" Love to." He caught at the pointed finger, kissed it. " Goodnight."

She went out with the twins, when Gale had brought his car around. She waved to them when they drove off. The light shone down on her. Her daffodil draperies blew in the breeze. She watched the car until it was out of sight, her breath coming quickly, her eyes shadowed.

CHAPTER IV

ON A BALCONY

WHEN the two girls reached home, they found their mother awake and reading in bed. The bed seemed to Theodora to overflow the room. It was enormous, Brobdingnagian, like the things in " Gulliver's Travels."

" Mother," she said explosively, " suppose some one had come up with us and found you in bed! "

Her mother was calm. " It is nearly two o'clock," she said. " If anybody had come up, he would have had to go down again."

" Like the King of France and forty thousand men," Sandra contributed.

" Oh, you two! " Theodora raged. " You think its funny — and it isn't. It is tragic to live like — chickens in a coop."

" You chose this apartment, Doady. We might have had a bigger one in a less stylish street."

" It was the best we could do." Theodora was restlessly prowling the limited space about the bed. " It was the best we could do and not be ashamed to invite our friends."

" Friends," said Sandra, " will come and see you if you roost in the top of a tree."

" Not the kind I want! " Theodora was still raging.

" Sit down," Mrs. Claybourne commanded. " You

act like a caged lion, Doady. What happened to make you so upset? Didn't you have a good time?"

The caged lion stopped in her tracks. "Good time? Well, if you want to know we were — wallflowers."

Mrs. Claybourne's dreams crashed. "Wallflowers?"

"Yes. Nobody wanted to dance with us."

Sandra, still preoccupied with the humor of the situation, supplemented, "We stepped on the men's feet." She began to rock with silent laughter. "Mother, it was awful. You should have seen our partners, folding their tents like the Arabs."

Theodora made a sharp interruption. "Sandra, I wish you wouldn't quote things. It is so archaic. But you don't care what people think of us. You don't care if we act as if we came out of the ark."

Theodora was getting hysterical. Her mother, recognizing the signs, shifted the subject.

"Well, Stephanie was nice to you, wasn't she?"

"She was polite enough, but she was sorry she asked us."

Sandra protested. "You don't know that, Doady. Her manner was perfect."

"So were her clothes. Everything is perfect about Stephanie Moore. But just the same she had us on her hands, and she didn't know what to do with us."

Mrs. Claybourne surveyed her daughter with speculative eyes. "Doady," she said, "there's some lemonade in the refrigerator. You'd better drink it and go to bed."

"I don't want to go to bed. I want to stay up and talk things out. Mother, you should have seen the refreshments. Just a teaspoon of salad and a square inch of ice. When I think of the parties we had at Windytop — platters of chicken and freezers of ice-cream. We'd have called this stingy."

" The Moores were never generous providers," Mrs. Claybourne remarked. " That's probably the reason they are rich. We've never been a saving family. Perhaps, if we had, we'd have more to show for it."

" Well, we're going to have something to show for it. I am going to start out early tomorrow morning and get something to do. Stephanie asked us to come again, but we can't unless we have some clothes. You can't imagine how out of place we looked tonight, and awkward. We were dreadful."

" My dear, you couldn't be that."

" But we were! Sandra knows it. But she won't face facts. She's like you. I have to fight both of you to make you see anything as it is. You'd stay in a rut forever."

She was very much in earnest, and very pretty and appealing. Sandra knew these moods of her sister's. Doady would go on endlessly arguing, asserting, complaining. Mrs. Claybourne had infinite patience. She sympathized, commanded, and comforted. And eventually brought her tense, accusing offspring to reasonableness and relaxation.

Taking no part in the conversation, Sandra had changed her dress for a white cotton kimono and now stood in front of the mirror, brushing her hair. Mrs. Claybourne's eyes rested on her with satisfaction. There was no difference in the mother's love for her two children. But she had to admit that Sandra was less difficult. She was more of a child than Doady, but such a wise child, going through everything with an air of irresistible gaiety. Half-turned, with parted lips smiling, her wide gray eyes surveyed the two of them with a sparkling sidelong glance; with the rose and ivory of her skin framed by the richness of her hair, she seemed to shed about her an atmosphere of youth and radiance.

Leaving Theodora still proclaiming her wrongs, Sandra stepped out on the balcony. A late wedge-shaped moon was poking its nose among the clouds. She stretched herself in an old deck chair which occupied most of the space, and gazed up at the silver sky.

In one of the apartments below, John McCormack's voice poured forth from a phonograph a passionate love-song. Sandra, with her hands under her head, listened and gave herself up to dreams. She had really, she decided, had a very good time at the dance. Set against the humiliation of the moments when she and Doady had been marooned on the gold bench were those other moments with Gale Markham. She liked him immensely. He was sincere and simple. She had a feeling that she had found a real friend.

Gradually the lights went out. The phonograph was silent. The moon hid itself behind a bank of clouds. Sandra sat up. It was time to go to bed. She leaned her chin on the rail and looked down.

Across the court and on the floor below the Claybournes' apartment straight, dark curtains hung on each side of the long window, outlining an illumined oblong through which could be seen a section of a wide table, a shaded lamp, and a man's hand writing steadily.

Perched on the table, sphinx-like as it watched the pen travel across the paper, was a great white cat. Utterly motionless the cat watched, except when the pen stopped and she bent her head to the long, slender fingers which ruffled her fur.

The man's hand was all that could be seen of him. He might be old or young, short or tall. But his hand told something of his mental make-up and of his characteristics, for he wrote quickly, as one who knows his subject, and the fingers which ruffled the cat's fur were kind.

And now Theodora was at the window. " We're having something to eat," she said. " I'm half starved."

Sandra would have preferred to stay outside. The tight little rooms oppressed her. Like her mother she sighed in the hot night for her own boughs at Windytop. But she felt the utter futility of rebellion. Things were as they were, because they had to be. One might as well be cheerful about it. Doady wasted a lot of energy in fighting windmills.

Mrs. Claybourne had made some sandwiches.

Sandra said with some compunction: " Why didn't you let me do it, mother? Oh, we shouldn't be keeping you up so late. You've got to go to work in the morning."

" I can go to bed early tomorrow night," Mrs. Claybourne said.

She was tired. But her daughters were her daughters. She lived for them; felt no task too hard if it contributed to their happiness.

Sandra, eating her sandwiches and drinking her lemonade, was aware that Doady's tense mood was over. Having shelved for the moment the memory of to-night's fiasco, she pushed on to plans for the future. She had found an advertisement in the evening paper. She read it aloud: "'Well-known art dealer requires energetic and trustworthy assistant with some knowledge of old china and glass, young, well-spoken, and willing to make himself generally useful. Call at Room 41, Stocks Building, before ten A.M.'"

"It's worth trying for," she said as she laid the paper down.

"But they want a man," her sister reminded her. "It says 'himself.'"

"I don't care what it says. There's no reason why a woman wouldn't do as well."

"And how much do you know about old china and glass?"

"I've read a lot, and I can learn."

"Getting a job," Mrs. Claybourne interposed, "isn't as easy as you think."

"Getting anything," her daughter said cocksuredly, "is putting your mind to it."

Sandra, listening, was glad that she wasn't restless like Doady. She didn't in the least care about getting a job. She got a lot out of small happenings, so that each day seemed to promise interests of its own, without going forth to seek them. It was perhaps the thing which gave zest to the life of Sandra Claybourne that she could, after those thrilling moments in the moonlight when John McCormack sang, give herself absorbingly to the eating of her sandwiches and the drinking of her lemonade. All was grist that came into her mill — a little walk to the butcher's, a little chat with the baker, a little cake to make for Doady and her mother, a little dusting and sweeping before she allowed herself the luxury of an hour or two on the balcony with a good book. Yet there was this about it all — the little things satisfied her not because of themselves, but because back of them were the dreams of youth, which leaped forward into the future and visioned splendors which might never come to pass, but which were none the less believed in and expected.

Theodora had no patience with Sandra's states of mind. She liked a good dinner and ate it with an appetite unlooked for in one so lissome, but she did not want to get the dinner. She did not want to hobnob with the butcher or chat with the baker. She did not want to bake a little cake or sweep a room. The things Theodora wanted had to do with getting on in the world. She did not believe in being content to go to market and to dream on the balcony with a book. Theodora did not care about the splendors of the future. She wanted things here and now. She felt that Sandra and her mother drugged themselves with dreams.

She was too tired, however, for further argument. So she kissed her mother and went to bed. Early in the morning she would go forth to seek the family's fortune. She had a sense of importance, as one who grasps at opportunities which others miss.

Sandra, too, kissed her mother. "Good-night, precious."

"Good-night, my darling."

It was a little ceremony sacred to the two of them. They always waited until Doady was out of the way before they performed it. Sandra had begun it on the night after her father died.

In bed and ready for slumber, Sandra found that
her eyes would not close. The room was warm, and at
last she again went out on the balcony. Wrapped in
her white kimono, she leaned over the rail. About the
court all the windows were dark. The moon shone wan
and pale. It was almost morning.

Suddenly her eye was caught by a figure on the balcony below. A man stood by the rail, the white cat
which she had seen between the parted curtains on his
shoulder. His face was upraised, and in the spectral
light his features showed plainly. His profile was as
thin as a silver dollar; his dark hair was tossed back
from his forehead; he was as still as a statue.

The moon touched Sandra, too, with light. As she
leaned on the rail, she was possessed by a sense of the
romance of the moment. She saw herself as Juliet
. . . the man as Romeo — " *Oh, she doth teach the
torches to burn bright!* " She was no longer little
Sandra whose partners had flapped their wings and
flown away. She was Beauty in a garden — " *Her
beauty hangs upon the cheek of night like a rich
jewel!* "

Her heart beat to suffocation!

The moon went behind a cloud. Sandra returned
to realities, fled through the window, shut it behind her,
and stood blushing in the dark. She wondered if the
man had seen her leaning on the rail. She felt that he
must have heard the beating of her heart. How silly she
had been! How silly!

Chapter V

GRISELDA!

MRS. CLAYBOURNE and Theodora started out together the next morning. The older woman had to be at her office at nine, and Theodora wanted to be first to answer the advertisement.

It was hot and close, and Mrs. Claybourne felt herself unequal to the long day. But she did not tell her girls. She was glad Theodora was so hopeful of getting a position. It would be dreadful to have her disappointed. But then, of course, such things happened.

She sighed a little as she pulled her plain, black hat down over her graying locks. Temperamentally she was placid, but this morning she had a sense of deep depression. Here she was at forty-five without having got ahead. Perhaps Doady was right: she and Sandra dreamed too much; they did not seize the moment and make it their own.

One might have thought, however, seeing Sandra at her morning's work, that she was making the most of the moments which were hers after the others had gone. She washed the dishes, straightened the rooms, changed her dress, and a little after eleven went out on the balcony with her book and a basket of sewing. With the awning down, she had some effect of privacy and a delightful sense of coolness, for the sun did not shine in the court until later in the day, and there was a soft breeze blowing.

Once or twice she peeped through the rails of the balcony to that other balcony below and across, where last night she had seen the man and the cat. But neither of them appeared this morning, and she told herself it was perhaps as well. Nothing would seem as it had seemed under the moon. And one did not play Juliet in broad daylight. She found her mind running on it, however . . . *"How silver-sweet sound lovers' tongues . . . "*

Sandra had a way of dressing up her thoughts with verse. Mrs. Claybourne adored lovely, singing sounds and had rocked her babies to sleep with rich, murmured cadences: *" The isles of Greece, the isles of Greece, where burning Sappho loved and sung "*; or *" This maid she lived with no other thought Than to love and be loved by me "*; or *" She was a phantom of delight, When first she gleamed upon my sight."*

Later they had learned by heart pages and pages of poetry. Theodora had cared less for it than Sandra. Theodora fed her eyes upon Beauty; Sandra fed her heart. There had been times at Windytop when Sandra had run with the wind, chanting ecstatically to the trees, the skies, the flowering fields, some passionate, perfect thing: *" And o'er the hills and far away, Beyond the utmost purple rim, Beyond the night, across the day, Through all the world she follow'd him."* Or *" She is coming, my own, my sweet, were it ever so airy a tread . . . My heart would hear her and beat, had it lain for a century dead! "*

It came to her now, as she sat under the awning on the

cramped little balcony, what Windytop would be on a morning like this, with a flutter of young leaves, the warm smell of the pines, a thousand roses in the garden, and Doady and herself with their fancy-work on the wide porch, and their mother reading aloud to them.

She had a little catch of her breath at that vision. It was dreadful to think that her mother, who loved the out-of-doors, should be caged in an office. With her fingers busy, Sandra's brain worked to find some way out for all of them.

She was roused from her thoughts by a commotion in the court. She looked through the bars of the balcony, then jumped to her feet and hung over the rail. The other little balconies were crowded with people. Everybody was looking down, there were excited cries of " Let her alone . . .," " Gee, he's got her . . .," " Can't somebody call him off . . .? "

On the opposite side of the court a cat had been cornered by a dog. The cat was a silver-furred thing with a tail like a fox. The dog was a hard-muscled brute with a brass-studded collar — a police dog, mad for his quarry, kept back only by the indomitable courage of the high-bred little creature who faced him.

Her right paw was busy. She struck at his nose again and again. He yelped, but did not give way. He had the better of it. Her back was to the wall; her blazing eyes saw no avenue of escape.

Sandra heard herself saying, breathlessly, " Oh, oh! " She wrung her hands helplessly . . . she couldn't stand it if anything happened to that pretty creature . . . why didn't somebody . . . why didn't somebody . . .

Then the heart-stirring thing happened. Out from between the curtains where the night before Sandra had seen a man writing came the man himself. He vaulted the rail of the balcony, climbed lightly down from one iron support to another, reached the ground, and crossed the court yard on a run.

The cat saw him and gave a frantic yowl. The dog did not see him, and plunged and bayed as his collar was caught by a strong hand. The man spoke to him in a foreign tongue. At once the excited brute ceased plunging and cocked his ear. The cat streaked away to safety. The man, without a glance at the crowded balconies, continued talking in a low voice to the dog.

There was great applause from the watching audience. It was like a scene in a play, with all the people looking down at the man and the dog in the court. Sandra's blood was pounding in her veins. What a picture he made, smiling quietly and without self-consciousness while the people clapped! He was without a coat, and his soft, white shirt was open at the neck. His hair, brushed straight back from his forehead, was dark and shining. His eyes, too, were dark and were lighted when the continued applause compelled him to look up and acknowledge it with a gleam of sardonic mirth. Where had she seen a face like that? Whose portrait? Booth, perhaps. Or was it Barrymore? Both of them — dark, vivid, with that sardonic touch.

Some one called from a balcony: " That dog needs a beating. He almost caught your cat."

The tall man laughed. " He won't get it from me.

It is as natural for him to fight a cat as for the Germans to fight the French. I must keep my cat at home."

The voice from the balcony persisted, "You spoke to him in German?"

"Yes." No more than that. Crisp. Decisive.

The cat appeared on her own balcony. The tall man looked up at her. "Shall I let him go, Griselda?"

Griselda. What an adorable name for a cat! Sandra was enchanted. The cat, moon-eyed, glanced down at her master, then began calmly to smooth her ruffled fur with her little pink tongue. Everybody laughed. Tragedy had been succeeded by comedy.

The tall man released the dog, and the big brute leaped away. The people on the balconies began to go in. The tall man entered the house by the regular route, and presently Sandra saw him again at his table, writing.

She had a thrilled sense of adventure. She settled herself in her chair, but found it hard to get her mind on her book. She was young, and she had never had a lover. Boys had liked her and had told her so. But what they said had meant nothing to her. None of them had appealed in the least to her imagination. But here was one who appealed to it. As she lay with her eyes half-closed, her mind seemed to sweep back over the wide range of the heroes in the books she had read. Not one of them but could be matched in beauty and in prowess by the man across the way. *Ivanhoe, Alan Breck, D'Artagnan, Rudolf Rassendyll* — he had them all beaten. And the wonder of it was that every day she could watch him from her balcony, see him at night under the moon! It was characteristic of Sandra that the question of meeting him did not enter her mind.

He was like an actor to be looked at, dreamed about, fitted into those dramas played on the stage of her illusions, but which had no physical presentment. That was enough for her. The rest might come later. She was content at the moment with the shadow, not the substance.

She was roused from her meditations by a question asked by a woman on the balcony of the adjoining apartment. She was leaning over the rail, bridging thus a part of the distance, so that her voice carried clearly.

"Did you see that man down there?" she demanded.

Sandra sat up. "Yes."

"His name is Rufus Fiske," the woman informed her. "I saw it on the house directory. He's good-looking, ain't he?"

Sandra hesitated. Then said with some stiffness. "Yes, he is."

"He got the cat from me," the woman said. "My husband don't like cats, and I had to get rid of her. I don't like them much myself. But we paid a lot for her, and we wanted to get our price. He paid it. He seems to have plenty of money. I should think he'd live somewhere else. I bet I wouldn't stay in this stifling place if I had the price of the rent anywhere else. I should think you'd hate it. A young girl like you. Shut up."

"It isn't bad," Sandra said. She wished the woman would stop talking and go away. She seemed somehow to spoil the morning. She had short, blond hair and round, blue eyes and wore a soiled, pink bungalow apron. "Your name is Claybourne, ain't it?" she

Chapter VI

IN A GARDEN

THEODORA, reaching Room 41 of the Stocks Building, found five men ahead of her. They all sat in an anteroom and were ushered one at a time into an office beyond, by a uniformed boy who said, coming out and seeing Theodora,

"They advertised for a man."

"I know. But I'm going to have a try at it." She was tense and vivid.

The boy hesitated, but finally led the way. "Mr. Maulsby isn't easy to get along with," he warned, as he opened the door of the inner room.

It was not, however, the difficult Mr. Maulsby whom Theodora faced as she entered. A rather stout, pleasant-faced woman sat at the desk. She was well-dressed and had an air of authority.

"I am Miss Deakin," she said. "What can I do for you?"

"I came about the advertisement," Theodora told her, "for an art dealer's assistant."

"The advertisement expressly states that we want a man."

"Well," said Theodora, "I thought if I filled the other requirements you might consider me. I am young, and willing. And while I don't know much about old china and glass, I can learn."

Miss Deakin looked her over, " You're nothing but a child."

" I'm eighteen."

" You don't look it. It's the short hair and short skirts. What makes you think you would suit Mr. Maulsby? "

Theodora, even more tense and vivid than when she had talked to the uniformed boy, said, " Because I want to work for him more than anybody else in the whole, wide world."

Miss Deakin stared. " Do you know him? "

" No. And when I read the advertisement I didn't know it was he who had advertised. But ever since I came to Washington the windows of his shop have been meat and drink to me."

Miss Deakin tapped her pencil thoughtfully on her desk. " You speak his language," she said. " That's something. Windows have never been meat and drink to me, and that's why I'm good at the business end of things. But Mr. Maulsby would rather look at Irish glass than eat an Irish stew." She smiled and lifted her hands in a little gesture of amusement. " I'm the other way. I'm going to have Irish stew for my dinner."

Theodora didn't in the least care what Miss Deakin had for dinner. " Why not let me see Mr. Maulsby? " she suggested eagerly.

" I might," Miss Deakin decided. " All the others I have interviewed this morning are hopeless. You are the only one who has a bit of appreciation of the kind of thing we want. Mr. Maulsby has to have some one to look after special customers when he is away. And they must be pleasantly and tactfully served. I look after the business end of things, and we find it better to have the office and shop in different buildings. And the shop force is short just now. Mr. Maulsby had to send one man over to England last week to have a try at a set of Wakelyn candlesticks that are on the market, and another one left last night for one of the New York sales. There's a pair of Porcelain Marli horses that a customer wants. That's why we advertised, to get some one at once."

Theodora had never heard of Wakelyn candlesticks or Porcelain Marli horses, but they sounded delectable. " If you'll only let me try! " she begged.

" I'll write a note, and you can tell any one in the front of the shop that I sent you to Mr. Maulsby. And if he doesn't want you, you'll have his word for it and not mine. I'd be glad to have a girl with nice manners. That last man was impossible."

Theodora, speeding away with the note, beamed on the pessimistic office boy.

" I'm going to see Mr. Maulsby."

The office boy indulged himself in a bit of pleasantry. " Well, I hope you like him. I see him every day."

On arriving at the shop, Theodora was shown at once into the garden. Two men were there, one in a great Chinese chair, the other seated on the stone bench. There was the fragrance of roses, patches of clear sunshine checkered with shadows, and a bird bath, with pigeons flying back and forth from its rim to the top of the brick wall.

As Theodora appeared, the two men got to their feet.

" Mr. Maulsby? " she asked.

The older man said, " You wish to see me? "

" I have a note from Miss Deakin."

He read it. " Didn't she tell you that I want a man? "

" Yes. But, Mr. Maulsby — I'm simply dying to
. . . work for you . . ."

Tense and vivid! Both the men saw it, as the office
boy had seen it and Miss Deakin. Mr. Maulsby's keen
eyes studied her.

" Why are you ' dying' to work for me? "

" Because every time I have looked in your window
it has been — meat and drink."

She used the phrase deliberately. Why not?
Miss Deakin had said that she spoke his language.

He made her explain, however. " What do you mean
— ' meat and drink ' ? "

" Well, it's more satisfying than a — dinner at the
Mayflower! "

She brought it out with a rush, laughing, and the men
laughed with her. In the eyes of the younger one was
a sardonic light. Was she really as naïve as all that?

Maulsby, too, weighed her. " If you mean what you
say, you are what I am looking for."

" I do mean it."

" Good. As soon as I get through with Mr. Fiske,
we'll talk about it. You needn't leave us. I'll get a
chair for you.

It was young Fiske, however, who brought the chair.
Theodora sat down in it and listened while the two
talked. Mr. Maulsby was older than she had thought
he would be. He was abrupt in manner. But she liked
him. She felt it would be quite heavenly if she could get
the place.

As for the young man in the Chinese chair, he was attractive enough, but had nothing to do with her future. He was not even a customer. He had come to sell some ivory figures which were set forth on the stone bench.

" I've bought them," Maulsby explained to Theodora, " although it almost broke me to do it."

"You can sell them for more than you paid," the other man told him, " but you won't. You'll never want to let them go. I didn't. But I had to have the money."

" He's buying a house for his cat," Maulsby further elucidated. " I tell him he ought to get a wife."

" Griselda is kind to my faults," Rufus remarked, " and when I am tired of her I can have her chloroformed."

Maulsby rose. " Come in with me, Fiske, and I'll write the check." Then, to Theodora, " I'll be back in a minute."

They went in, and Theodora settled herself in her chair with a sigh of ecstasy. Could anything have been easier? Here she was, in Paradise! The little ivory figures still stood on the bench; a light wind blew rose-petals over them. The spired cedars cast shadows on the grass; the doves flew back and forth from the wall to the rim of the bath. Here was beauty brimming over! Meat and drink? Oh, the thing was nectar and ambrosia, food for the gods!

When Felix Maulsby returned, Theodora said to him: "Your garden seems a thousand miles away from everything. It is like one of Alma Tadema's paintings."

" Alma Tadema is out of fashion," Maulsby stated, "but a garden like this gives the lie to his critics. You've got an eye for things, and I'm glad of it. Most of the people I have about me might as well be in the shoe business, or soap. Now, you take Miss Deakin. She thinks I put her over into the other building because I wanted to get the office away from the shop, but that wasn't my reason. I simply couldn't stand her common-sense shoes and her marcel wave. As for Miss Carter out there in front, her horn spectacles almost drive me mad."

He sat down on the bench and began to put the ivory figures into their case. " I'm going to take these home and show them to my wife," he said. " I'm not keen about leaving them in the shop. Somebody may try to buy them, and Fiske was right when he said I'd probably keep them. That's the trouble with this business. I never buy a lovely thing without wanting to hold on to it forever."

" I'm afraid I don't know just why things like that are so valuable," Theodora confessed.

" I'll teach you. I am sure we are going to get on. I'm not a hard taskmaster. And now perhaps we had better talk about what I am to pay you."

He drove a rather sharp bargain. " You've a lot to learn, and you will grow toward what you're worth."

He asked a few questions about her family, and she told him of her mother and Sandra, of Windytop and the efficiency apartment.

" It's like a cage. I can't stay in it all the time, that's why I want to work."

" I see," he stood up. " Come on in, and I'll show

you the shop."

He showed it so thoroughly that it was after twelve when Theodora started home. She was aware, as she stood waiting for the street car, that the day had darkened. The air was filled with dust that blew up from the hot streets. Everybody looked moist and pink. The northwest sky was black.

" There's going to be a storm," Theodora told herself, and hopped on the car in a hurry.

Women were fanning themselves, and men were mopping their faces, but Theodora felt cool and crisp. With the news she was bearing home with her, the elements had no power to touch her. Tempests might rage, lightning flash, and thunders roar, but she was going to work tomorrow morning! Nothing less than an earthquake which swallowed up Mr. Maulsby's shop could quench her raptures.

When she arrived home, she fell into the arms of her twin. " Sandra, I've got it."

" Doady! Really? "

" Really."

" Where? "

" Maulsby's."

" Not the one with the lovely windows! "

" Yes."

" Oh, Doady! "

They were a sparkling pair, eyes bright, breath quick. " As soon as I change," Theodora said, " I'll tell you all about it. I didn't have an umbrella, and I had to run for it."

She laid a magazine on the table. " Mr. Maulsby loaned me that. It tells all about Wakelyn candlesticks and Porcelain Marli horses. Just the words sound fascinating, don't they, Sandra? "

" I'll say they do." It seemed to Sandra as if the air in the little room was electric with the spark that Theodora had lighted. Wakelyn candlesticks! Porcelain Marli horses! Splendid! Sumptuous! Stimulating!

" I'll have lunch ready by the time you get into dry things. There's just the tea."

The storm had brought with it a change of wind and coolness. Sandra had raised the awning, and the room was filled with silver light. With the tray between them on a little table, the two girls, shut in from the outside world by a curtain of streaming rain, were aware of the deliciousness and delightfulness of the moment.

Theodora, relating her adventures, began with the office boy and Miss Deakin. She progressed to the garden and her meeting with the two men. She told of the beauty of the spired cedars and the checkered sunlight on the sward, of the fragrance of the roses, the birds flying back and forth. She described Felix Maulsby:

" He's delightful, Sandra. Magnetic. He makes me feel that there's no end to what I can do for him."

Her meeting with Fiske was not emphasized. He became important only as the owner of the ivory figurines. " The loveliest things, Sandra. The Five Senses. Mr. Maulsby paid two thousand dollars for them. He says they are worth more than that. But he wouldn't tell Mr. Fiske of course."

" Mr. — Fiske? "

" The man who sold them to him. Rufus Fiske. He's rather young and good-looking."

The thing came like a thunderclap! *Rufus Fiske,*

Rufus Fiske, Rufus Fiske . . . !

Sandra wondered why she did not say to Doady, "Oh, Rufus Fiske, he lives across the court."

But she did not say it. She simply sat there listening to Theodora's voice and to the rain which played a beating accompaniment. How queer life was! A few hours ago she had not heard of Rufus Fiske. And here he was running, as it were, along the road of life beside her. Perhaps he would run on ahead and she would never catch up. Yet she had a thrilled sense that this was the beginning!

Chapter VII

" WANTED — TO FIND! "

WHEN Mrs. Claybourne reached home that
night, the news of Theodora's good fortune
was like wine to her weary soul. All
through the hot day, as she had worked in her office, she
had longed for Windytop. For the wide and comfortable spaces. The big room where one might be alone.
The hill at the back of the house, with the exquisite stillness of the little grove that topped it. Oh, for an hour
in that grove tonight, with the rising moon tangled in
the branches of the trees, and with the plaint of the wood
dove intensifying the stillness. Sanctuary. It had
seemed to her, riding home in the crowded trolley, as if
she could not face the narrow confines of the apartment,
the lack of privacy, the girls' problems.

And now here was Theodora making her incredible
announcement. " Eighty dollars a month, mother, and
more to come if I am what he wants."

" My darling — how wonderful! " The reaction
brought faintness. Mrs. Claybourne's lips were white.
She caught at a chair.

The twins were solicitous. " Lie down a bit, dearest,"
Sandra said. " I won't hurry things, and you'll have
time for a bath before dinner. I'm having an omelette
and mushrooms, and Doady ordered ice-cream. We're
going to celebrate! "

Sandra sang under her breath as she beat up eggs, and broiled the mushrooms. Theodora had put on her hat and had gone for flowers for the center of the table. It was a big extravagance, but they had decided the occasion warranted it. " It will perk up mother, poor dear. She misses the garden."

Roses and ice-cream and Rufus Fiske! That was the way Sandra's thoughts ran. She hardly dared look out of the window. She would wait until dusk came. Until the moon rose.

While Theodora was gone, Gale Markham called up.

" I want the two of you to lunch with me on Saturday. Have you anything else on hand? "

Sandra told him frankly, " We never have anything on hand."

" I'll come at one, then. And we'll have a ride afterwards."

" I'll have to ask Doady. She's got a job."

" A — what? "

" A place to work. At Maulsby's. The art shop. She adores it. She says Mr. Maulsby is marvellous."

" He is more than that. He's a personality. Not always an agreeable one. But never a bore. He married his wife because she looked like Sir Peter Lely's Duchess of Portsmouth. At least, that's what he says. She doesn't look like it now, but she thinks she does. She is as odd in her way as he is in his. People like to get invitations to her dinners. Stephanie's quite mad about them. Goes there a lot. Once upon a time I went, but I'm too poor to keep the pace. Look here, suppose I come over tonight and congratulate your sister. And meet your mother. May I? "

" Of course."

" I won't keep you up late. You'll need your beauty sleep after last night."

Last night! As she hung up the receiver Sandra wondered if it had been only twenty-four hours since she had stood on the balcony like Juliet, under the moon!

Theodora, arriving with six pink roses in a white paper, heard the news. " Gale Markham is coming."

" When? "

" Tonight."

Theodora's eyes swept the crowded room critically. " I wish he had given us a bit more time to fix up. But the roses will help."

" Men aren't critical, Doady. And he knows Mr. Maulsby."

" Does he? "

" Yes. He says Mrs. Maulsby is as interesting as her husband. And that people fight for invitations to dine with them."

" I knew they were like that. I can't believe in my luck, Sandra."

Mrs. Claybourne, appearing at that moment, remarked, " Down our way we don't fight for invitations from shopkeepers."

" Mother," Theodora protested, " nobody pays any attention to things like that in these days."

" Perhaps not." Mrs. Claybourne felt that it wasn't worth the argument. Why spoil their little feast with a discussion of worn-out social standards? But a Claybourne was a Claybourne. Subconsciously she had a feeling of resentment that Stephanie Moore and these

Maulsbys, whoever they were, might think they could condescend to her daughters.

When Gale Markham arrived, he brought more roses.

"Mother cut them from our own bushes. She sent them to you, Mrs. Claybourne. She remembers having met you years ago. She was Betty Ballard."

Mrs. Claybourne, too, remembered. "She was the prettiest thing."

"She is still pretty," said Betty Ballard's son. "And she is more than that. She is the bravest woman I know."

He did not explain why he called her brave, nor did they ask him. But Sandra, having heard him say it with a deepening of his young voice and an added brightness in his blue eyes, felt her heart warm toward him.

"Mother hopes you'll have tea with her some afternoon," Gale continued. "It is hard for her to make calls. She's rather an invalid and rarely gets out."

When Gale got around at last to talk of the Maulsbys, he said to Theodora: "You'll love his house. It's a charming place."

"I may not be invited. You see, I'm just a girl in his shop."

"Maulsby isn't like that. All he asks of his guests is that they are interesting. He has no patience with banalities. You can't cross his threshold just because you've got a lot of money or a string of ancestors. He gets together all sorts of freaks and celebrities. There's always an amusing crowd."

"I shall never be able to keep up with Doady," Sandra stated. "She came home today talking about

Wakelyn candlesticks and Porcelain Marli horses. It is all Greek to me."

It was not, it seemed, Greek to Gale. He knew a lot about it. " We sold Maulsby loads of things after Dad died. Mother says our house looks like the Whistler room in the Freer Gallery — all shelves with nothing on them."

He said it lightly, so that they were not aware of the tragedy that lay behind his words. At his Dad's death had come the revelation of an estate mismanaged and utterly without value. All the beautiful things that had been sold were to have gone into the home which Gale had planned for Stephanie. There had been one chair in which he had dreamed of her by his fireside. It had been sent to Maulsby's with the others. And that had not been the worst of it. Losing the furniture had been a little thing beside the fact of Gale's loss of faith in the woman he loved.

Mrs. Claybourne, in her best dress of thin black, leaned back in one of the big chairs and listened to the chatter of the young folks. She decided that she liked Gale. Already she was linking him in her mind with romance. Which of her daughters would be crowned with his favor? Sandra with her dreams, or Doady with her driving ambitions? Either of them would make him a good wife. Of course, he was poor, the girls had told her that. But then his mother was a Ballard. One need go no further than that for distinction.

When Gale went away, all the plans had been made for Saturday. He was to call for Sandra and pick up Theodora at Maulsby's.

Theodora confessed: " We've nothing to wear."

" Nonsense! " Gale's eyes went from one twin to the other. " I've told you, you're a pair of pretty things. Why worry about accessories? "

" Wait till you see us with our new haircuts. And I'm going to wear rose-colored smocks in Mr. Maulsby's garden — and learn to dance the Charleston." There was laughter in Theodora's eyes, but earnestness in her voice:

" You'll see. At Stephanie's next dance Sandra and I won't be wallflowers."

" Speak for yourself, Doady." Sandra, too, was smiling.

Mrs. Claybourne asked, " Were they really wallflowers? "

" It was my good luck that they didn't dance. Otherwise I shouldn't have had a look-in."

When Gale went away, he left them with a fine sense of his friendliness. They were all to have tea with his mother on Sunday.

" I shall feel safer if I have you tied up for two engagements," he told the twins. " And I shall never be able to call either of you ' Miss Claybourne.' I'm old enough to be your — godfather. You won't mind my calling them Sandra and Doady, will you, Mrs. Claybourne? "

" I think he's an adorable person," Sandra announced as she brushed her hair.

She said it frankly, because she wasn't in the least self-conscious. She had no blushes or heart-beats when she thought of Gale. She left her tremors and thrills for Rufus Fiske. She could not have spoken Rufus' name aloud if she had died for it.

It had grown warm again, and when a little later Sandra stepped out on the balcony, the world was flooded with silver. She stood by the rail and looked across the way. No one was there. The window was dark.

Oh, well, the night was heavenly . . . She flung herself down in the long chair, and gazed up at the sky . . . "*that orbed maiden . . . with white fire laden . . . whom mortals call the moon . . .*"

There intruded presently on her consciousness the sound of voices, and she became aware that two men were standing in the court below

" If I have a house, I must have a car. See what you can do for me, Williamson. Second-hand."

Williamson's voice had a youthful quality. " Sounds like matrimony to me. A house and a car."

" Only fools marry."

" Woman-hater? "

" No. But I have eyes to see. And there's so much unhappiness."

" And so much happiness. I'm going to make a try for it when I find the girl. If she'll have me."

" You can get any girl, if you really want her."

" That's easy enough for you to say. You've got the looks."

" Do you think I want to be married for my looks? "

" Well, you might be."

" Heaven forbid. I'm domestic enough with Griselda. I have money enough to support a cat, but not a wife. So why muddle things up."

" Some day you'll fall in love."

" Which has nothing to do with the case. One may fall in and out again."

" No," said Williamson stoutly, " if love is worth anything, it is for one woman. Men who squander sentiment on a half dozen don't know love when they see it."

Silence for a moment. " You are fortunate to think
that."

" I do think it. Constancy is the best gift of the gods.
Men and women who haven't it miss a lot."

" One may have it and yet not find an object on which
to bestow it."

Silence for a moment, then Williamson said: " You'll
wake up some day and want a home. A wife. Children."

" My dear fellow, I'm not romantic. And poverty
dims the glamour. Do you think I'd want a wife
getting red-faced and out of temper over the gas stove
on a night like this? I ate broiled fish and a salad three
miles out at a charming inn. I couldn't have afforded
it for two. And all Griselda asks for is a bit of salmon
from a can."

" Isn't there something in having a face on the other
side of the table? "

" I have a book to read. A cat to pet. That's enough
for me."

" I don't believe it. And I've got to be going, Fiske.
It's getting late."

" Come on up to my apartment. I've some pale dry
ginger ale on ice, and there's a bit of cheese and some
biscuits."

" You say that like an Englishman."

" I went to school in England. Two years there and
two in Germany, worse luck. I learned to speak German so well that when the war came they got me into

the secret service. The only good I'll ever get out of
that is a book I'm writing of my experiences. Some of
them seem pretty rotten when I put them on paper.
Things are expedient in time of war which don't quite
sway level in times of peace. I'm staying in Washington
because I can get some of the stuff I want up at the
Library of Congress. I go up there in the afternoons
and write at night. I want to get out in the country,
where I can have quiet. My nerves got touched up a bit
by the war. But it was worth it."

"Well," Williamson's voice was modified by distance
as he walked beside the other across the court, "I was
too young for it. But I'd give half I possess to have
been in it."

"That's what a neurotic world can't understand,"
Rufus Fiske said, "that death and terror were balanced
by bigger things. That the evils of peace at this
moment are worse for young men than war. You know
Noyes' 'Victory Dance.' That's what I mean —
'Back to the jungle the wild beasts prance!'"

Sandra strained her ears to hear more. But there
was no more coming. The two men had entered the
house.

After that it was quite like a pantomime, with the
two men crossing and recrossing the space between the
parted curtains. They ate and drank, and at last
Williamson left. And Rufus Fiske sat at the table
writing.

Sandra, watching him, thought of the things he had
said. He was hard. A cynic. She hadn't imagined
him like that. Yet his hand had been kind when he
stroked the cat.

Her mother came to the window. " Aren't you ever going to bed? "

" I'm not sleepy." She rose, however, and went in. " I feel as if I should never shut my eyes. I'll take something to read to bed with me. Perhaps it will make me drowsy."

She picked up one of the magazines that Theodora had brought, and carried it with her. Propped up on her pillows, with a low lamp flooding the pages with light, she found the book interesting. It had many colored illustrations and was packed with advertising of antiques and art objects.

Turning the pages idly, her eye was caught by a line of print:

" Wanted — To find a set of ivory figurines, Seventeenth Century, representing the Five Senses. Taken from private residence in Santa Barbara. Suitable reward for information or for return. Address L2. Care of this magazine."

The blood all seemed drained from Sandra's body. She spread her hands over the staring words to shut them from her sight.

After a while she grew a bit calmer. Snapped off the light and lay wide-eyed in the dark.

The thought which had frightened her was preposterous. A man like that couldn't. Yet what did she know of him except that he was kind to a cat and had a head like a Ganymede? And there was that impossible person in the pink bungalow apron.

" My husband says, ' Where does he get his money? ' "

Chapter VIII

SIXTY MINUTES

A T NOON on the day after Sandra read the advertisement, Rufus Fiske came into the great Library on Capitol Hill and made his way to an exhibit of etchings on the second floor. He would see them before he lunched, then settle down to a season of work in the alcove in the reading-room where a desk had been assigned to him.

He was to meet Williamson later and complete the purchase of a cheap little car, then ride out into the country to inspect such small houses as might promise shelter for himself and for his cat.

The etchings were worth seeing, and it was one o'clock before he left the gallery where they were displayed, walked to the top of the grand stairway, and stood looking down at the sightseers below who studied the signs of the Zodiac set in the floor, or stared up at the mural decorations and at the procession of enchanting marble children which decorate the balustrade.

Gradually there emerged from the midst of the indefinite individuals who composed the crowd, the very definite figure of a girl. She was standing on the lowest step of the right wing of the stairway. She had the air of waiting for some one. She kept looking this way and that and up and down.

It was during one of these ocular excursions that

she glanced up and caught Rufus' gaze. She gazed back for a startled moment, then a burning blush swept over the whiteness of her cheeks.

Rufus wondered why she blushed. His glance had been casual. Yet there had been that startled response to it. Oh, well, she was probably some self-conscious little thing waiting for her lover, all a-flutter with the thought that the world was watching.

Without seeming to observe her, he was aware that her small, close hat was green and that her tie was of the same clear hue. Shining locks of copper-colored hair came out from under the bright hat. As she had looked up at him he had noted the long-lashed eyes as unclouded as a child's.

She began to ascend the stairway at the same moment that he began to descend. They met half-way, and astoundingly she spoke his name.

" Mr. Fiske! "

He stopped at once, " I beg your pardon? "

" Mr. Fiske . . .! May I talk to you for a few moments? "

How frightened she was! He could see her heart beat in her throat.

" Mr. Fiske, I live in the same apartment house that you do, on the other side of the court. My sister works for Mr. Maulsby. Last night, when she came home, she brought a magazine. I read it. And I found an advertisement I think you ought to see."

He reflected, somewhat cynically, that her method of approach was at least original! He found himself murmuring bromidically, " An advertisement? "

" Yes. I have it in my bag."

She opened her bag and began to search for it. He was aware of her embarrassment and aware, too, of a certain excitement which made her awkward in separating the paper she sought from the others in the bag.

Rufus, looking down at her, had a sense of something familiar in her aspect. Where had he seen her? Suddenly it came to him. She was the little girl who had waved to her mother! The one who looked like " The Boy in Red! " He hoped he was not going to be disappointed in her. She had seemed such a child, yet here she was, apparently making an opportunity to meet him.

She found the paper and handed it to him. He read a marked paragraph, and when he raised his head, his eyes were blazing.

" Has anyone seen this? "

" No."

" Why did you bring it to me? "

" I thought you ought to know. Doady told me about the ivory figures. That you had sold them to Mr. Maulsby. I haven't said a word to anybody. I was on the balcony and heard you tell your friend that you came up here in the afternoons. It seemed better to speak to you away from home."

While she thought out her halting sentences, his blazing eyes seemed to challenge her motives.

" What do you think? That I am trying to hide something? "

" No," steadily. " I shouldn't have come if I had thought that. Mr. Fiske, I don't know just why I came. I only felt that you would want to see it before other people did. So that you could explain."

" There isn't anything to explain to you or any one."

" Oh," breathlessly, " I'm sorry — I bothered you."

" There isn't anything to explain," he repeated. " The whole thing is preposterous."

He was being brutal, and he knew it. The child was an honest little thing, who for some unknown reason had interested herself in his affairs. He acquitted her now of forwardness in her approach. She was too much in earnest, too unconscious of any effect she might be making. Yet — why couldn't she have let him alone? Why face him with a thing he wanted to forget? The chances were that Maulsby might not have seen the advertisement, or any one else who knew that he had sold the ivories . . .

Of course, Sherry was at the bottom of it. She wanted to hold him up to the world's scorn. She might even now be telling the story to the members of her set. Giving her own version of it.

Well, let her give it! If she wanted a fight on her hands, she could have it!

He came back to the child with the burning cheeks.

" It was good of you," he forced himself to say, " and I am grateful. May I keep the paper, and may I ask you not to speak of it? "

The blush faded. A hot light came into her eyes. " Do you think," she demanded, " that if I had intended to tell about it, I would have risked being misunderstood by coming here? "

She turned and started down the steps. He followed.

" I'm sorry," he said. " I am afraid I have been very rude. And please don't think that I misunderstand." He was finding himself unexpectedly on the defensive. " Won't you wait a moment while I tell you that it was a brave and beautiful thing for you to do? "

They had reached the lower floor, and as she stopped and turned toward him, he saw that her eyes were wet.

" It was a silly thing for me to do," she said. " I am always doing silly things and being sorry for them."

" You mustn't be sorry for this. You have really done me a great favor, although for the moment I was so disconcerted that I forgot my manners."

If he had hoped to win immediate forgiveness, he was disappointed.

" That's all," she said stiffly, " I must be going."

" No," he stepped in front of her so that he barred the way out. " You are not going. I want you to stay. I feel that I owe you an explanation about this advertisement. Will you let me tell you all about it? "

She stood like a bird poised for flight. " I don't expect you to tell me all about it."

" Please. And won't you forgive me? And, I'd appreciate it no end if you would have lunch with me. It's a long story, and we can talk better upstairs."

" Oh, I couldn't! " — breathlessly.

" Why not? "

She came back honestly: " What would you think of me? What would I think of myself? "

He swept that aside. " The whole thing is unconventional. You know it, and I know it. But I have said what I think — that you have done a brave and beautiful thing. I couldn't possibly misunderstand your motives. And I want you to know that while I have asked you to lunch with me, you need never speak to me afterward if you don't wish it. If you will give me an hour. Just enter my world for sixty minutes? After that, I promise you, you can cut me dead, if you like, and I'll — take my medicine — "

Sixty minutes! An hour of enchantment! It was like a gate swung back with gardens beyond. Or a door opened into a king's palace. Sandra was not strong enough to resist.

"Oh, well," she said. "Why not?"

"Why not, indeed?" he was smiling down at her. "And now we'll go upstairs, and I'll find a quiet table, and you shall tell me what you like to eat."

Like one in a dream she let him lead the way. They went to the top floor, and Rufus ordered food which sounded to Sandra's unsophisticated ears complicated, but delectable. And when the waiter had gone, he said:

"Do you know you are really not a stranger? That I've seen you before?"

"When?"

"The first time was years ago. I was sixteen. I saw a painting of you."

"Oh, you couldn't. No one has ever painted me."

He enjoyed her mystification: "A great artist did it. Before you were born. I saw the original in an art gallery, and the artist was Vigée LeBrun. I went back again and again to look at it. And the other day at Maulsby's I saw a print of the painting. And the other night, as I sat on my balcony, I saw two girls going to a party. And they stopped under a lamp, and one of them looked up and waved to her mother. And the one who waved looked like the picture in the famous gallery and like the print in Maulsby's. And after that, when I thought of the girl who waved, I called her ' The Boy in Red.' "

" Me? "

" You.   Do you like it? "

" Love it."   The wide-lidded eyes were lighted.

" Have you ever seen the picture? "

" No."

" Some day I'll take you to Maulsby's."

She shook her head, " Everything ends in sixty minutes."

" Do you really mean that? "

" It was you who set the time."

" I may beg you to give me an extension.   And by the way you haven't told me your name.   Your sister is Theodora Claybourne.   You see, I remember.   So you must be Miss Claybourne.   But what's the rest of it? "

" I'm Sandra."

" Sandra Claybourne?   It suits you.   I should have hated it if you had been Susan or Sarah."

The soup came.   A delicious soup.   Rufus took a taste or two, then forgot it while he talked.   " There's a lot back of that advertisement.   More than I have time to tell.   But I'd like you to know a little of it. Those words brand me as a thief.   And I'm not a thief.   The ivories are mine.   But I haven't a scratch of the pen to prove it.   The whole thing sounds like a something out of a book.   But it is real life as I have lived it since my mother died."

Leaning forward, he spoke in his low and pleasant voice, clipping his words a little in the English way.   As his story progressed Sandra hardly knew what she ate. It seemed incredible to her that she should be sitting

opposite the man she had first seen from her balcony
in the moonlight, while he poured out to her the tale
of the tragedy which for years had thwarted his life.
She felt that the confidence he was reposing in her
bound him to her in some subtle fashion. That even
if their acquaintance ended in sixty minutes, they would
still be united by a sense of spiritual understanding.
It was as if the little lad of whom he was speaking had
suddenly thrust his hand in hers and had asked her to
hold it tight.

When Rufus finished his story, the hour was almost
up. In that time the despairing waiter had brought
four courses of delectable food and had taken it away
scarcely tasted. It was, he reflected, as he went back
and forth with impassive face, a pity to waste gastro-
nomic perfection on young lovers. He thought them
that because of their preoccupation. He hoped for the
solace of a generous tip. The girl was unsophisticated,
but the man showed signs of the kind of cosmopolitan-
ism which knows how to bestow largesse for expert
service.

Dark and brooding, Rufus demanded finally, " You
see? "

" Oh, yes."

" Do you wonder that I have lost my faith in everything? In God? In man? "

She sat staring at him. Then, " Oh, don't you
believe in anything? "

A thousand people might have asked that of him,
and he would have flung back a savage " No." But
something puzzled and appealing in her earnest face,
made him say, " I wish I did."

Not for worlds would he have admitted that to any one else. For years he had covered his hurt with a protective shell of hardness. No one knew how passionately he yearned for the thing he had lost, for the dreams of the boy he once had been.

He was not to know until he looked back upon it later that this was the supreme moment. It was to hold in his life something of the significance of the dove flying above the waste of waters, or Blondin singing under Richard's window, or of the day when America first set her foot in France.

It was, in other words, rescue from the loneliness of his own unfaith. Neither of them knew as yet that Sandra had lighted at that moment the small taper of her belief in him that was to illumine increasingly his darkness as the days went on.

He asked her, hanging on his words: " What made you come to me? Most people would have let it pass. Wouldn't have cared — what happened."

How could she tell him? That for her he was Romeo on a balcony, Galahad, Apollo Belvedere, Ganymede, Booth, Barrymore, Ivanhoe — all the heroes of a romantic girlhood rolled into one. She had come to him that morning with an impassioned sense of adventure, such as had carried the happy princess beyond the purple rim, or Evangeline on her trackless pilgrimage. After that one dreadful moment on the stairway when Fiske had seemed to fail her, she had been swept on by his dominant demands. She felt at this moment that if he had asked her to set out with him on an endless quest, she would have followed him — forever —

Yet, thrilled and swept by the moment's exaltation,

this was what she said to him: " I saw you from my balcony. And I liked the way you treated your cat."

" So you saved Griselda's master because of Griselda? " He did not think her remark trivial, he saw her heart beating again in her throat, and having dealt much with women, knew something of the things that stirred her.

" Griselda's a great comfort. And a great care. I am hunting a house to keep her in."

He talked then of his plans. At last he said: " The hour is up. But it's got to be more than sixty minutes."

" I'm not sure it ought to be."

" Please. Can't you make it possible for me to meet you according to the mode? I might drop in at Maulsby's some day when you are to be there with your sister. We'll keep today to ourselves, and what I have told you. But if you'll give me permission to meet you properly, I'll ask you to lunch with me once a month."

All her gaiety, and the sense of humor which had been submerged by the sentiment of the situation, came back to her in a rush at the thought that this was not the end.

" How can I promise a thing like that? " she demanded. " Without a time limit? Twelve lunches a year? Twenty-four in two years? Sixty in five years? "

He flung back with amusement, " It would be almost like being married."

" And you'd only have to see a woman's face once a month on the other side of the table." She caught herself up, then confessed: " I have been eavesdropping. I was on my balcony, and I heard what you said to your friend."

" Williamson? He believes in romance. Poor fellow! "

" Don't you believe in it? "

" Only in books. It reads well. But one can't live by it."

" I am going to live by it. Mother does. Outside she's just tired and middle-aged and up against things. But inside she calls them ' other-world' dreams. I am sure she sees my father always in a garden, and herself walking beside him."

He admitted: " Sometimes I see my mother like that. But I know it is only because I want to think it, not because it is true."

" How do you know it isn't true? "

" It can't be proved."

" Nobody would believe the world was round before Columbus proved it. Skeptics never achieve anything. It is the dreamer who builds worlds."

He shelved that to ask again: " But romance? Don't you know that it is only in books that men are heroes and women angels."

" Who wants them to be heroes or angels. Romance isn't that. It isn't thinking people perfect. It is the adventure. It is courage and laughter and beauty . . ."

Surveying her with appreciation, he was aware that she typified the thing she spoke of. Gallant, vivid, impetuous, one felt that she would follow the road of life light-heartedly, singing a song.

" You ought to be a page with a feather in your cap, and a *viola-d'amore*." He was leaning back, smiling at her, his darkness gone.

" Perhaps some day I shall start out and sing for my suppers. And I shall be Xander and not Sandra."

Delicious fooling. She was like a child at fairy-tales.

He asked for his check, and while he waited for his change, he reminded her:

" You haven't accepted my invitation. I have asked you to lunch with me every month — twelve times a year — one hundred and twenty times in a decade."

" How can I accept an invitation like that? It's too fantastic. Each time must be a new engagement."

" Then you will? "

" Wait until we've been introduced. When our sixty minutes are ended, I am not supposed to know you."

He laughed. " When are you going to Maulsby's? "

" Oh, well — Saturday. We are to lunch with Mr. Markham. He and I will pick Theodora up at the shop."

" Good."

He gathered some bills from the little silver tray which the waiter was presenting, and rose. The waiter fluttered around them as they went. He reflected that he had not been mistaken in his man. His tip crackled in his pocket.

When they reached the first floor, Fiske took the longest way to the entrance. He was loath to let Sandra leave him. She was like some bright and lovely star which flamed across the darkness of his soul. He knew that when she was gone, all the past would surge upon him. There would be Sherry — as he had last seen her, in a red coat and white breeches and three-cornered hat. He hated the way she managed a horse, but she had made a picture of herself against the blue of the sea and the pale gold of the sands.

Passing through a dim corridor, Sandra stopped. " I love these paintings. Don't you? "

There were the boys of the poets in the lunettes along the walls — Adonis, a white and lovely figure dead in the forest with a wound in his side. Ganymede on his eagle, Endymion asleep under the moon, Uriel, Comus, The Boy of Winander . . .

" ' *There was a Boy: ye knew him well, ye cliffs* . . . ! ' " Sandra, quoting the verse, stopped in the middle. " Doady hates to have me do it. Recite poetry, I mean. She says I sound as if I came out of the ark." She was smiling up at him, her boy's chin tip-tilted. " Doady's adorable. But now and then mother and I find her trying. It's our own fault, of course. We don't want to move as fast as she wants us to."

She held out her hand to him. " Please don't go any farther. I have a feeling that I shall meet all my friends, and they'll ask me if I've been introduced to you."

He took that confiding hand in his. " Will you wave to me now and then from your balcony? "

" I'll wave — to Griselda," she showed him how she would do it, a charming gesture, then went away, leaving him among those lads of whom the poets dreamed, the dead Adonis, the scornful Uriel, and that Boy beside the lake of stars.

CHAPTER IX

SECOND THOUGHTS

T HERE is no reason," Rufus said that night
to his cat, " why a man should be a fool."
Griselda opened her pink mouth in a noiseless
mew. Her tail waved its triumphant plume. Rufus,
with a can-opener in his hand, was master of her fate.
If he chose to call himself a fool, she could not help it.
She loved him, but her mind was on salmon and her
much-delayed supper.

Rufus had dined with Williamson and had bought the
salmon on the way home. He had also bought the second-hand car and had agreed to buy a house.

With so many things between this hour of midnight
and the noon hour he had spent with Sandra, the glamour of her presence had faded. Old memories had
stirred in him. Old hatreds had stalked through the
dark recesses of his mind. What right had he to burden
that child with the whole story? He might have made
a partial explanation and let it go at that.

He had said to Williamson: " I'm afraid I am very
poor company. Something came up today that roused
a lot of sleeping devils."

Williamson was sympathetic. " Have 'em myself
sometimes."

" Not like mine. You're too young."

Williamson did not argue. He wished that he might

ask questions, but he dared not. He adored this new friend of his — this charming, cynical friend who seemed to know so much of the world, yet who dwelt like a hermit with his books and his cat.

Hesitating a little, the boy said: " Why look back? Why not look ahead? Do you know," he stammered a bit, trying to express his thought, " do you know, I like to think of you as you'll be when you are fifty. In the full use of your powers."

" How do you know I have any powers? "

" You have only to use them. I'd give ten years of my life to possess your brains and looks."

It was so sincerely said that Rufus was touched: " I wish I believed in myself as you believe in me."

They swung after that into more cheerful talk, and when dinner was ended, they drove out to look at some little houses which Williamson had on his list.

None of them suited Rufus. " They're so cramped," he complained, " and the grounds are no bigger than pocket-handkerchiefs."

" Well, what do you expect? " Williamson demanded. " A château? "

" I want something away from people. All these have neighbors."

Williamson considered that. " There's a man out in Maryland. It's twelve miles from the city. I'm not sure what we shall find."

" We'll try it. And the farther from the city, the better."

The man in Maryland had two cottages, as like as two peas, close together, and all fresh white paint with green blinds.

" They're pretty," Rufus said, " but too close together. Aren't any bigger than boxes."

The owner said, " What do you want? "

" I hoped for at least one big room, and a lot of
ground."

" Have you any furniture? "

" No."

" I don't know but I've got what suits you. It's
a bit rough. It is really a barn I built on a site where
I expected to build my home. But my wife thought it
was too far out, so we came down here. We lived in the
barn one summer, and there ain't never been an animal
in it. Now and then some campers come out, and we've
kept it furnished. If you wanted to live in it in winter,
I could put a stove in."

" The winter can take care of itself," Rufus said.
" Let's go over and look at it."

It was almost dark when they reached their destination, but the deep rose of the afterglow was back of the
hill on which the barn stood. The rich color showed
between the trunks of the pines which topped the hill,
and as the men left the car and took the path toward the
house, there was the soft singing of the trees, and the
fragrance of them, and the needles underfoot.

" Heavens, why didn't you show me this in the beginning? " Rufus' tone was querulous. " I'll take it, no
matter what the house may be."

The barn had been painted a dark green and was a
somewhat ungainly structure with its lines softened by
the vines which grew over it, and lightened at this season
by the bushes of bridal wreath which threw their veils
of whiteness against its gloom, and by the masses of

climbing roses, pink as the sunset sky.

There was a big barn door, and a smaller one. When a lamp within was lighted, and the doors were flung wide, the golden shadows of the interior seemed to merge themselves into the mauve shadows of the night, so that one had a sense of great space, as if the house were a part of the groves which surrounded it, and had grown there with the trees.

" We used one end of this as a living-room and the other as a dining-room. There's a room to correspond overhead, which can be divided by curtains. I built on a kitchen and a bathroom and had water piped up. The furniture isn't much, but most of it is strong, and there are grass rugs I can put in if you should decide to buy it."

" I have decided," Rufus said. " I decided it outside, and now that I am inside I want it more than ever."

He was standing in the great barn door. Beyond the pines there was a sweep of meadow straight to a twilight sky of amethyst.

He drew a deep breath. " I'll come on Monday. And I'll mail you a check tonight. Williamson can give you references."

" That's all right. And I'll have it cleaned for you."

The owner of the house was turning off the light. Outside were ghostly shadows. When Griselda came, Rufus reflected, she would be another ghostly shadow among the slender, sighing trees. How she would love it — the mysteries that matched her own! The sense of freedom. On a night like this he and she might walk for miles and meet no one.

It was not until he reached home that he thought

Chapter X

AGAIN THE BALCONY

SANDRA had been late on the balcony because of Ione Morton. Ione had unexpectedly come to spend the evening with the Claybourne family. " I am so lonesome," she had confessed, standing in the door. " Do you mind? "

They did mind. They preferred infinitely their own company. But what could they do? The hospitality of the Claybournes was a tradition and a sacred trust. Guests, however intrusive, were never turned away. So it happened that Ione Morton, crude and commonplace, and utterly unconscious of any social difference, thinking herself as good in every way as this plain, grayhaired woman and her shabby little daughters, was admitted, and sat on the edge of her chair, and talked all the evening about her neighbors.

And as she talked, Sandra began to see the house in which she lived as something less than the pleasant place she had thought it. She had met none of the people, but she had liked to look at them, to watch the young mothers sewing on their balconies, the young fathers coming home at night, the babies gay in the grassy court. She had thought it all very domestic and charming if a little crowded, and she had known of nothing sordid or scandalous or even sorrowful in the histories of any of them.

But Ione Morton knew. She did not see things in the least as Sandra saw them. The babies did not seem to her gay, or the mothers contented, or the fathers happy. She was not very gay herself, and she did not want other people to be gay. She was not contented, and she felt that others must share her discontent. She was not happy, and she envied the happiness of others; she refused, indeed, to believe in it. She did not like books; she did not like her day's work; she was satiated with cheap pleasures, and so, with nothing to fill her mind, she got a certain triumphant satisfaction in finding flaws in the lives of those about her.

Mrs. Claybourne listening with shocked politeness, tried to lead the conversation into other channels. Sandra and Theodora, less shocked perhaps, but feeling that the thing had gone too far, aided and abetted their mother.

Ione, however, refused to talk of anything else. And she came at last triumphantly to a climax.

" You know that Mr. Fiske? Well, he's moving away."

" What Mr. Fiske? " Theodora demanded.

" Rufus Fiske. Across the court. Your sister knows who I mean."

Sandra, trying to seem at ease, said: " Mrs. Morton told me the other day that Rufus Fiske lives in this house. I don't think I mentioned it to you, Doady."

" No, you didn't." Theodora turned to Ione, "Mr. Fiske comes sometimes to the shop where I work."

" What kind of a shop? "

Theodora told about it. Ione found it hard to understand what Maulsby sold.

" I don't see why anybody would pay such a lot for old things."

Sandra was glad Theodora did not mention the ivories. She was sure Ione would have found something sinister in Rufus' possession of them. As it was, she said with sharpness:

" I don't see why a man should want to go out and live in a house alone. It ain't natural. I heard he was leaving here from the manager."

Having made the most of her conversational ammunition and still unaware of the unfavorable impression she had created in the minds of the Claybournes, Ione rose to go.

" I hate to leave. When my husband ain't home, it's dead lonesome. Say, I wish you girls would let me take you to a movie sometime. In the afternoon. I'd pay for the tickets, and I'd like the company. What do you say about Saturday? "

She was wistful about it, and for the first time Sandra saw her as pathetic. Ione, in that limited life of hers, lacked friends and did not know how to win them. Sandra wondered what such a woman would be if she had spent her childhood at Windytop and had had a lovely mother. It made, after all, a difference.

Theodora was saying: " We can't possibly go on Saturday. We are lunching with a friend."

" On Sunday then."

" We are to have tea with some people in Georgetown."

" Do you mean supper? "

" No. In the afternoon."

" I've heard people talk," Ione said, " about serving

afternoon tea. But I never did it. What's the difference between that and supper? "

Mrs. Claybourne elucidated. " Giving your friends a cup of tea is a nice, easy way to be hospitable."

" I'm afraid I ain't hospitable. It's always such a lot of trouble to have people in to eat. And my husband would laugh if I gave anybody tea. He'd want to mix cocktails for 'em. You know men are like that. He don't feel he is doing anything if he can't offer a highball or something."

When Ione had gone, Theodora said hotly: " Oh, she is dreadful, Sandra. How did you happen to meet her? "

" She spoke to me from the balcony. I think she is dreadful too, Doady. But I feel sorry for her."

" Why should you feel sorry? "

" For being so dreadful. Now and then she seems rather simple and sweet."

Mrs. Claybourne agreed. " But I hope she won't come again. We'd hate to hurt her feelings, but I can't have you making such friends."

" Of course not," Theodora emphasized. " Sandra, how funny that Rufus Fiske should live in this house."

" Isn't it? " Sandra, to hide her agitation, seemed to stifle a yawn. " I'm going to bed."

" So am I in a minute." Theodora's mind was still on Rufus. " It might be pleasant to ask Mr. Fiske here some time when we have Gale Markham."

" You heard Mrs. Morton say he's leaving."

" Oh, well, that wouldn't prevent his coming now and then. And from what I've seen of him, he seems good company."

Good company, indeed! Oh, what would they say if they knew she had lunched with him, was to lunch with him again? Twelve times in a year . . . sixty times in five years . . . Oh, how silly to think of it . . . !

Having brushed her hair and donned her white kimono, Sandra lingered in her mother's room. " There are moments," she said, " when I wish we had never left Windytop."

" Homesick, my darling? "

" A little."

" I know how you feel. These June days . . . with the rose-leaves blowing . . ."

" And the breeze in the pines! Mother, some time you and I will run down and sniff the roses."

" Some day we'll go back forever," her mother said with fervent emphasis.

And suddenly Sandra in a panic knew that she didn't want to go so far that she couldn't have lunch with Rufus Fiske. Twelve times! Sixty!

With her hand on the latch of the long window, she said, " I'll have a look at the moon."

" It's too late for the moon, dearest."

" Oh, well, I'll get a whiff of air."

" You are a perfect Juliet," her mother informed her, " hanging over that balcony."

For one breathless moment it seemed to Sandra that her mother was clairvoyant. Then Mrs. Claybourne added:

" But there isn't any Romeo. Come here and kiss me ' good-night.' If you are going to stay out there long, I shall be sound asleep."

So they had their little ceremony. " *Good-night, my precious.*" " *Good-night, my darling.*" Then Sandra stepped out to meet enchantment.

All about the court was darkness. Peering down into the blackness, she thought she saw the spark of a cigarette on Fiske's balcony. Was he there? Looking up?

Presently she knew! For a light flared, and she saw Rufus standing against the glow of it. She saw his hand go up . . . his salute . . .

She wished she might call down to him. That they might speak, as long ago those other lovers spoke. But here were a thousand ears! These balconies were not made for trysts. They were travesties on that one which years ago o'erhung a garden . . .

Yet he was there. And she was here. In the dark she blew him a kiss. He would never know. And no ears could hear or eyes could see. Her eyes feasted on him standing tall and splendid in the lighted space.

Chapter XI

IN WHICH STEPHANIE SPOILS A PARTY

SATURDAY morning!

Sandra was not sure whether she was glad or sorry that she was so soon to see Rufus. The thing that faced her was, in a way, stupendous. In all her life she had never hidden anything from her mother, and now she must keep to herself the fact that she had lunched at the library with a perfectly strange young man; had promised him her friendship, future meetings.

After this, of course nothing would be done clandestinely, yet she had an uneasy feeling that her compact with Rufus might have results beyond her control. Having told her his secret, he had asked that she keep it to herself. She was linked to him by a promise which had for its basis a bit of deception which made her uncomfortable.

" I wish mother knew," she told herself soberly as she put on the green hat and green tie and surveyed herself in the mirror.

The reflection pleased her and drove her worries for the moment from her mind. She wondered how she would look in red. She had been thrilled by Rufus' talk of her resemblance to the portrait. She had always been somewhat healthily unconscious of her charms, but now, seeing herself with Rufus' eyes, she linked herself romantically with the lovely ladies of Reynolds and

Romney and Gainsborough. She did not, of course, belong among them, but if Rufus put her there, why question his right to do it?

Gale, calling for her a little after twelve, sensed in her some new quality. A deepening of the girlish prettiness into something like beauty. He thought it might be the way she was dressed, the tender color she had chosen to wear.

" I like your hat," he said, as he took his place beside her in the rackety car.

" Oh, do you? Doady and I treated ourselves on the strength of her new job."

" Is her hat green? "

" Blue. You'll see how nice she looks."

" I see how nice you look."

When they reached the shop, Maulsby was out, and Theodora was busy. Fiske had not arrived. Gale and Sandra wandered through the rooms. Sandra knew what she was looking for, but she said not a word about it. Her eyes went from wall to wall as they passed through, and she was glad when Theodora joined them and said,

" Let's go out to the garden."

" You two run along," Sandra told her. " I'll come in a minute. I want to roam about a bit."

When at last she came upon what she sought, she had a pang of deep disappointment.

" Do I look like that? " she demanded of herself with something of dismay.

For here was no romantic beauty. Just a madcap boy, with a sidelong glance and a cocky turn of the head.

As she continued, however, to gaze upon the picture, she was aware of certain charms which had escaped her. The fresh youthfulness of the little lad, the lovely parted lips, the exquisiteness of the flush on the smooth cheeks, the limpid beauty of the laughing eyes.

Suddenly she heard a voice behind her, " You see? "

She whirled around and faced Fiske. " Oh! " she said, and that was all.

" So you hunted him up? " There was amusement in his voice. " Do you like him? "

" I didn't at first."

" Why not? "

Her honesty was matched by her sense of humor. " I hoped I was better-looking."

His shout of mirth reached Gale and Theodora, who had stopped to examine some Irish glass in the adjoining room. They turned and came back.

" I didn't know you two had met," Theodora said. " This is my sister, Sandra, Mr. Fiske."

Fiske answered her without a moment's hesitation. " We were introduced by ' The Boy in Red.' I found your sister standing here and was struck by her resemblance to the portrait."

Gale and Theodora looked at Sandra and looked at the print.

" Sandra's much better-looking," Theodora decided.

" That's what I said," Sandra informed her. " And Mr. Fiske laughed at me. I think the boy is frightfully attractive, but I had hoped for something prettier, like the Princes in the Tower."

" There's something more in that picture," Rufus assured her, " than mere prettiness."

Gale agreed with him. " There's youth, and a sparkling quality as if he drank of the wine of life."

Theodora interposed: " I don't believe you men know each other. Mr. Fiske, this is Gale Markham. Shall we all go into the garden? I can't leave until Mr. Maulsby comes."

Maulsby, arriving a little later, was told by Gale: " I am taking your new assistant to lunch. Have you any objection? "

" None, except to be sure that she is back on Monday morning."

"I'm glad you feel like that about it," Theodora said, and presented him to her sister. " Mr. Fiske thinks Sandra looks like Vigée LeBrun's ' Boy in Red.' "

" Take off your hat," Maulsby directed, " and let me see."

When it was off, Maulsby stated: " Fiske's got an eye. The resemblance isn't apparent at first glance, but it grows upon one. But he shouldn't tell you such things, Miss Sandra. They aren't good for little girls. Too many compliments."

They let him rattle on for a time. The four of them were perfectly content. The garden was all blossoming fragrance; the birds were flying; the sunshine made shadows under the trees. The day was wonderful.

At a quarter after one Gale rose. " We must be getting on. I told Stephanie to meet us at the restaurant."

" Stephanie Moore? " Maulsby asked.

" Yes."

" She's dining with us tonight. We are giving a dinner to a visiting antiquary. He's rather unusual.

A Scotsman, and young. So we're asking some young people to meet him."

" Your wife asked me. I'm sorry I couldn't accept. But I have another engagement."

Fiske saw Markham and the twins to the rackety car. He wished that he might have been asked to join the party. But of course he couldn't expect that. Nobody knew who he was. Except Sandra. And she was pledged to secrecy.

He went back to give Maulsby his new address and found him at the telephone. When he hung up the receiver, Felix said: " My wife's been disappointed in not getting enough men for her dinner. I wonder if you'd do me a great favor and accept a belated invitation? I can promise you a rather interesting time. And some charming people."

" My dear man," Rufus told him, " you are taking a sporting chance in asking me. You don't even know that I have a dinner coat."

" I have eyes," Maulsby said. " And I know a gentleman when I see one."

" I don't go to dinner parties."

" Go to this one," Maulsby entreated. " Marcia has put it up to me, and all the men in our crowd are out of town or at the country club on Saturday afternoons."

Rufus consented reluctantly. He was letting too many things encroach upon his solitude. First, Sandra, and now this demanding person who had to have a guest for dinner.

Passing through the rooms, they came once more upon the print of " The Boy in Red."

" I want it," Rufus said. " I have always liked it, and now that I have bought a house, I can hang it on my walls."

He told of his cottage. " It is as quiet as the grave and as restful as a monastery. You must come and see it."

" I will. I've always yearned for a thing like that, but I've married a wife."

The touch of cynicism was echoed in Rufus' mind: a wife was a millstone about a man's neck, thwarting him. Or if she was gentle and clinging, masculine brutality broke her heart. As he went toward home, he told himself that there must be no philandering with this child, Sandra. Waving one's hand on balconies didn't last. Romance was fleeting. The Romeos and Juliets got the worst of it. The sooner he packed his bags and got away, the better. Among the pines he and Griselda would find peace without entangling alliances.

He bought the print, however. Maulsby gave it to him at a bargain price and threw in the frame. Rufus reflected that it would be a reminder of the gay little girl when he saw her no more and she had forgotten him.

Meanwhile Sandra, unaware of the decision which would have darkened her day, was riding with Gale and her sister along the narrow streets back of the old market.

The news of Stephanie's inclusion in the party had been dampening to the spirits of the twins. It had seemed a great adventure to go with Gale, and they had felt no lack in themselves. Happy and contented in their little new hats and white dresses, they had looked forward to their outing without a cloud to darken their anticipation. But with Stephanie and her elegancies imposed upon them, they were aware of a new aspect.

Theodora indulging herself in one of her unspoken staccato conversations, was indignant. *If we had known she was coming, we might have spent more money on ourselves. We're nice enough for Gale. He's the kind of man who looks beyond clothes. But Stephanie has an air of putting it over on us . . . I wish he hadn't asked her.*

They found the restaurant, when they came to it, on the second floor above an old commission house. It was a simple, pleasant place, and in the low-ceiled room which they first entered were well-scrubbed tables, counters covered with white oil cloth, and on the counters bright, nickel-plated urns, colorful bottles of condiments, and big blue bowls of crackers.

Gale led them beyond this room to a veranda which overlooked the river and the piers where the Norfolk boat and the excursion steamers stood at rest. To the right was the tall shaft of the Monument, to the south the wide sweep of the Potomac. A fresh west breeze blew in their faces; the water was ruffled by it, and the flags on the boats fluttered.

Gale pointed out to the girls the small boats bringing up fruits and vegetables to the market.

"In winter they have cargoes of oysters. There are soft and hard crabs coming now, and of course there will be watermelons in a month, with the boats sunk to the water's brim with the weight of them.

Nothing is so picturesque as it used to be, for there are fewer sails, with the motor engines doing everything with more speed. And many of the crops are brought in motor trucks over the good roads."

Their table was set on the veranda under a wide awning. The linen was coarse, the china and glass heavy, but everything was clean and shining.

" I told you things might be a bit crude," Gale said to them, " but the food is delicious."

Stephanie, arriving, seemed somewhat out of tune with her surroundings. It was not that she was too elaborately fine, but that she was too elaborately simple. A coat of rough, white homespun covered a plain frock of white silk. A white felt hat, white shoes. Mauve stockings, white suède gloves. Exquisite, nothing to criticize. Yet the twins positively squirmed with a sense of their own contrasting cheapness. Stephanie was like a snowball from a spring bush, or a cloud in a summer sky. Like thistledown on a May morning.

She stood poised for a moment in the doorway which led out on the veranda, then she said, " Gale, what an adorable place! Why haven't you brought me here? "

Not waiting for an answer, she came forward, two young men followed her.

" You said to pick up two," she told Gale, "and here they are."

She introduced the young men. Their names were Smith and Darrow. It didn't in the least matter, Theodora decided, whether they had any names. They were obviously Stephanie's satellites. They were there because of Stephanie, and for no other reason. If they spoke to the twins, it was with an air of not seeing them. If the twins spoke, they seemed to listen with one ear, or perhaps a half of one. If, on the contrary, Stephanie spoke, they hung on her words. She was the goddess. They tended her altar. Other flames might flicker and die. They neither knew nor cared.

It was Gale who kept things going. He drew out the twins delightfully. He refused to have them over-looked. They found themselves gradually at their ease. And with the ice once broken, they gave of their best in gaiety and girlish chatter.

The lunch was delicious. Crabs browned in their own red shells, a basket of French bread. A crisp salad.

Stephanie's praise rang with a sincere note. "I never tasted anything better than these crabs. Why haven't you found this place for me before, Gale?"

"I was afraid you might spoil it," he told her honestly.

"Spoil it?"

"Yes. By making it fashionable."

She was flattered. "Well, if I could, why not?"

"Heaven forbid! In a week they'd be having blue candles and Batik. Do let us have one bit of American atmosphere amid all the welter of foreign effects. If you try to change this place, Stephanie, I'll drop you from my list."

She flashed a smile at him. "I dare you."

"I am warning you. If you bring jazz and Russian tea down here, I shall cast you off without a shilling."

"Oh, well . . . Of course, I like it this way, Gale. But you'll have to confess it is crude."

"That's its charm. It is clean and has delicious

cooking. I don't miss pink lights and a saxophone."

" Pink lights and saxophones have their place."

" Perhaps, but their place isn't here. This is the last outpost of old-time simplicity."

" I am not sure that I care for simplicity."

The astute Theodora became increasingly aware that below this argument was something which did not appear on the surface. Gale's manner was heated as he flung out,

" Oh, well, you're a bit of a snob, Stephanie." The twins held their breath. Such plain speaking! And rather rude of their friend Gale. Smith and Darrow bent down to their goddess solicitously. But Stephanie leaned over and brushed Gale's hand with the tips of her fingers. It was hardly more than the touch of a butterfly's wing, but it had the effect of a caress.

" Don't be so cross," she said.

" We might not have been there at all," Theodora told Sandra that night, with some indignation. " I never saw anything so — unblushing."

Sandra, indignant too, but immensely interested, said, " He didn't seem to notice it any more than a fly — or a mosquito."

For Gale had calmly countered: " I'm not cross. It is only that you don't like the truth about yourself."

" What is the truth? "

" That you are wrapped in cotton-wool."

Stephanie kept her temper. " Tut, tut," she said. " If you don't stop saying such things to me, I shall run away."

She rose and turned to the twins. " May I drop you anywhere? " she asked.

Before they could speak, Gale interposed. " I am taking them for a rubber-neck ride. We are going to see everything."

" Why can't we all go? In my car? "

" You'd be bored stiff. You'd better run along with Smith and Darrow, and I'll deliver these pretty things at their own front door."

For the first time her composure was ruffled. " You'll do as you please, of course. You were always high-handed."

" Not always! " His tone was significant.

Stephanie flushed. " That's not quite — fair."

She went away soon after that, with her two satellites. And after she was gone, Gale stood looking out over the sun-lighted river.

" I am sorry," he said at last, " that I lost my temper. I am afraid I said things I shouldn't. But Stephanie . . . doesn't fit in . . . She is a very lovely person . . . I am always trying to make her fit . . . and then losing my temper because she doesn't . . . ."

" It was more," was Theodora's later deduction, " as if he were apologizing to himself than to us. Of course, there's something behind it. I wonder if he's in love with her."

Sandra shook her head. " She's in love with him."

" How do you know."

" Because if she wasn't, she'd never forgive him for the things he said to her. Yet she had forgiven him before she went away. I saw her touch his hand again with her finger-tips."

" It's as if she draws him," the wise Theodora remarked, " and he doesn't want to be drawn. As if he is fighting against something that he is afraid may conquer him."

There was no doubt about it that Stephanie had in a way spoiled the party. Gale gave them a wonderful ride, but they were subtly conscious that something had gone out of him when Stephanie left — he fell now and then into fits of abstraction. His eyes had a far-away look.

" I'd be willing to bet my hat that when he got home he telephoned to her and apologized," Theodora told her twin. " He had it on his mind."

Sandra agreed. " I know it. But I hope he didn't say he was sorry. He was rude, but Stephanie isn't the kind to understand an apology. She will put her foot on his neck and keep it there."

CHAPTER XII

A GUEST OF HONOR

A S HE got into his dress clothes, Rufus asked himself why he had promised to dine with the Maulsbys. He didn't want to do it. What he wanted was to sit at his table and fill page after page of yellow paper while Griselda sang at his elbow, and there were no disturbing humans to trouble his soul.

Tonight should end it. After that he would seek the solitude of the pines. Williamson might now and then bear him company, or at a pinch, Maulsby. But there must be no other interruptions. Even the little girl, with her engaging charms of youth and naïveté, must be thrust out.

He drove to Maulsby's great place in the suburbs in his own small car. He smiled as he parked modestly among the limousines and was aware of the arrogance of the liveried chauffeurs. He envied no man his grandeur. Sumptuous motors and smart drivers had nothing to do with happiness. It was a gift of the gods. That shabby child who had lunched with him could more than match any woman of fortune in her air of gaiety and good humor.

As he ascended the steps of the terrace, he told himself that Maulsby's taste in residences was as impeccable as in antiques. The gray stone edifice was set in a formal garden; a fountain played, and there was a statue here and there; an old-world atmosphere of quiet loveliness.

Entering the doors, Rufus found a pale illumination which seemed to repeat the enchantment of the out-of-doors. The drawing room was in gold and ivory. The ceiling was high, and there was a crystal chandelier. The wide stretch of polished floor glimmered like a pool under the moon.

Mrs. Maulsby proved to be a rather splendid person. No longer young, she carried herself with the complacence of a one-time beauty. She had brought a large fortune to her husband, and she adored him. The price of her adoration and of his augmented income was a continued demand on him for the attentiveness of a lover. If at times this attitude wore on him, he did not let her know it. He conceded to her her aura of romance, and she moved, glorified, in the midst of it.

"I am giving you Stephanie Moore as a table companion," Marcia Maulsby told Rufus. "She's the most attractive girl here. And I thought you deserved a reward for helping us out."

He smiled at her. "I need no reward."

Marcia began to be sorry that she was not to sit beside him. She thought him extremely good-looking. Felix had not told her that. He had simply assured her that her guest would be presentable.

Stephanie wore orchid tulle and some lovely pearls. Rufus found her easy to talk to. She was, he at once divined, socially expert. She chattered about trivial things, feeling her ground, as it were, for some common interest.

"I've had such a day," she said. "I lunched at a

quaint place down by the river. But I'm not to tell about it."

" Why not? "

" For fear it may get to be fashionable, and that would spoil it."

" I'll promise not to make it fashionable."

She gave him the address. " You may not care for it. I am not sure that I do. I don't mind going now and then to such places, but as a rule I want things like this — " A wave of her hand indicated the center-piece, a tall, silver dish filled with green and purple grapes and pomegranates, with the candlesticks of carved Dutch silver set foursquare and holding pale green candles.

" Marcia has perfect taste," Stephanie continued. " Nobody else would have thought of putting those little ivory figures along the table."

Rufus looked, and with a leap of the heart saw the five nymphs. The light of the candles flowing over them gave them an almost fluid quality as if they moved and breathed.

" Aren't they adorable? " Stephanie was asking.

" They are more than that." He did not say that they had once been his. " Which do you like best? "

She studied them for a moment. " The one with the rose."

" Why? "

" Oh, fragrance is such a tangible thing to me. When I get a whiff of the perfume of certain flowers, I am carried back; wet violets, and my first lover; roses, and my first big dance; honeysuckle, and renunciation."

" Renunciation? You should never be sad."

" Why not? "

" Oh, the world should belong to beautiful women."

" We have our — tragedies — "

The eyes she raised to his were, he felt, too calm and cool for any knowledge of acute suffering. Yet the touch of pensiveness added to her attractions, and she knew it. She was not ingenuous, although she gave the effect of it. She was, in fact, playing a game to which sentiment added piquancy. It was not unpleasant to play the game with her. He leaned forward a little.

" Tonight there are no flowers. No fragrances. How will you — remember? "

Her pointed finger traced a pattern on the tablecloth. " I shall remember — Will you? "

She flashed a smile at him, then turned and talked to the guest of honor on the other side of her. Rufus was filled with admiration of her expertness. How perfectly she understood the effect of challenge. When she turned again to him, she would expect him to go on playing the game.

Well, why not go on playing? She was delightful to look at, delicate, sophisticated, with a thousand subtle perfections. And he was not dead to such charms.

Yet why should he be held by subtlety, sophistication? Women like Stephanie were the same the world over. The child in the cheap little hat was, on the other hand, as individual as if a mold had been made for her and broken. She had no arts with which to augment her attractions. Only a fundamental sincerity. Only a faith in God and man that made his throat ache when he thought of it. How quickly she had taken her place

in his life! And now she must go out of it. Must.
There was no alternative.

Stephanie, turning back to him, found him unresponsive. At last she said,

"A penny for your thoughts."

"I am sorry. Was I being rude?"

"You were not being interested. And I am not used
to it."

Again there was that effect of challenge. Oh, well,
he might as well give her, for the moment, what she
demanded.

Marcia Maulsby watching the two of them, said to
the young antiquarian,

"Isn't Miss Moore charming?"

"Oh, very. I talked to her a bit but she likes the
other chap better. He knows how to say pretty things.
I know nothing but antiques."

"But you know them so well."

She smiled at him brilliantly, but knew in her heart
that she was bored. The young antiquarian was not
a success. He might be famous, but he was excessively
one-ideaed. She didn't in the least blame Stephanie for
preferring Rufus.

However, she had to talk. No hostess could sit dumb
and unresponsive with a celebrity at her side. She
grasped at anything.

"Did you notice my table decoration?"

"The ivories. Yes —" He stopped there.

"They are really quite worth while. Felix brought
them home today." She reached for one of them, set it
before him. "The five senses. This is the loveliest.
It represents Touch. That hand smoothing the leopard

skin . . . Do you see? "

He was examining the little figure through his glass.
" By Jove! "

He seemed after that so preoccupied that Marcia
turned from him to the man on her left. She was glad
that they had reached the last course and would have
coffee on the terrace . . . Felix, at the other end of the
table, was as fresh as a daisy. But then he had on each
side of him a vivacious young matron. No dry-as-dust
antiquary. On the terrace they could dance — with
the radio furnishing the music . . .

The ices were being eaten. Pale green in silver
shells. Stephanie, finishing hers, said to Rufus:

" But I must talk to this other man. He's here to
be lionized. And he won't like being neglected."

" He's perfectly happy," Rufus informed her. " He
has nabbed one of those nymphs and is cataloguing
her in his mind."

Stephanie turned to the antiquary. " Are you? "
" Am I what? "

" Cataloguing that little figure? Or are you planning
to carry it off when Felix isn't looking? "

" Neither. I was trying to decide something? "
" Really? "

" Yes. The ethics of a thing. Whether I ought to
tell my host something that I know about these ivories."

" Tell me, and I'll decide for you."

He shook his head. " What does a pretty woman
know about ethics! "

" That's the first compliment you've paid me."

" Well — you American women are spoiled." He
smiled at her. " I can't compete with that chap on

the other side of you. How long have you known him? "

" We met — tonight."

" And already you're making love to each other."

" Oh, no, we're not. It's just a game. I know it. And he knows it. But it's great fun."

The young antiquary decided that she was really very beautiful. He bestirred himself. " Suppose you teach me — the game? "

" Now? "

" We're having coffee on the terrace. Mrs. Maulsby said so. Perhaps you'll say some of the things to me that you've said to that young — gamester on your right."

Behind the young antiquary's glasses his eyes twinkled. He was really not so dry as Marcia had deemed him. And there were other things in this world besides antiques. But he rarely thought them worth going after.

There was no moon, when at last Marcia and her guests assembled on the terrace, but there were many stars. Marcia made Rufus sit beside her.

" My guest of honor seems to have waked up. He has carried Stephanie down to the lower end of the garden."

" She is teaching him a game," Rufus said with a note of laughter. " He asked her to. She told me."

" What kind of game? "

" The one she was playing with me."

Marcia was impatient. " I don't understand."

" The game lovely women like to play. I may have to go down, when I finish my coffee, and rescue her."

Stephanie, however, needed at the moment no help. The young antiquary was being told about fragrances. *Wet violets, and my first lover; Roses, and my first big ball,* and all the rest of it.

The young antiquarian refused to be impressed even by *honeysuckle — and renunciation.* "Flower perfumes are commonplace," he informed her. "I have memories — of amber and myrrh, spices and sandalwood."

"Tell me about them," Stephanie entreated. It was one of her assets that she could make men talk about themselves. "You must have had some marvellous adventures."

He had. He gave her something new — exotic. She found herself listening, forgetting that she had promised Rufus to come back. Forgetting that she had agreed to dance with him. Even as Rufus had played the game with her, so she had played it with him. But here was something that went beyond the game, a vivid history of a man's achievement. Stephanie's brains were better than she believed them. She had an intelligence which as a rule she refused to exercise. Society demanded certain things of her, and she gave them. Out here in the dark, it was pleasant to relax for a time and listen to the sure, young voice which had so much to tell.

She was almost startled when he stopped and said:

"I've talked enough — and now, since you've taught me the game, I must give you a souvenir." In the dark he reached for her hand, laid something in it. "All the odors of Araby are in it," he said.

"What is it?"

" I'm afraid I can't tell you. Nobody knows. Do you like it? "

" Oh, it is heavenly."

" I took it from the hand of a mummy. A queen we found in a great tomb. It was wonderful to think that all these years her little hand had held it."

" A bit — gruesome."

" I think not. She has been a thousand years in Paradise."

" Oh, if you look at it that way."

" What other way can I look at it? Death is not the end."

Marcia and Rufus were walking in the garden. " Stephanie," Marcia said, stopping in front of the absorbed couple, " you have missed three dances."

" Well, I'm having such a gorgeous time."

" Come on into the house. Felix has some new things he wants everybody to look at."

Stephanie, walking beside Rufus, said: " I really liked our antiquary. And I really listened. Usually I don't."

" Don't what? "

" Listen when men talk intelligently."

Rufus wondered if, after all, there were some depths in her he had not sounded. Perhaps, having only trivial things to give her, he had received only trivial response.

" Let's have one dance," he said.

The terrace was deserted, but the radio was still broadcasting. They danced in perfect step. Rufus enjoyed it.

" I hate to go in," he remarked when they had

finished.

"But we must. Felix won't like it if we don't look at his treasures."

As they came into the drawing-room, they found the guests grouped around their host, who had one of the ivory figures in his hand.

"I want all of you to see these at close range," he was saying.

Stephanie crossed the room and dropped down in a chair beside the young antiquarian, who looked up and smiled at her. Rufus, falling back to the edge of the group, wished that he might go home. He had had enough. Stephanie in orchid tulle under the crystal chandelier was a being who did not belong to his world. Nor did he want her to belong to it.

Maulsby, with another of the nymphs in his hand, also stood under the crystal chandelier. "It is hard to decide which is the most perfect."

The young antiquary spoke, "Where did you get them?"

"Bought them. A few days ago."

"Who sold them to you?"

Maulsby's lips twisted in a shrewd smile. He did not intend to tell that he had bought them of Rufus. Such things were between the parties of the sale and were not to be talked about.

"I got them of a man who said they were heirlooms."

The young antiquary leaned forward in his chair. He had, apparently, at last decided what was the ethical thing to do. "I have an idea that you've been fooled, Maulsby."

"What do you mean?" sharply.

"Well, I read an advertisement yesterday in one of the trade magazines. It describes those figurines perfectly and says that they were stolen from a private residence."

Rufus heard. Back of them all, listening.

"Nonsense!" Maulsby was saying. "It couldn't have been these."

"My dear fellow, I'm sure of it. Perhaps I shouldn't have said anything . . ."

Marcia's voice interposed. "Felix, where did you get them?"

There was a moment's hesitation, then Felix said: "I bought them of a man whose honor I cannot question. If they were stolen, he is not the thief."

His guest stated with some cynicism: "We are all thieves. Is there any honor among antiquaries?"

Rufus had risen. He came forward and stopped under the glittering chandelier. He was aware of Stephanie, of the pale beauty of her gown, of her fair hair shining under the light.

He was aware too of the startled faces turned up to him.

"The figures were mine," he said. "I sold them to Maulsby on Thursday morning."

Chapter XIII

THE OPEN GATE TO ROMANCE

RUFUS' head was flung back, his chin up, his tall figure at ease. Debonair, with that sardonic gleam in his eye, he faced the startled group, while the echo of his astounding confession broke against their silence.

Then Maulsby began an excited protest. " My dear fellow, you needn't have told that."

" Why not? " He said it lightly, and how could they know he hated it, this pose of insensibility, when his blood was boiling?

" Why shouldn't I? " he went on. " The figures were mine until I sold them to Maulsby. And that's all there is to it, except that I am sorry to expose a family skeleton. The ivories are heirlooms. More than one of us wanted them, and the others won't admit my right of ownership."

The young antiquarian helped out by saying: " Look here, old chap, I'm half sorry you didn't steal them. All's fair in our game. We're rather a ghoulish lot. We rifle tombs and all that."

Rufus smiled at him. " Probably some of you are asking why, if I wanted them so badly, I was willing to sell them. Well, that's another family skeleton."

He stopped then, knowing their curiosity was at high pitch, but not willing to gratify it. He stepped down from the stage and dropped into a chair beside Stephanie.

"Are you willing to speak to me?" he demanded.

"It was thrilling."

"Well, there was nothing else to do, was there? I didn't want to embarrass Maulsby."

The people about them were examining the ivories with more attention than they had heretofore given them. In low tones they talked about Rufus. Opinion was divided. Some of them felt that he would have done better to hold his tongue. "It would have been much less spectacular."

Rufus, giving an eye to his critics, said to Stephanie, "Not all of Maulsby's guests approve of me."

"I hope you don't care. And I hope you are coming to see me."

"After all this? I feel like a sort of self-discovered Dick Turpin."

"You shouldn't. And I really mean it. Why not go to tea with me tomorrow in the garden of an old friend? She always lets me bring people, and you'd love her."

"Sorry. But I'm moving into the country."

"Really."

"Yes. I've bought a house. With the loot from the ivories."

"So that was the reason you sold them?"

"That, and to spite another member of the family."

"You're frank enough about it."

"Well, the truth is in me, and why lie to lovely ladies?"

She laughed and stood up. "Sometimes lovely ladies

like to be lied to. Oh, I must be going, and tell Marcia what an enchanting evening we've spent. You've helped her out. During dinner it promised to be stupid. I could see her getting worried."

As he walked with her toward their hostess, she persisted: "You haven't said you'd have tea with me tomorrow. Why should you take all day for your moving?"

He didn't want to go, but he agreed to do it. He told himself that it was the easiest way out. And after he got into his new quarters, he could shut himself away from the world.

It was toward morning when he reached home. But he sat up long enough to write a letter:

"You may be interested to learn that your posting me up as a sort of amateur Raffles has resulted in publicity enough to exceed your wildest expectation. Or shall I call them hopes, Sherry? Yesterday I sold the ivory nymphs to a dealer. Tonight at his dinner table somebody recognized them as those which had been advertised. My host, to save me from embarrassment, would not tell where he got them. So I told, laughing as if it were a light thing. But it was not a light thing, and I felt like a fool. I fancy that will please you. So you have had your revenge.

"Maulsby will write to you because I have urged him, not because he doubts me. You can tell him what you like. So that's that, and is all I have to say about it. Perhaps I shouldn't have said anything. But the ivories are sold, and I have the money for them. I can't go farther than that, can I? Unless you should sue for them, and then you'll have to prove ownership — and you can't."

He signed it simply, "Rufus," sealed it, and addressed it to "Mrs. Rufus Fiske," went out and dropped it in the house letter-box, and came back to look up at Sandra's balcony. She was asleep, of course, untroubled by the things which had made his evening a humiliation, and which had again blackened his heart with hatred.

But Sandra was not asleep. On the other side of the court she lay wide-eyed in the darkness, her mind on a thousand things. Life had traveled fast for her in the past few days. It had all begun with Stephanie's party. Before that, there had been no break in the monotony, and now here she was, linked to Rufus Fiske by a knowledge of his past, and thrilled by the thought of the bond.

She did not know when she would see him again. It was enough that she would see him. There was uncertainty, perhaps, about the time and the place, but there was no uncertainty about another meeting, and another, and another . . .

The future which she conjured up held her imagination; her dreams reached forward . . . ! So the dawn came to silver the sky, and she became aware that Theodora, too, was awake.

"Sandra," from the other bed.

"Yes?"

"I can't sleep. I keep thinking about tonight."

"Tonight?"

"This afternoon. At Mrs. Markham's. Stephanie

Moore will be there."

" How do you know? "

" I heard Gale ask her."

" Oh." Sandra sat up. " Did she say she'd come? "

" Yes. And she'll spoil things."

Sandra knew what Doady meant. She didn't want to admit that Stephanie could spoil things. It sounded small-minded, as if they were jealous. But they were not jealous. It was simply youth's rebellion at being set aside. Some intuition told them that to Stephanie they were all the things she had voiced to Gale — country mice, white elephants.

" We'd have a better time without her," she agreed, " but we might as well make the best of it."

" I'm not so philosophic as you," Theodora said petulantly from among her pillows. " That sort of thing never gets anybody anywhere."

" Where do we want to get? "

" You may not know where you want to get, Sandra, but I know. I want the time to come when everybody will say, ' There goes Theodora Claybourne,' and turn their heads to see."

" Mother would say that ladies don't want to be looked at."

" Oh, well, they do! Only they're not frank enough to admit it. I intend always to be frank with myself. I shall face my defects and do away with them, and if I have any charms I shall emphasize them."

Sandra, turning on her elbow, surveyed her twin. " Where did you learn all that, Doady? "

" I've been watching Stephanie Moore. She does it. Why shouldn't I? "

" It sounds frightfuly sophisticated."

" It isn't. Only I'm the one member of the family who thinks we can improve on the original stock. Mother lives in the past, and you live in the present. The past doesn't do me a bit of good, and I'm not satisfied with the present, so I'm going to grab the future and get as much out of it as I can."

" If I thought you meant it — " Sandra began.

" I do mean it. I want to be distinctive. But I haven't quite decided on my type. I've been lying awake wondering whether I dare wear Mother's crêpe shawl and brush my hair back in the Spanish style like Raquel Meller."

" You're too fair. And anyhow it sounds theatrical to me."

Theodora, small and tense among her pillows, said, " All the women whom the world has heard of were theatrical — Helen of Troy, and Lady Hamilton, and Madame DuBarry."

" Oh, well, of course," Sandra murmured, " that kind."

" I don't have to be like them. But I can learn of them. Now, you are different. You don't have to emphasize your personality. You've got something that everybody recognizes — Mr. Fiske did yesterday, and Mr. Maulsby and Gale Markham when they compared you to that picture. But did any of them look at me? They did not. I'm not complaining " — Theodora sat up. — " I'm not complaining. Only it is left to me to do things. You couldn't pose if you wanted to. But I can, and I'm going to do it. Stephanie does, and look at her."

"Doady, you won't be half so nice."

"I don't want to be nice. I want to be distinctive."

There was no doubt but Theodora was working herself up. Sandra recognizing the danger signs said soothingly: "If I were you, I shouldn't worry about this afternoon. You'd better shut your eyes and go to sleep again. I'm going to have a bath and take a walk. I'll come back in time to get breakfast for you."

Theodora, relaxing a bit, yawned, "I wouldn't take a walk this morning for a million dollars."

"Wouldn't you?"

Sandra was standing now by her sister's bed. There was a radiance about her, which made Theodora say:

"I never saw anyone like you. You get so much out of nothing."

But Sandra was not getting much out of nothing. She was getting a great deal out of something which had changed her world. She reflected, as she turned on the water for her bath, that a walk to Doady this morning would be just a walk. To Sandra it was an open gate to romance. She wanted to swing down Sixteenth Street in this silver light, turn off at Rhode Island Avenue, and drop into a church which was not of her faith. She wanted to link its candles and its quietness with her exalted mood. She wanted to come out again, to be wrapped in the sunlighted warmth. She wanted to go on and on, alive with the ecstasy of youth and its dreams.

A little later, she found herself crossing the court to the arched entrance. It was deserted except by the cat, Griselda, who was taking the air, as dainty a white pussy as the world might see, utterly at her ease as if no dogs had ever chased her, placid as a pool at dawn, her tail like a plume, her step unhurried.

Now, to Sandra, Griselda was more than a cat. She was the sign and seal of Rufus' chivalry. Sandra set against the sardonic gleam in his eye, the bitter words on his lips, his tender consideration of this little creature. His defense of her, the whimsical note of tenderness in his voice when he spoke of her, seemed more than to balance his skepticism, his apparent hardness.

So Griselda became the receptacle of mysterious forces. Like some of the small Egyptian gods she was haloed by divinity.

" You beauty," Sandra whispered, and knelt and in a hushed voice called her.

The white cat responded. Came up and ducked her pretty head. Sandra lifted her, and held her close.

" You beauty, you beauty," she whispered again.

Then she looked up and saw Rufus standing on his balcony.

" Where are you going? " His voice, too, was hushed.

" For a walk."

" May I go with you? "

" Oh! Of course."

" I'll be down . . . in a second . . ."

She walked on and waited in the shadow of the archway. She felt that all the windows must have eyes. That Ione Morton might be there in her pink bungalow apron. Oh, well, she didn't care. She didn't care who saw her, since Rufus was to walk with her.

CHAPTER XIV

"MORNING'S AT SEVEN"

IN his heart of hearts, Rufus knew he should have
let little Sandra go for her walk alone. But seeing
her from his window with Griselda in her arms,
the temptation to speak to her had been too great, and
the rest followed. In the night he had dreamed of
her; it seemed now as if this might be a part of his
dream, to be sharing with her this ineffable morning.

Wise in the ways of women, he knew the happiness
his presence brought her. There were all the signs —
shining eyes, flaming cheeks, the quick-pulsing beat
in the white throat. She was as dewy as the morning,
as innocent as Pippa. " *The year's at the spring . . .
the day's at the morn . . . morning's at seven . . .*"
The lilt of the lines kept time to his swinging step.

" Where were you going? " he demanded.

" Anywhere." Before she met him she had known
where she was going. But now she would go where
he led. " Anywhere," she said.

" I know a place where we could have breakfast
together."

" I told my family I'd be back."

" Can't you call them up? "

" I'm afraid not."

" You could tell your mother you met me, and that
I asked you, and that it's a lovely place under the
trees."

She shook her head. " Mother wouldn't like that."
" Why not? "

" Well, she has conventional inhibitions." The cock
of her head, the sidelong, sparkling glance were a
reminder of the picture to which he had compared her.
" I'd ask you to go back and breakfast with us," Sandra
went on, " but the exigences of our apartment do not
permit unexpected guests. We have to set the stage
with our revolving scenery."

He liked her frankness, her sense of humor. " If
you won't go to breakfast with me, we'll ride out to
Rock Creek Park. It isn't much of a walk to the
garage, and I want to show you some deer in the en-
closure. They have their new horns, and they are very
proud of them."

She was aware that he had not said, " By your leave."
He had a masterful way of taking things in his own
hands. And she liked the masterfulness.

The deer at the Park were confiding creatures. They
came up to the fence and nibbled the clover that Sandra
offered them. Their eyes seemed to hold unshed tears.

" Poor things," Sandra said.

Rufus protested: " Not poor at all. They have food
and drink and a wide space to roam. And no fear of
hunters. It is the creatures in the cages that I hate
to see. The great cats behind bars, with concrete
floors for the feet instead of the warm sands of the
desert or the tangled growth of the jungle."

She said somewhat bromidically, " You seem fond
of animals."

" People who have been lonely children always are,
aren't they? I had no brothers and sisters. My horses

and dogs, my rabbits and pussy cats, made up my world."

They sat down on a grassy slope from which they could watch the deer. Sandra had taken off her hat and laid it on the grass beside her. The sun shone through the leaves above her, so that she was dappled with gold. With her bright hair, the red and white of her, she seemed to belong to the greenness as the deer belonged, or as some nymph of the woodland might belong. Rufus wished that it might last forever, this tranquil scene and this charming child to share it. He had never known any woman who gave the same effect of serenity. Sandra seemed untouched by the things which had made his own life stormy. Even in those earlier days, before he lost his mother, there had been no peace, only a restless search for relief from the unhappiness which hung over the household.

He found himself telling Sandra about the Maulsby dinner and its dramatic climax.

"I never dreamed, when I said I'd go, that I'd get into a thing like that. Maulsby and I talked it over after the rest of his guests were gone, and I insisted that he write to Sherry. Then he'd know I was telling the truth as far as my relationship to the advertiser was concerned. Whatever she may say can't hurt me, because she simply can't prove her ownership. She'll want to buy the ivories back. But Maulsby has promised me no one shall have them until he gives me the option. He'll probably keep them in his own collection. But if they are sold, they shan't go back to Sherry."

"I should think," Sandra said with vehemence,

" that she'd hate herself."

His smile was grim. " Sherry's mind doesn't work that way. She is getting a lot out of making me uncomfortable."

There was a short silence. Then Sandra said, " Mother and Doady will be wondering where I am."

" Let them wonder."

" I must get back — "

" Sure you won't breakfast with me? "

" I'd love it. But I can't . . ."

He smiled at her. " That sounds as if you mean it. Well, I don't want this to end. You're a restful little person, do you know it? As comfortable as Sherry is uncomfortable."

Dimly Sandra was aware that his words raised a barrier between those dreams of hers on the balcony and their realization; that to be a comfortable little person was a far cry from being Juliet in a garden. Here was no Romeo swearing to the moon, but rather a tired warrior, made peaceful by the companionship of a faithful page, a Saul soothed by the song of a David.

Yet, with characteristic adjustment, she took what was given her, made the most of it. Surely this was more than she could have ever hoped for, to be here on this heavenly morning as his comrade and friend.

It was when, a little later, they drove up to the archway which led to the court of their apartment house, that Rufus said.

" And now, when shall I see you again? "

The flutter in her throat, the radiance in her eyes! " Any time. We hardly ever have engagements, except now and then with Gale Markham. We're going this afternoon to his mother's to tea."

" So am I."

" Really? "   How the world sparkled!

" Yes. Stephanie Moore asked me. She was at the Maulsbys' dinner."

A shadow across her brightness! *Stephanie! With Rufus in her train! A princess passes! Two country mice in a corner!* Sandra's mind might for the moment have been Theodora's, with its tense staccato comment.

In a moment, however, she reacted. What matter with whom he came, so that he was there and she would see him!

So once again her world sparkled, and when she arrived at her small apartment and found her mother and Theodora not only awake, but up and dressed, she met their inquiries with a gay air of adventure.

" Where have you been? " they demanded.

Her eyes were stars. " A-walking down the street with Rufus Fiske."

" Rufus Fiske! "   It had the effect of a chorus.

" Yes.   We went to the park — and we fed the deer — and we sat on a bank and talked — and he asked me to breakfast."

" Did you go? "

" No, I told him mother had — inhibitions! "

" Inhibitions? "

" Yes. It sounds dreadful, doesn't it? Like drugs or drink. But what I said was, ' conventional inhibitions," which would not allow me to breakfast at seven with a practically unknown person."

They laughed together, and then Mrs. Claybourne

said, " I'm glad you acted like a lady."

" Mother, would it have been not like a lady if I had eaten breakfast with him? Well, I wanted to."

" Do you like him? " Theodora asked.

Like him . . . !

Sandra managed to say with an effect of indifference: "Oh, he's really very nice. You'll see him this after-noon at the Markhams', mother."

" *The Markhams'*," Theodora emphasized. " Did you ask him? "

" Doady — as if I would! He is going with Steph-anie. He met her last night at the Maulsbys' dinner, and she — annexed him."

" She would, of course," Theodora stated. " He's too good-looking to escape her."

Mrs. Claybourne was scandalized. *" Doady! "*

Sandra took off her hat and began to get breakfast. When the others offered to help, she refused to let them.

" It's my job. Doady can help with the dishes. But you sit on the balcony, mother, and try to think of your-self as a lady of leisure."

As she peeled peaches and cut them up, and poached eggs and buttered thin toast, Sandra seemed outwardly the same Sandra who had done all these things a thou-sand times. But she was not the same Sandra. Never again to her mother and Doady would her heart be an open book. Henceforth she would shut away from them a secret delight, a something that would be profaned if even loved eyes looked upon it.

It was while they were at breakfast that it began to rain. Sandra, shutting the windows against a drench-ing downpour, said, " Who would have dreamed of a storm like this? "

" I was going to church," Mrs. Claybourne said.
" I ought to go anyhow, I never let rain stop me at
Windytop. But here I seem tired so much of the time."

" I am not going either," Theodora stated. " You
pray for both of us, Sandra."

Sandra was in a mood to pray for the whole world.
Not for anything would she have stayed home from
church. She wanted to sing hymns of praise for this
happiness which was in her heart. Yet it was characteristic of her that even in this mood of exaltation, she
found a place for practical things.

" I'm having a roast," she told her mother. " I'm
afraid I was frightfully extravagant, but I found such
a ducky little shoulder of lamb. It is all ready to go
into the oven, and there'll just be the potatoes to put
around it, and the peas are all shelled, and Doady can
set the table."

" When my ship comes in," Theodora announced,
" I'm going to have Sunday dinner at night. And I'm
going to have all my dinners at eight. And breakfast
in bed."

To Sandra, getting ready for church, Theodora's
desires seemed narrow and futile. Why think of dinners at night, and breakfasts in bed? There were other
dreams. Not of Juliet on a balcony, but of a page in
red, going deeply into a forest, to follow the fortune
of a tall knight with a gleam in his eye and a curl of
his lip, and with a white cat rampant on his shield!

CHAPTER XV

THE THING THAT HAPPENS

THAT afternoon to the Markhams, Theodora wore her mother's shawl. It was a lovely thing of coral crêpe, embroidered in its own color, and with its fringe knotted in an intricate pattern. With fair hair swept straight back from her forehead, a flat curl brushed forward on each cheek, and with her slenderness and almost childish grace, she was an arresting and charming figure.

" My hat doesn't fit in with the rest of it," she said with some discontent as she put it on, " but I shan't wear it when I get there, even if the others do. I am going to set my own pace this afternoon and see what happens."

" What could happen? " her mother asked.

Theodora shrugged her shoulders. The gesture belonged to the shawl and she knew it. She could see herself in the mirror, and admired her own dash and style.

" Anything," she answered.

" If you really want my opinion, Doady," her mother said, " I should say that the shawl is entirely too conspicuous for daytime wear."

" Nothing is too conspicuous," Theodora said, " if it makes people look at you."

Sandra took no part in the conversation. She was

glad Theodora could wear the shawl. It was not appropriate for the time and the place, but it was distinctly becoming. And Doady would play up to it. That was Doady, throwing herself into any part she elected to play.

As for Sandra she needed no decorations, for what did she care what any of them thought of her except Rufus? And he had said he liked to be with her. In spite of her shabby clothes and cheap little hat, he liked to be with her.

They took a taxi-cab to the Markhams'. It was an unheard-of extravagance, but there was no convenient trolley, and Theodora's crêpe shawl was impossible in the street car. Even in the cab, the glare of the sunlight made it gaudy, and she began to wonder a little how it would seem in Mrs. Markham's garden, and whether, if it happened to be hot, she would have to take it off.

Fate was kind to her, however, for as they reached their destination, the rain came down again, and tea was served in the dim, long living-room with its polished floor. In this setting Theodora's brightness was subdued and enriched. She laid her hat aside, patted the flat curls, and made a picture of herself in a window-seat, content to be alone for a moment, waiting her opportunity.

She forgot herself, presently, in a study of the room and of her hostess. She decided that Mrs Markham belonged to this background as a picture belongs in a frame. Slender, gray-haired, and in black lace, there was nothing new or fashionable about her, nor was there in the room, which had been furnished when Betty

Markham came to it a bride and had never been changed.

Before Rufus and Stephanie arrived, several people came in. An old gentleman sat down by Sandra, and a young one by Theodora. Another old gentleman joined Mrs. Claybourne and Mrs. Markham at the tea-table, and Gale chatted with two pretty girls.

Thus it happened that when Stephanie floated in, perfect in pale blue, she made the effective entrance which always belongs to the late-comer.

" Cousin Betty," she asked, " have they eaten up all the cakes? The storm kept us. The streets are running rivers. We needed a gondola instead of a motor car."

She bent and kissed Mrs. Markham. " I've been telling Mr. Fiske about your famous tea cakes. He's ready for a dozen of them."

" He shall have all he wants." Mrs. Markham held out her hand to Rufus. " I'm so glad you could come."

From the other side of the room, where Sandra sat with her old gentleman on a chintz-covered sofa, she could see Rufus and Stephanie standing by the tea-table. Her heart tightened. What a pair they made! She graceful and exquisite, he tall and splendid.

" My dear child," the old gentleman was saying, " let me get you tea and some of Betty Markham's cakes. They are plummy things, and scandalously rich, but none of us can refuse them." He got up on his stiff old legs. " You'll have one lump — two? And lemon? And I shall bring four cakes, two for each of us."

He was a nice old duck, Sandra reflected as he trotted off. But she didn't want to drink tea with him. She

wanted to drink it with Rufus. She wanted to stand
up on her toes and wave to him, and say:

"Here I am! Waiting!"

But, of course, she couldn't. The thing had to be
done decently and in order. Presently he would drift
her way and say, "Oh, here you are!" as if he hadn't
expected it.

But she hadn't reckoned with Stephanie. Stephanie,
who floated here and there, passing little cakes, lighting
candles as the storm darkened the room, talking to
everybody in her gay voice, pressing Rufus into service,
calling on him for cups of tea, more little cakes, thin
bread and butter, lemon and cream and sugar . . .

She kept Gale, too, busy, as other people came in.
Theodora, observing, made mental notes of Stephanie's
method: *She gives the effect of having both of them
at her feet. Of their being satellites. She's playing
them off against each other. And she won't let anybody else have them, if she can help it.*

After a time she saw Rufus approach Sandra, and
set a little table before her. Then he brought Stephanie, drew up a chair for her, brought a plate of the
plummy cakes, brought thin bread and butter, brought
cups of tea, and dropped finally into a chair beside
Sandra with an air of having put something over.

And the thing he had put over, Theodora decided,
was to keep from being dragged after Stephanie like
a slave at a chariot wheel.

She tried to show him off, rapped Theodora's brain,
and he wouldn't let her.

All about the room were other little tables with other
little groups, their voices lost in the crash of the storm,

so that they seemed to Theodora like actors in a pantomime. Everybody, apparently, knew everybody else.
Even her mother had an air of being at home with it all.

" She may be shabby, but she has an air of being born
to it," the critical little daughter conceded with a throb
of pride.

The young man who had brought her tea seemed not
in the least ruffled by Theodora's absorption in the
surrounding scene. He talked steadily about himself,
laughed at his own jokes, and ate more than his share
of the rich little cakes. He was apparently content to
keep Theodora company and was, perhaps, deluded
with the idea that he was making a permanent impression.

He was, however, making no impression. Theodora
had larger things in mind than the conquest of callow
youth, things which had to do with taking the center
of the stage away from Stephanie, who was again on
her feet, floating about in heavenly blue.

In one corner of the room was a piano, an old-
fashioned instrument with yellow keys. Theodora had
had her eye on it from the first, and when the callow
youth, whose name was Mark Beveridge, stopped for
breath, she said to him,

"Let's walk over and look at that old piano. I
believe it's a Chickering." It was a Chickering. Inset
with mother-of-pearl. Theodora, having duly admired
it, sat down and ran her fingers over the keys. One or
two people looked up and looked away again. The
thunder rolled incessantly, and in the midst of the noise
and rush of the storm Theodora began to sing. She
sang precisely as if she had no listeners, as if what she

was doing was done for herself and for her own pleasure, without a thought of those about her.

The song she sang was an old Spanish tune; her slender figure swayed as if to the beat of castanets, the coral shawl, caught at one shoulder by an old cameo brooch, fell about her, her hands coming out of it slender and ringless. Her voice had a throaty quality and was very sweet and true. It had, too, a deep emotional appeal which made up for lack of training. She did not try to sing above the storm, but rather under it, so that the clamor was like a great accompaniment of brasses and drums and bass viols.

One by one people stopped to listen, their eyes focussed on that charming figure amid the shadows — the coral shawl catching the candle-light, the golden head flung back, the vivid face with its pointed chin.

"Who is she?" they asked. And gradually the murmur ran from one to another, "Theodora Claybourne."

Sandra, hearing it, felt her heart leap! Doady was doing it! And how clever of her! And how the storm had helped! Nothing could have been more effective than the gay contrast of the shawl and the surrounding darkness.

Stephanie, having returned and waking all at once to the fact that one of the small white elephants was emerging from oblivion, said to Sandra, "I didn't know your sister sang."

"Oh, yes. Daddy taught her that Spanish thing."

"She sings like a native," said the gay old gentleman, "and I'll bet her little feet could dance it. Jove, how I used to love to see those girls in Granada."

"Do you sing? " Rufus asked Sandra.

It was the first word he had addressed to her for some time. Stephanie had kept him busy with her chatter about things that had happened at the Maulsbys' dinner. She had left Sandra to the gay old gentleman. And Sandra had been content to be left, for a wonderful thing had happened! When Rufus had brought the little table, he had dropped into her lap a small red rose.

"Your color," he had said, and had smiled down at her.

After that, while she drank her tea, she held the rose in her left hand under the table, her fingers curled about it.

And now, when Rufus asked her, "Do you sing? " she said,

"Doady has all the accomplishments."

Stephanie, breaking in, remarked: "How queer. Twins usually do the same things, don't they? "

"Doady and I don't," Sandra said. "She says that I dream about things and she does them."

The gay old gentleman interposed: "She's getting up from the piano. Why doesn't some one ask her to give us another song? "

He rose to his feet, but Gale Markham was saying eagerly, "Everybody is asking for more, Doady."

"Oh, well." Theodora gave a moment's effect of modest hesitation, then sat down.

Again her fingers rippled over the keys. Once more the haunting voice sang beneath the storm. *In the gloaming . . . oh, my darling . . . when the lights are dim and low . . . and the quiet shadows falling . . . softly come and softly go . . .*

It was an old song, frankly sentimental, belonging to her mother's girlhood. Yet there was about it a poignant quality, and Theodora made the most of the sentiment and poignancy. Except for the storm, the room was still. The gay old gentleman openly wiped his eyes.

Sandra, leaning back in her chair, her eyes on Rufus, saw his chest rise and fall, his throat contract in a sudden spasm.

When the music stopped, the gay old gentleman rose: " I must go and tell your sister . . . we old fellows sang that years ago to our sweethearts."

Stephanie floated after him. And Rufus and Sandra were left alone together.

" I have been waiting for this," he said.

Silence.

Then he asked, " Have you? "

" Yes."

His hand found hers under the little table. " Sandra," his voice was husky with emotion, " it is unbelievable, the thing that has happened to us."

She did not ask what had happened. She knew. The thing that had happened to Romeo when he saw Juliet. The thing that happened to Aucassin and Nicolette, the thing that happened to Dante! The thing that happens to all those who find love at first sight!

" Even this morning," Rufus went on, " I thought it was friendship that I wanted. And when I brought you the rose, it was because, as it nodded to me from a vase, it made me think of ' The Boy in Red.' But something in your eyes as you looked up at me . . . and when

your sister sang . . . that song my mother used to sing
. . . Sandra, I knew then, and you knew! "

She was trembling. " Please . . ."

" Oh, I know I shouldn't be saying it. I thought
I should never say it to any woman. Sandra, give me
your hand — the other one."

The one with the rose! Oh, the kindly darkness of
the storm which hid them from inquiring eyes. The
sweet color in her cheeks . . .

" Sandra, Sandra! "

" Rufus, please."

"I know. I mustn't . . . not here! But when?
Tonight? When can I see you? Where? "

Where? Oh, there was only the stuffy little apartment with her mother and Theodora. What chance
for romance?

But Rufus' mind had leaped forward and found a
way. " I'll take Stephanie Moore home and come
back for you. We can dine at a charming place in
Maryland."

" Oh, but I couldn't."

" Why not? "

" Mother wouldn't hear of it."

He was not to be thwarted. " Would she hear of it
if I asked your sister and Markham? Well, then, we'll
make it a party of four, and after dinner, we'll drive
on, and I'll show you the house I've bought. Such a
queer old house, Sandra! I want you to see the hill and
the pines."

Chapter XVI

" THERE GOES THEODORA CLAYBOURNE! "

GALE MARKHAM, leaning on the piano, said
to Theodora,
        " Why have you been hiding your light
under a bushel? "

" My light? "

" Yes. Why didn't you tell us you could sing like
that? Do you know you've had all the women wiping
their eyes and all the men blowing their noses? "

She knew! And besides hadn't Mark Beveridge
told her, and the gay old gentleman, and the others
who had come up to congratulate her? And now here
was Gale, waiting his opportunity until he could have
her to himself, adding his voice to the rest.

She dared not let him see her eyes, lest they betray
her exultation. " I'm afraid my songs are frightfully
old-fashioned," she said demurely.

" Old-fashioned. My dear child, don't you know it
is quite the thing to be mid-nineteenth century? Sentiment is coming in, and sophistication is going out. Just
watch and see. We're tired of jazz and noise. The
age of realism is dead. And it's dead because it isn't
interesting. Life has a lot more thrills than the critics
are willing to admit. We like to laugh and cry. It
relieves our complexes. Nations who can laugh rarely
see red revolution. Their sense of humor prevents it."

She was not listening. What did she care about realism or red revolution? What she cared about was the applause of the multitude. Taking the center of the stage from Stephanie, who came up at this moment, like a heavenly visitant, bringing two blue candles in silver holders. "Don't you need more light?" she asked, and set one on each side of the music rack.

"I've been telling this child," Gale said, "what a success she is. Doady, I'm so soppy with sentiment that I shall be making love to Stephanie, if she doesn't watch out."

"It wouldn't be the first time," Stephanie retorted.

Gale laughed. "Dear girl, if you aren't careful you'll reveal your past."

Stephanie's restless fingers were twisting the fringe of Theodora's shawl.

"Oh, well, all the world knows it; why shouldn't Theodora? What Gale is trying to tell you, Doady, is that once upon a time he and I were engaged, and when he lost his money I threw him over, and he thinks and the world thinks that it was because he lost his money. And they won't any of them forgive me, and under their breaths they are calling me a mercenary wretch, though they don't dare say it to my face."

"I dare," Gale told her, "only I don't do it, because you are too pretty to have your feelings hurt."

Were they in earnest? Theodora was not sure. They seemed to take it all so lightly. Yet there was beneath the surface an undercurrent of seriousness.

"Your mother is my friend," Stephanie was saying: "she believes in me."

"My mother," Gale flung back at her, "is an angel.

She loves you, and that's the end of it."

"It isn't the end. Her faith in me is just . . . the beginning."

Theodora, thirsting for knowledge, broke in. "If you weren't mercenary, what were you?"

"Sensible," said Stephanie.

"She believes, in other words," said Gale, "that romance must be tempered by thrift."

"I believe nothing of the kind," Stephanie asserted with some heat, "but I believe it must be tempered with a certain amount of common sense."

"She felt that she couldn't give up her facials and fur coats, and that I wouldn't be happy if I had to look after the furnace. So there you are. She still has her facials, and I look after the furnace. And neither of us is — happy." No lightness there! His blue eyes like steel!

"I beg your pardon, Doady," he said, looking down at her. "We have no right to impose this discussion of differences on you. But your song got under our skins, you see. And the storm . . ."

Stephanie, still twisting the fringe of Theodora's shawl, said:

"Gale, I'm asking Rufus Fiske to go home with me to dinner. Ruth O'Malley has just telephoned she's motoring from Baltimore and will spend the night with me. And I want you to make the fourth."

"Sorry."

"You mean you won't come?"

"Not tonight."

She flushed. "You might at least have invented an excuse."

They faced each other for a moment, then Stephanie touched Gale's coat with the tips of her slender fingers.

" We're not quarreling, are we? "

" I don't care what you call it," he said with a touch of rudeness, and her hand dropped to her side, and she turned and left him.

He stood for a moment, saying nothing, then he told Theodora, " You see, she still has power to hurt me."

" Why do you let her? "

" Because that's the man of it. Holding on to that which is withheld." He seemed to gather himself together. " Poor taste, I call it, to be talking like this to you. Aren't you going to sing us another song? "

" Haven't you had enough? "

" Not I. Nor the rest of them."

Came just then a crack and a crash; the lightning lit the room with a lurid glare; the thunder seemed to shatter the world.

Some of the men jumped to their feet, one or two of the women cried out . . . a sort of thick silence followed . . . and out of that silence came Theodora's voice in an old sacred song, a cry of human hearts for help.

The wind was furious now. The trees were bending and breaking under it. The rain streamed; the lightning flamed and flamed again; the cannonade of thunder was continuous. And Theodora sang!

It was her moment of triumph. About her everything fell away. She did not see the room, nor the men and women in it; she did not hear the noise of the storm. She heard, rather, far off, the echo of a thousand voices: *" There goes Theodora Claybourne! There goes Theo-*

dora Claybourne."

Forgotten for her were the deeper meanings of the great hymn, forgotten everything but the effect of her acting upon her audience: *I'm like a picture . . . sitting here between the two blue candles . . . in my coral shawl . . . like something by Fra Angelico . . . or was it Lippo Lippi?*

As the last note died away, there was a burst of applause. Theodora smiled, let her hands drop from the keys, stood up.

" What a child she is! " said everybody.

The callow youth, who had hovered in the background, now came forward. " Gee," he said, " you've made a hit! "

Theodora with becoming modesty said, " Oh, well, the storm helped a lot."

" Your sister wants you," Mark Beveridge went on; " she asked me to bring you over."

So across the room went Theodora, slender in her coral shawl, swaying a little as she walked, her head upheld.

It was that upheld head which caused the catastrophe — that and her high heels, and the waxed floor, with its shining length from the piano to the corner where Sandra sat.

Theodora taking no thought to her heels, or the waxed floor, or her haughty head, felt the world slip suddenly away from her. There was no grace in the fall. It was simply an ignominious tumble.

It was not the callow youth who picked her up. It was Gale Markham, reaching her at a bound, lifting her, saying,

"Little Doady, are you hurt?"

She didn't know whether she was hurt or not. There might be bones broken, but she didn't care. The blow to her self-esteem was crushing.

"Take me away, take me away," she whispered, her eyes hidden against Gale's shoulder.

As he carried her through the hall to the library, she sobbed and sobbed, her slender form shaken.

He laid her on a couch and knelt beside her. "Where is the pain?"

"It's my . . . pride," said Doady.

"Bless your heart, nobody cared."

"I cared."

He tried to comfort her. "My dear, don't cry."

But she would not be comforted. "It served me right," she said, and kept on sobbing.

Other people came, her mother and Sandra, and Mrs. Markham, and after a while they induced her to go back to the others. Her nose was red, but she powdered it. Her flat curls were out of place, and she put them back again. When she reached the living-room people crowded about her. To them she was the same Theodora who had played and sang. But she knew herself a chastened spirit.

It served me right . . . it served me right! said the well-brought-up Theodora. *It might have been lightning instead of wax on the floor.*

Chapter XVII

TWO MEN LIKE THAT

MADGE CLAYBOURNE had supper with her friend, Betty Markham, and stayed late. Rufus Fiske had carried off Gale and the two girls, and Mrs. Markham had refused to let Madge leave. "We'll have a pleasant, quiet time, my dear, talking over old times."

But what they really talked over was their children.

"Since his father's death, Gale has been everything to me," Mrs. Markham said.

"You have a younger son?"

"Truxton? Yes. Gale is keeping him at school at a great sacrifice. But all the men of our family have gone to Exeter, and we hated to break the line."

After that the two proud mothers chanted antiphonally, "Gale" . . . "Sandra" . . . "Theodora" . . . "Trux."

"I thought I should never get over the disappointment when Gale's engagement was broken. But Stephanie was right, although I am afraid Gale will never forgive her. He thinks her cold because she let common sense rule."

"I agree with him," Madge said heatedly. "How could any woman give him up?"

"But, my dear, he isn't able to marry."

"Then she should wait for him."

" Girls don't do that in these days."

" My girls would."

Betty Markham shook her head, " Don't be too romantic for them, Madge. Modern life exacts so much, and love in a cottage has gone out of fashion."

They argued it — Madge, the dreamer, and Betty, the worldly-wise.

" Oh, I don't want my girls to be practical," Madge flung out at last. " Betty, I've been poor, but somehow I've always gilded the poverty. And looking back, I wouldn't change things."

Betty Markham leaned over and patted her hand. " Dear girl," she said, " we won't quarrel about it. And perhaps you are wiser than I."

On the way home Madge reflected that Betty Markham's poverty was not like her own. Betty was cared for, protected by the tenderness of her son. But Madge had the world to face without such protection. The girls were, of course, her shield and buckler against discouragement, but it was she who must be the real wage-earner, although what Doady could do would help.

When she reached her apartment and put her key in the lock, the door of the adjoining apartment opened, and Ione Morton stuck her head out.

" Did you go to your tea? " she asked.

" Yes."

" If I come in, will you tell me about it? "

Mrs. Claybourne's consent was given reluctantly. But Ione came. And sat down and began to talk.

" That man Fiske moved out this morning," she said

finally. " Bag and baggage. Carried his cat in a basket."

" He was at the tea," Mrs. Claybourne informed her.

She started to say that her daughters were at that moment motoring with him, but fortunately refrained.

" Well, I don't see how he got into high society," said Ione. " Do your friends know anything about him? "

" They must, of course, or they wouldn't have asked him." Madge said sedately, then remembered with a sinking of heart that she had asked Betty, when Sandra had said he wanted them to ride, " What do you know of Rufus Fiske? "

And Betty had said: " Nothing. Stephanie brought him."

Yet he was charming, and he had seemed so glad to meet Sandra's mother, and had promised as he left her:

" I'll deliver your daughters safe at your front door, Mrs. Claybourne, at ten. So you are not to worry."

After they had gone, Madge had said, " Down our way, we still have chaperones," and Betty had shaken her head and answered, " Our girls won't have them, and Gale is as good as any old woman."

It had seemed to Madge wonderful that her daughters should be escorted by a pair so gallant as Gale Markham and Rufus Fiske. Gentlemen. It would be ridiculous to worry, with Doady and Sandra in such good hands.

And now here was Ione Morton raising the question. Mrs. Claybourne decided that she wouldn't talk about it. So she told about Betty Markham's tea.

" It was a dreadful storm," she said, " but we were

all so cozily shut in that we didn't seem to mind it."

" I shouldn't know how to act," Ione said, " at a place like that. Some day I'm going to buy an etiquette book and study it. You'd think it would be simple enough to go and drink a cup of tea somewhere, wouldn't you? But I wouldn't know . . . I wouldn't know anything . . ."

Mrs. Claybourne reflected that all the etiquette books in the world wouldn't make it possible for Ione Morton to drink a cup of tea properly at a place like the Markhams'. She was so obviously common, yet there was as Sandra had said, something wistful and appealing in the lonely creature.

When Ione had gone, Madge made her preparations for the night. As she pulled down the folding bed and arranged her pillows, she wondered if Gale's heart would be caught in the rebound. Would he, having loved Stephanie, find solace in Sandra or Theodora? There was no reason why, having loved one woman, he could not love another. Even Romeo had another lady before Juliet swept before his ravished eyes. Madge, doing her hair up in kids, beamed in the mirror. It was not her own reflection that she saw — a middle-aged woman with gray hair in little horns, it was, rather, a figure in satin and pearls, with dark curls under a peaked cap. The Juliet of Madge's day had been Julia Marlowe, dimple in chin, lovely of voice, blooming with youth and beauty.

Comfortable finally on her pillows, Madge read her book. Why worry? Two men like that . . . gentlemen!

Promptly at ten the girls arrived. Sandra, laughing in a sort of breathless way, bent and kissed her mother.

" It was glorious! "

She was glowing, beautiful. Madge stared at her. Sandra had never been like this!

Theodora, also glowing but less effulgent, began at once: " I'll say this for Rufus Fiske — he knows how to do things."

" Tell me about it, darling."

" We had dinner at the loveliest place. Out-of-doors — and the most delicious food. But it wasn't that. It was the way he made us feel, and Gale. They're both of them darlings."

This from Theodora! Sandra silent, taking off her cheap little hat, taking off her cheap little dress, taking off her cheap little shoes, a Cinderella back from the ball! But a Cinderella with a difference. For she had left with the prince not a glass slipper but a heart.

In a dream she heard Doady telling her mother all about it. Presently, when Doady was in bed, Sandra would have things to tell her mother. Things so astounding that it seemed incredible they could have happened!

" And Gale wouldn't go to dinner with Stephanie, but he went with us," Theodora continued. " I heard her ask him."

" Betty said it nearly broke his heart when Stephanie threw him over."

" Were they engaged? " Sandra asked.

" Yes. And when he lost his money, she wouldn't have him."

" He's a thousand times too good for her," Theodora

flamed; " he's the kindest man I ever met."

She meant every word of it. Whatever Gale might think of Stephanie, he had set his mind on helping Rufus give the twins the time of their lives. And Theodora had confided in him. How she had hated being a wallflower on the night of Stephanie's dance, she and Sandra. She had brought her story up to date, even telling him that the effect at the piano was premeditated. " I wanted everybody to say, ' There goes Theodora Claybourne.' "

He had shouted at that. " So as Gilbert and Sullivan would say, you were ' dissembling ' ? "

" Yes."

They had said all these things to each other while they sat in Rufus' shadowy living-room, while the other two went to the top of the hill to see the after-glow.

Theodora, curled up in a chair with a great many cushions, had stated. " I'm all over bruises. And it serves me right."

" My dear child, why? "

But Doady stopped there. For how was she going to explain that something within her had been shocked by her exploitation of a song which had always had for her a deep and solemn sigificance?

" When I get home, I'll take a hot bath," was her prosaic way of side-tracking further discussion, and presently Sandra and Rufus came back, and all the way home she and Gale sang college songs, while Rufus and Sandra on the front seat listened.

Having related all this to her mother, she decided it was time for the bath and got up from the bed:

" Sandra will tell you the rest of it. I've got to go

and pet my black-and-blues."

Sandra waited until she had gone. Waited until they could hear the water booming in the tub. Then she whirled away from the mirror, knelt beside the bed, and laid her bright head on her mother's breast.

Silence for a moment, then she whispered, "Mumsie . . ."

"Yes, dear."

"Rufus . . . loves me."

Madge's heart seemed to stand still. It was all very well to dream dreams and see visions. But this precious child! Why, when had she seen the man? Once? Twice? When had she met him? Yesterday?

"Oh, Sandra!" she said. "How could he? You don't know each other."

"Oh, mother, we do. Better than you think. At first, it was a secret. But tonight he said I might tell you."

A secret? Her little Sandra? Again that stab at the heart. Who was this man with whom her child had had a secret understanding? A prince? A gentleman?

But Sandra, still kneeling, was relating an incredible story. Of the ivories. And of the advertisement. And of her telling Rufus at the Library.

"I don't know how I ever had the courage, mother."

And then the things Rufus had told her. That he was the son of a rich man who had made his mother unhappy. And he had been unhappy, too. And of his mother's death, and the installing of a stepmother not much older than himself. Of the stepmother's enmity toward the boy, their growing hatred of each other. A hatred which darkened everything. And then his father's death, and an unjust will.

"But the ivories were his, mother. His grandfather gave them to him when he was a child. But they had always stood in a cabinet in the drawing-room, and Sherry wanted them because they belonged to Rufus. And Rufus wouldn't let her have them. And he brought them here and sold them, and Sherry advertised him as a thief."

"Sherry? You're going too fast. Who is Sherry?"

"His stepmother, dearest. She isn't much older than he, and all his life she thwarted him because she wanted his father's money. And he has seen so much of unhappy marriages that he felt he would never marry. But now he wants to marry me."

Chapter XVIII

SHERRY

THE white cat, Griselda, wandered in a Paradise of aromatic fragrances, with a carpet of pine needles under her paws. Above her the plumes of the tall trees were swept by a slight breeze, and the floor of the little grove was sprinkled with gold, where the sun filtered through the branches. Now and then a butterfly, drifting in the still air, roused her to action. She emerged, as it were, from a puff-ball effect of rotundity into a lithe, springing creature, eager-eyed, avid. Then losing her quarry, she would pad along once more, contentedly, at the heels of her master. As they went deeper and deeper into the wood, she uttered now and then a mew of protest, and when at last Rufus sat down on a log and lighted his pipe, she stretched herself lazily on the cushioned pine, panting, her tongue showing its pink tip.

Rufus smiled at her. " Tired, old lady? "

She answered him plaintively. She was really very comfortable, but with feminine instinct she took sympathy when she could get it.

He smoked for a moment in silence, then he said: " Your nose is out of joint, Puss Cat. There's some one else . . . I love . . ."

He said it with quick breath. Even now, after the three weeks in which he knew that she loved him, he could not speak of Sandra without that quick beat of his heart. He hoped he would never think of her without it. With his face uplifted to the singing branches, he said it again,

" There's some one else . . . I love . . ."

Three weeks! And every day he had seen Sandra. Their meetings had been carefully planned. Since no one knew of their romance except Mrs. Claybourne, they had thought it best for Rufus not to come to the house too often. But there had been lunch once or twice at the Library restaurant, because of that first luncheon; a visit to the Zoo because of that radiant Sunday morning; a drive one night with her mother out to Rufus' house, when Doady had a dinner engagement at the Maulsbys'.

For Doady had not been told. Never before had Sandra kept anything from her twin. But this must be kept.

" Doady would never understand," Sandra had told her mother, " how it happened so soon."

Mrs. Claybourne agreed. For herself, she understood perfectly. She believed in love at first sight. And why not? Hadn't half the world loved that way? And was the other half, which had taken second thoughts, and third, and even fourth and fifth thoughts, any happier for its prudence?

At every moment and at every meeting, Rufus had been conscious of the change which was transforming him. Life had become all at once a thing not of bitterness and morbid brooding, but of love and laughter and lightness of heart. Sandra with her youth and gaiety was like new wine to his spirit. Looking forward to a future in which she would be beside him, he put thoughts of the past resolutely behind.

There were things which he had not yet told her. Some of the things she must know before he married her. Things which might startle and shock her, but which, please God, would not make her love him less. Perhaps he could bring her out some day to this cathedral stillness. How she would love it! Shut in by the trees, one seemed to breast emerald depths in which the branches of the pines waved like giant seaweed.

In a week or two they were to tell the world. That had been decided. By that time people would have grown accustomed to seeing them together. Once or twice Rufus had gone with Sandra and Doady to the Markhams', there had been tea in the garden of Maulsby's shop to which they had all been invited, and a Sunday supper at Stephanie's when her Baltimore friend, Ruth O'Malley, was visiting her.

Rufus was for an early marriage. " I'll give you a month to get ready, Sandra."

" But August, Rufus! Nobody is ever married in August."

" We'll set an example."

" September will be much nicer."

" Do you really think that, or are you just — saying it."

Her blushes had been beautiful. " I'm just — saying it."

And he had put his finger under her chin, and turned her face up to him and said, " Love me, Juliet? " And had lifted her off her feet in a little whirl of triumph when she answered, " Yes."

He called her " Juliet " because of the balcony. She was not quite sure she liked it.

" Things ended for her so tragically."

" I'm not sure it was tragic. Death isn't the worst. She and her Romeo suffered no disillusionment."

But she had shuddered: " I want to live a thousand years — with you, Rufus."

She was very frank about her feeling for him. There was no coyness, no coquetry. It was to him beautiful that she should be like that. He had seen so much of artifice and worldly-wiseness.

So the little house was to be ready for her. As he walked back toward it with Griselda at his heels, he made his plans. He had been getting his own breakfast coffee, with a woman coming in later to clean for him and set out his lunch. He had dined where he pleased; at the Inn not far away, or in town, and of late, once or twice with the Claybournes.

It had delighted him to see Sandra at her domestic duties. She had seemed to add luster to them. She was so deft, so much in earnest. " With the decks cleared," as Doady put it, in the crowded apartment, Sandra would set the table with its centerpiece of flowers, fragile as butterflies, its tall white candles — its thin green glass, inexpensive but effective, picked up by the discriminating Doady.

Then, having provided background, as it were, for the feast, Sandra would bring on dishes suited to the hot day — a cool jellied soup, delicate fish in a blended sauce, new vegetables, fruit for a finish, with crisp little cakes. It was all, Rufus decided, an art in itself. The lovely art of housewifery, of which he had known nothing. His boyhood had been spent in a house full of servants. He had never seen his mother in the kitchen. She had never made for him a slice of toast or a cup of coffee. He had always associated housework with drudgery. Yet to see Sandra wash dishes! With a big pan full of bright suds, her little hand mop, her rack to dry them in!

She had tied him up in a white apron and had made him help her. "Oh, Romeo, darling," she had said, surveying him, "you look delicious!"

This had been, of course, on one of the nights when Doady was out. With Doady present there was no talk of Romeo and Juliet. Only a thrilled sense of the things that Doady didn't know, and which they knew, he and Sandra, and dear Madge Claybourne, who entered understandingly into their romance and kept their secret sacred.

It was strange that Theodora had guessed nothing.

"She would," Sandra had said, "if she wasn't so absorbed in her own affairs. Just now, she feels that if she is going to have anything she must go out to get it. She says she is not like me. That things come to me . . . fall into my lap like ripe fruit. While she has to climb the branches."

Rufus had made up his mind, that when Sandra came to him there must be a maid. There would be necessity for economy, but not such economy as would make things difficult.

He had not planned to see her tonight. She had lunched with him, and that, she had told him, was enough. He had some work to do, and he must do it.

Yet he knew that if he called her up, she would see

see him again if he said so; and at the prospect of a meeting there would be that lilting note in her voice, as a bird answers its mate.

When he reached the house, he opened his door, and stood in the big room into which now streamed the slanting rays of the sun. The dining-table which had been pushed back into a corner, and on which his work was spread, became suddenly important for other uses. He would get some strips of linen, a set of quaint Russian candlesticks, and Theodora should find him a bowl for fruit. And there must be fresh covers for the chairs — something with a flash of scarlet — Sandra's color.

He had hung " The Boy in Red " above the table where he worked. He loved to look up at it, to meet the laughter of the eyes under the long lashes. It was a better picture, he felt, than any he could ever have of Sandra, for the artist had caught something of the spirit of youth with the brush of a master, and had shown that which no photograph could ever reproduce.

He picked up the receiver and gave a number.

" Juliet? "

" Oh . . . *Rufus* . . . ? "

" Yes. I want to see you."

" When? "

" Tonight."

" But I saw you — today."

" What difference does that make? May I come? "

He could. Doady, she said, had gone to Baltimore on the late afternoon train to try to sell some old silver to a difficult customer. Sandra and her mother were having an early dinner and would then go to a movie. " Mother needs an outing."

" At nine then? "

" Yes.　The picture begins at seven."

" I'd come in and go with you, but I can't make it."

Rufus whistled softly as he changed his clothes and set Griselda's dish of salmon before her.

" You'll have to keep company with the bats and owls, Puss Cat," he told her, " I have on hand other and more important matters."

He walked to the Inn and after dinner returned to the house to get his car to drive to the city.　Following the winding path through the woods, it seemed to him that life had never been so serene as now, with all the loveliness of the twilight about him, and ahead of him the thought of his meeting with Sandra.

He found Griselda much occupied with the activities of the night-flying creatures — a great beetle booming against the screen back of which Rufus had left a dim light burning; a moth seeking the same light.　The white cat's eyes were shining, her tail twitched; when a late crow cawed overhead, she chattered her teeth at him.

Rufus laughed.　" You're a bloodthirsty little beast," he began, and did not finish, for his eyes were caught by a splash of color against the green.

Far down the road, at the end of the winding path, a big motor car had stopped, and a woman was coming toward him under the trees — a slender woman in a coat and hat of a daring shade of pink.　The hat hid her face, but there was no need to see her face.　Rufus knew her by her walk.　She carried a cane enameled in the same pink color, and touched it lightly to the ground, swinging her body with the swaggering air one sees in the paintings of famous beauties or on the stage in old costume plays. Whatever else Sherry might lack, she did not lack a sense of the picturesque. Tilted on her high heels, she made her mincing way — a modern Lady Sneerswell, a short-skirted Pompadour. And behind her the last of the sunset provided a gold back-drop for her magnificence.

And with her coming Rufus' house of cards crashed down. Oh, fool that he had been to think he could build in so frail a foundation a romance for himself and Sandra! He might have known Sherry would blow it away with a breath, or demolish it with a touch of her pointed finger!

He stood as if paralyzed. In a moment she would be near so that he could see her face — that impudent face with its hard, hazel eyes. He would have to wake from this nightmare which froze his tongue.

But she spoke first. " I had your letter," she said, as she came up to him, " and I have come to talk about it, Rufus."

CHAPTER XIX

THE CAT AND THE MOUSE

W ILL you come in? " Rufus said.

Outwardly he seemed absolutely at his ease. But within he was seething. That Sherry should come here! Could he never escape her? Would she always pursue her relentless course? Yet, looking at her, frivolous in her pink, he wondered that he should make such high tragedy of it. She hardly deserved to be dignified by the rôle of malevolent fate. She was, rather, a mischievous marplot, ingenious as to her methods, seeming to do nothing with seriousness, but accomplishing her ends.

" Why go in? " she asked. " Can't we sit out here? These trees are heavenly."

He fetched chairs. She posed herself against the one with a fan-shaped back. The sunset was dulled, but there was still gold enough to light her.

" I got your address from Mr. Maulsby. His letter came with yours."

Rufus said nothing. He was leaning against a tree, his eyes on Griselda, who, in pursuit of a beetle, flashed here and there like a white flame.

" What an enchanting cat! " Sherry said.

" I have called her ' Griselda.' "

" Is she as meek as that? "

" I thought she might be. It was too much to expect, of course."

"You are always expecting too much, Rufus, of people as well as pussy cats."

"That's an open question, Sherry, which I refuse to argue." He had regained his poise and was smiling.

She said impatiently: "Sit down. I want to talk to you about the ivories."

"What is there to talk about?"

"I mean to have them. Of course, you know that, Rufus."

"I told you I had sold them to Felix Maulsby."

"I shall buy them back."

Rufus gave a short laugh. "I think not. He has promised not to sell."

She shrugged her shoulders. "How silly to promise anything!"

"Felix is a man of his word."

"He thinks he is."

He refused to discuss Maulsby's state of mind. "Sherry," he demanded, "why do you want them? And why should we act like two children grabbing for a toy?"

The new note in his voice arrested her attention. The well-remembered bitterness was not there, but rather a grave challenge.

"I want them," she said, "because they were your father's."

"No," he said, "you want them because I want them."

"That's utter nonsense, Rufus."

The old argument, flung back and forth — how often they had been at it! One might have thought the world was at stake instead of five small ivory figures. But the thing at stake was something more than that. His will against hers. If she bent him now, she would break him. And he would not bend.

The gold had gone out of the sky. Sherry's pink was dimmed to amethyst. Her impudent little face under her hat was a blank, white oval.

He dropped into a chair opposite her. Griselda jumped to his knee. He ruffled her fur, and she stretched herself at her ease, purring her contented song.

" Next winter," Sherry said out of the darkness, " I am going to live in Washington."

The hand that was smoothing the white cat stopped. " What for? "

" To be near you."

" That isn't the truth, Sherry."

" Well, then, to get the ivories." There was laughter in her voice.

For years she had laughed at him like that. And he hated it. He hated the thought, too, that she would be in Washington. Through all the years since his mother's death, Sherry had been an octopus with a tentacle always out to drag him down when he strove to reach the surface. But now he had not only himself, but another, to strive for. Having once cast off his stepmother, and the influence she had for so many years exerted, he would float free on the sea of Sandra's devotion.

So he said with an effect of calmness: " I don't care where you are or where you live. My life is my own. I shall do with it as I please."

" But what if you should want to — marry, Rufus? "

He had braced himself for that, knowing she would fling it at him. "Well, if I should want to, what then?" he flung back.

"The game would be mine."

A long silence, in which he gathered strength to tell her the truth. It came at last. "I have met the girl, Sherry."

He was aware of a quick movement. She was leaning forward, and the fragrance of the exotic perfume she used came to him.

"You mean you are going to marry her?"

"Yes."

"And let me have — everything?"

"Yes."

She was eager. "Tell me about it."

"There is nothing to tell."

"What makes you say that, Rufus? There must be something of course. Where did you meet her? And what have you found in her so — incomparable that you are willing to lose the game to me?"

"Why talk about it? When I send you a wedding invitation, you can play your trump card, and that will be the end of it."

"When will that be?"

"As soon as she will set the day."

She was on her feet. "Congratulations."

He, too, rose. "Thank you."

"And — Rufus — what are you going to live on?"

"My plans are my own."

"Oh, well," her voice held still that note of triumphant eagerness. "When I came, I didn't expect such good news as this. I am almost inclined to give you the ivories for a wedding present."

" They are not yours to give."

" Perhaps they may be by that time, and — I shall want to meet the bride . . . Have you a picture of her, Rufus? "

" No."

" Haven't you really, or are you just putting me off? "

" I have no picture, but if you want to know how she looks, I've a print on the wall that will give you an idea."

An uncontrollable impulse had come to him to display his treasure. He had a wicked satisfaction, too, in feeling that Sherry had never heard of Vigée LeBrun. She had a shrewd way of disguising her ignorance and a certain knowledge of the commercial value of antiques, but of the culture which presupposes a background of books and travel, she had had none when his father married her, and she had acquired none since.

Rufus led the way into the house. There were no overhead lights, so he held up a lamp, and its rays streamed down upon the picture. " It is called ' The Boy in Red, ' he informed Sherry, " and it is considered a masterpiece."

Sherry looked up at it and laughed contemptuously. " A child like that! "

" Yes . . . with a child's youth and innocence. She has given me back my faith in life, Sherry."

" Has she? " Sherry laughed. " Well, will you thank her for giving me back a fortune? "

Her head was up, the hazel eyes triumphant. The great diamond on her finger glittered — the diamond his father had given her.

Rufus had a sudden revulsion of feeling. His marriage was what she wanted, what she had schemed for. And now he was losing the game to her, and he had sworn he would not. That he would play it to the end. At whatever cost to himself, he would play and win!

He hardly knew what he said after that, something trivial, and presently Sherry went away. He walked with her to her car. It was her own car, with a Japanese chauffeur she had brought from the Coast. Rufus recognized him and spoke.

" You are far away from home, Ito."

Ito smiled. " Too far. Some day are you coming back, sir? "

" Some day."

They drove off, and Rufus went home through the dark grove, Griselda pattering behind him like a little white ghost.

He sat for a long time in the darkness, thinking. At last he entered the house and telephoned Sandra.

" My dear, I can't come."

" Is anything the matter, Rufus? "

" Yes. I am writing."

" But, Rufus . . ."

" Sandra . . . when you say your prayers . . ."

" Yes . . .? "

" Think of me."

He flung himself then down at his table, and began to write his letter:

" My little Sandra:
" Sherry has just been here. She got my address from

Maulsby. When I saw her coming up the path under the pines, I knew nothing good had brought her. If she had not arrived at that very moment, I should have been on my way to you. But since she came and I have talked with her, I feel I must write to you some of the things I have withheld, and which will supplement what I told you that first morning at the Library.

" As I said then, I was ten years old when my father married Sherry, and my mother had been dead less than a year. But what I did not tell you was that for five years before my mother's death, Sherry's presence in my father's office was a shadow on my mother's happiness. It isn't necessary to go into it any farther than that. I had never liked Sherry and could not affect a liking when she came to the house. My close association with my mother had made me sensitive to all that concerned her. Sherry hated me from the beginning. She was jealous of me because I was my father's son, and because I might be a menace to her full inheritance of his fortune.

" My father loved her. There is no doubt of that. She has a sort of hard prettiness; he liked the prettiness, and the hardness was a challenge to his strength. When Sherry wanted a thing, she fought for it, and the battle was a constant stimulus to his interest. Now and then she would let him win, and he would glow with triumph at his conquest. She lived a frivolous, rushing life and kept him amused. She was shrewd enough to feed his vanity. She made him feel he was still young, virile, handsome. He did not reflect that no young woman marries an old man unless he has something to give her — a house, a fortune, ease of living.

"So gradually she gained a complete ascendency over my father. He had a certain pride in me. I was strong in body and in out-of-door sports more than a match for most of my mates. I made good averages in my studies. I was, in fact, a thoroughly normal boy, except for a growing fear of my stepmother, a fear which had nothing to do with physical cowardice, but which had to do with my affections. I was such a little lad, Sandra, and as I look back I am sorry for the boy who was myself. Sherry was always finding ways to hurt me through the things I loved. There was an old dog which I adored and which had been my mother's pet. One day, when I had set my will against Sherry, she gave the dog away. It nearly broke my heart, and after that I was afraid to fight her. If I did, she would retaliate by selling something in the house that I cherished because of its association with my mother — a chair in which she always sat, a teapot from which she poured. One day she went farther than that and discharged a faithful servant because I had defended him from her injustice. Now and then I checkmated her, as when she sent the dog away. I found out where he was, and bought him back and gave him to a friend. He was an Irish setter, and I can see him now waiting at my friend's gate and being wistful when I went away.

"As my father grew older, he became, I thought, a little gentler toward me, but Sherry saw that I was sent East to school and college, and though in my holidays I tried to show something of affection for my father, Sherry always came between us. And at last I stopped trying.

"They had been married ten years when the war

came. I had four years of it, and I think even my father was proud of the record I made. I can say that I fought with the best of them, and I won some honors. I am telling you this in no spirit of egotism. I only want you to know that I can fight anything — except Sherry.

" After the war I stayed in Europe for some time. There were things I could do for our Government, and I did them. I was not dependent on my father. I never asked him for money, though he had offered me an allowance.

" Then one day the news came to me of my father's death. I went home to learn that he had left me half of his fortune, the other half to Sherry. But in a codicil it was expressly stated that if I married, my share would go to Sherry. It was really a fantastic thing for him to do. I have often wondered why he troubled to put it that way. He might have left everything to her at once, and that would have been the end of it. I can only think that Sherry herself influenced the wording of the will, so that she might have a hand in my future. She wanted to play with me as a cat with a mouse. She wanted me to be always stabbed by the knowledge that if I took the money, I couldn't have a wife, and if I took a wife I couldn't have the money.

" So you see, dearest heart, that if I marry you, Sherry wins. She will be victorious in the battle which we have fought so long. I care nothing about the money. In proof of that I can tell you that in the two years since my father's death, I have spent not a penny of the income on my half of his estate. I have a small legacy from my mother. I have lived on that and on what I can make with my pen.

"And now . . . I come to the thing that is hard to say. Sandra, I can't take you into my life. To do it would be to shadow you with the things which shadow me. Sherry would find a way to hurt us both. She has always hurt the things I love, and I will not have you hurt.

"So I am going away. Tomorrow. Without seeing you. I had no right to woo you, but I was swept on by a tide too strong to stem. You will say, of course, that love is worth while only when it fights for the beloved. But one can't fight the intangible. Sherry is my Old Man of the Sea, I can't shake her off. When I am with her, I become not the man you know, not the man my men knew in France, but the little boy of ten, seeing his old dog sent away . . .

"I shall give the keys of the house to the man from whom I bought it, and shall leave Griselda with him. I wish you'd look after her. She's a loving little creature and will miss me.

"I shall not ask you to forgive me. Whatever judgment you pass upon me I must endure. But always, through all the years, I shall think of Juliet on her balcony, my lovely child — leaning down . . ."

When he came to the end, Rufus dropped his head on his outflung arms and was very still. The white cat, who had slept while he wrote, waked up and gave an inquiring murmur. Still with his face hidden, his hand came up and caressed her. Even in the midst of this bitter moment, his hand was kind.

Chapter XX

THE SILVER MILK POT

THEODORA, starting out that afternoon for Baltimore, was a cocky little figure in dark blue with touches of white at the throat and wrists, her slim legs in beige stockings, her shining pumps of patent leather.

Felix Maulsby eyed her approvingly. " I don't see how you do it," he said.

" Do what? "

" Make such an effect on so little."

" Well," Theodora told him, " I put my mind to it. The trouble with most women is that they buy too much. Dressing well is a part of my job. I've got to get on in the world, and that's one way to do it."

Felix had never known a woman quite so practical in her methods, and he found Theodora amusing. He felt he was making no mistake in sending her to besiege the Difficult Customer in Baltimore. Her enthusiasms carried her a long way in dealing with people. She had made sales where he himself had failed.

He was entrusting to her a precious silver milk pot, engraved by Nathaniel Hurd, and she was to hint at other treasures. " There's the plated tea-board, and the bullet tea-pot, and the trencher salts, and the Jacobite goblets."

" I know," Theodora sighed rapturously. " I'm

simply mad about the goblets, and I've studied up on all of them."

"She's disagreeable to deal with," Felix warned her, "and you'll have to keep your temper. I couldn't, when I last discussed things with her, and that's why I am sending you. You have tact, and here's a chance to show it. You'd better come home on the nine o'clock train and take a taxi up to our house. Marcia wants you to help plan the decorations for the garden party. It's the last one she'll give before she goes to the North Shore, and she was much pleased with the way you arranged the porcelain room in the shop."

"I rather liked it, myself," Theodora admitted.

She had no false modesty. And her arrangement of the porcelain room and the results therefrom had been somewhat of a triumph. Things had been too crowded, so when a rich collector was expected, she had swept everything out, and put pink gladioli in a pair of old Deft vases, backed them with an eighteenth century mirror, had draped a length of chintz which repeated the pink and blue, and had sold the vases, the mirror, the table on which they stood, at a price that had amazed Maulsby.

Thus Theodora, having found the thing she could do, was doing it whole-heartedly. Doing it, perhaps, a bit too cocksurely, but youth was to blame for that, and age would tame her.

When she finally entered the chair car on the late afternoon train, she carried a magazine, a leather hand-bag, and the milk-pot in a square box. For the first time in her life she was traveling in state and elegance. Her expenses were being paid by her employer, and there was no reason for economy. And with the Claybournes there had always been the necessity to stint and save.

When the train started, she opened her magazine and began to read. Her eyes strayed now and then, however, away from her book, to her pale silken stockings and the slim and perfect slippers. She liked very much the look of her feet. There was something unmistakably high-bred about them. Her mother would have said they looked as if they belonged to a lady. People who clumped came from peasant stock and wore awful shoes. Thank goodness, she and Sandra . . .

At this moment, the complacency of her thoughts was disturbed by the sudden emergence of another foot into her line of vision. Up the aisle a chair had twirled slightly, and a silver-gray stocking and an ineffable gray shoe were posed on a hard, green-plush floor cushion which the porter had pushed into place. Theodora was sure she recognized that foot. Where had she seen it?

A hand, dropping over the arm of the chair, gave her the key. Stephanie! No mistaking her. She wore a ring that Theodora remembered, and there were besides those pointed fingers!

Theodora's conceit went out of her like a collapsed balloon. Stephanie always had that effect on her. Gone was the glory of her blue frock, her shining shoes. She felt that Stephanie would never have worn a shoe that shone. She affected always an air of simple elegance which drew eyes to her, yet seemed not to bid for the attention it attracted. Even now, as she leaned forward to speak to a friend across the aisle, she seemed utterly unconscious of the eyes upon her.

The friend to whom she spoke was Ruth O'Malley, the Baltimore girl, whom the twins had met one night at dinner. She was, they had thought, delightful, with her frank manner, her deep laugh like a boy's. Theodora made up her mind that she would if she could, get away without speaking to Ruth or Stephanie. They would probably be met by the O'Malleys' car, while the best she could hope for was a taxi.

When the train reached its destination, Theodora made her exit through the rear door. She took with her the leather bag and the magazine, and it was not until she was in the taxi and had started on her way that she discovered she had left the milk-pot!

She leaned forward and spoke to the taxi-driver. "Go back," she said. "I've left a parcel in the train."

Her voice was cool, but she was in a state of excited dismay. The milk-pot was, from a collector's point of view, priceless.

As she hurried down the platform, she forgot Stephanie, she forgot Ruth O'Malley, she forgot everything but the thing she sought, so that it was almost with the effect of coming out of ether, or of having been dead and being resurrected, that she was aware of a voice crying,

"Doady Claybourne, how did you get here, and what in the world has happened?"

It was Stephanie, of course, flanked on one side by a red-cap with her bag, and on the other side by the O'Malley chauffeur with Ruth's bag, and Ruth was laughing and demanding as Stephanie had done,

"What happened?"

"I can't stop," Theodora, poised for flight, flung at them. "I've left something in the train. A milk-pot."

They stared after her in amazement. " What does she mean by a milk-pot," Ruth demanded.

" Some of Felix's stuff," Stephanie decided.

" We'd better wait for her."

" Oh, well . . ."

When Theodora returned, she was radiant. She carried a square box and waved it while she was still at some distance.

" The porter had it," she exclaimed breathlessly. " I am sure he thought it was candy and hated to give it up."

" Is it one of Felix's things? " Stephanie asked her.

" Yes. And he has set a high price on it. This woman I am to visit wants it awfully, but she isn't willing to pay for it."

" Where does she live? " Ruth asked. " Can't we give you a lift? "

" Charles Street."

" It's just a few blocks."

So Theodora sat between Ruth and Stephanie on the wide back seat of the big car, and Ruth asked to see the milk-pot, and said when it was shown:

" When you come again, you must let mother see some of your antiques. She's wild about old things."

Theodora hardly heard the remark. She was suffering from a reaction of her exaltation of the morning. The glory had gone out of her day. Here she was bound for a great house where she must try by hook or crook to sell her wares to a customer, and here were these other girls sweeping on to join a crowd of young folk at the country club, and sweeping back for a dinner dance at Ruth's.

"Gale's coming," Ruth vouchsafed.

Well, there it was! Ruth and Gale and Stephanie! Young! Having good times!

Yet when at last she was shown into the drawing-room of the Difficult Customer, her spirits rose. The thrill of conquest was upon her. If she sold the milk-pot, and the tea-board, and perhaps some other things, why should she care if Stephanie danced?

Now, if this were anything but a true chronicle, Theodora would have been made to lead the Difficult Customer to defeat. She would have come off with flying colors. But neither of these things happened. The Difficult Customer proved to be even more unpleasant than Felix had prophesied. She was dressed for dinner in impeccable black lace and amethysts, and she had a butler and three maids and had always had them, and she had always lived on the northwest corner of that particular block near Mount Vernon Square, and she had always had people do things the way she wanted them, and she wanted Theodora to take just two hundred dollars less for the milk-pot than the price asked.

"It's outrageous!" said the Difficult Customer.

"Not at all," said Miss Theodora Claybourne of Virginia, who wouldn't have spoken to any pickananny at Windytop as the Difficult Customer had spoken. As if there were a gulf between you. Not to be bridged by those who didn't have a butler and three maids and a house on the northwest corner of old North Charles!

"Not at all," repeated Miss Claybourne of Windytop. "It's really cheap at the price."

The Difficult Customer rose. "That's nonsense of course, and you can tell Felix Maulsby I told you."

She was imposing in her impeccable black lace. "I had intended," she said, "to show it to some friends who are coming to dine with me. That's why I had you bring it at this hour. But I shall not show it."

Theodora had risen also. She was not in the least impressed by the black lace and the amethysts and the butler and maids and three-score and ten years of residence on Charles Street. The things that daunted Theodora were beauty and the arrogance of youth as expressed in Stephanie. What did she care for this withered aristocrat with her years upon her?

So she said earnestly, and with an air of meaning it: "I am sorry. I should have liked to sell it to you. But since you don't want it, it will go to another collector."

"What other collector?"

"She lives in Baltimore and is having a dinner dance tonight. But I am sure she will see me, and if not, I can come over tomorrow."

"What's her name?" the impeccable black lace demanded.

"That," said Theodora, "I am not permitted to tell. Mr. Maulsby never allows me to speak of one customer to another."

"What a snippy little thing you are," said the Difficult Customer with biting tongue. "Mr. Maulsby shouldn't have sent you."

"He sent me," Theodora told her, "because I worship the lovely things he has in his shop. And I'd hate to see them go into the hands of any one who didn't worship them."

The impeccable lady knew she ought to stop the

conversation right there — that it was beneath her dignity to bandy words with this cocksure little creature. But she wanted to bandy words. So she said:

" I have made a study of old silver for years. But I don't worship anything but God."

The words were no sooner out of her mouth than she had a feeling that she had gone too far.

" Oh! " said Theodora, and that was all.

But the impeccable lady was left with a sense of having done something underbred and awful!

Theodora, being shown out a few moments later by the impeccable's butler, held her head high. She had failed with the Difficult Customer, but she had other worlds to conquer. There was Ruth O'Malley's mother, the " other collector " of whom she had spoken. The remark of the daughter had made little impression at the time it was spoken, but now it came back as significant.

She went into the big hotel, which was only a block or two away, and found the O'Malley number in the telephone book. She asked for Mrs. O'Malley and was told she was engaged. " May I take a message? "

" Will you tell her I'm a friend of her daughter, and I have some old silver to show her."

Presently the man came back. " Mrs. O'Malley will see you if you can come at once. She is entertaining at dinner at eight."

Mrs. O'Malley was as plump and pleasing as her daughter. She was resting on a *chaise longue* after having her hair dressed, and was drinking iced chocolate.

" My dear," she said, when Theodora was seated,

" it's a dreadful thing, isn't it, to drink chocolate before dinner? Especially when one needs to lose pounds! But it is a rule of mine not to be hungry at my own dinner table. It hampers one dreadfully to want to eat when one should be interested in one's guests. And now, won't you have a cup of chocolate with me? "

Theodora was glad to have it. The dày was hot, and her passage at arms with the impeccable one had left her somewhat shaken. It was delightful to rest at ease in the chintz-covered chair, while the pleasant person on the *chaise longue* alternately sipped her iced drink and talked about antiques.

Here was, Theodora discovered, no cold collector. Mrs. O'Malley was glowing, responsive.

" Irish glass is my specialty," she confided, " because of my Irish blood. But I love these little, old silver pieces."

She handled the milk-pot with reverent fingers. " I want this. And I'm coming over to look at some of the other things. Tomorrow? We leave the day after for the North Shore with Stephanie."

Theodora rose. "We'll have tea in the garden. You'll adore it, Mrs. O'Malley. And you'll never get away without the Jacobite glasses."

Theodora, emerging from Mrs. O'Malley's room, found the whole house waiting as it were for the arrival of the guests. As she descended the wide stairs, she seemed to sink into a sea of rosy light. There were flowers everywhere, and their fragrance. Men and maids moved here and there giving last touches. None of the family had come down, but in the drawing-room was one guest who said with an air of astonishment as Theodora reached the last step,

" Doady, how did you get here? "

" In my new slippers." She was sparkling.

Gale surveyed her with interest. " My dear child, you look as if you had picked a star from the sky."

" I've picked a whole constellation."

" Tell me about it."

" Oh, I mustn't stay. I'm not invited. Mr. Maulsby sent me over with a piece of old silver to sell to a customer, and I didn't sell it. And on the train I had seen Stephanie and Ruth O'Malley, and they said Mrs. O'Malley was interested in antiques, so I came here . . ." she flung out her hands as if she would embrace the world, " and she saw me, and she's a darling."

Gale laughed. " You're a darling," he told her lightly. " And you've enthusiasm enough to sell anything. How do you do it? "

" Do what? "

" Keep yourself running at such speed."

" I've always had to do things. I'm the dynamo. Sandra and mother are the dreamers."

" Don't you ever dream, Doady? "

There was a startled look in her eyes, "Oh, sometimes — when I let myself."

She was standing on the step above him, and at that moment, down the stairs behind her, came Stephanie — slim and white in her sleeveless dinner dress, a lily on a stem.

" Doady," she said with a touch of sharpness in her voice, " how did you get here? "

" That's what Gale asked me." Theodora vouch-safed, " and I said in my new slippers. But it was really because of what Ruth told me, that her mother liked old silver. So when my other customer wouldn't meet my price, I came here, and I sold the milk-pot."

" To Mrs. O'Malley? Really? "

" Yes. And now I must run on, for the guests will be arriving."

" Don't go," Gale urged. " Stephanie asked me to come early, and here I am, and here you are, and there's no reason why you can't stay till the others come."

But Theodora knew there was a reason. And the reason had nothing to do with the arriving guests. It had to do with the fact that three's a crowd! Stephanie wanted Gale to herself. And she didn't want Theodora.

Gale insisted, however, that she wait until he called a taxi. Then, when it came, he went out to put her into it.

" I'd much rather be going back with you," he said, holding the cab a moment to talk to her, " than eating dinner with Ruth's gang. Look here, let's run away tomorrow and dine somewhere all by ourselves. Shall we? "

Theodora had a fleeting vision of Stephanie waiting in the rosy light, slim and white like a bride.

" Yes," she said with the wicked joy of one who triumphs over an adversary. " Yes, I'd love it."

Chapter XXI

THE GIRL THAT RUFUS WOULDN'T MARRY

WHEN Theodora reached home, it was very late. From the train she had gone out to the Maulsbys' and had talked for a long time with Marcia and her husband. She found that they had more to discuss than the matter of the decorations. Felix had opened a branch on the North Shore and wanted Theodora to take entire charge of the Washington shop for the summer.

" The people I have here haven't any idea of doing it properly. You know my requirements, and I shall be free from worry."

Theodora was still tingling with the excitement of it all when Marcia's big motor car set her down at her own doorstep. She went on tiptoe through the dim halls and turned the knob of the door of her apartment with caution. She expected to find her mother reading in bed and Sandra asleep. But her mother was not reading. She was lying high on her pillows, breathing with difficulty, and Sandra was bending over her.

At once Theodora's own affairs fell from her. " Oh, what's the matter? "

" She had a faint spell," Sandra said. " I've sent for the doctor."

Mrs. Claybourne tried to reassure them. " It's nothing . . . I shall be all right . . . presently . . ."

But she was not all right presently, and when the doctor arrived, he gave one look and got out his hypodermic.

"I'll have you comfortable before you know it," he said cheerfully, and bent to his task.

She relaxed in a moment, and the color came back to her cheeks.

The doctor surveyed her. "Been working too hard?"

"Perhaps. And it's so hot. Sandra and I went to a movie, and when we came back we were sitting on the balcony, and suddenly everything was black before me."

"I see. Well, you must stay in bed tomorrow."

"I ought to go to work."

"Not until I let you."

He wrote a prescription and said he would leave it at the drug store. "She must be kept quiet," he told Sandra, who had followed him into the hall.

Sandra asked, "How serious is it?"

"I can't be sure. If her heart is involved, she may have to take a long rest."

Sandra told Doady later what he had said. Madge had gone to sleep, soothed by the drug which the doctor had given her. The two girls lay side by side in their little beds and talked in low tones.

"If she takes a long rest, it means giving up her position," Theodora said.

They considered that in dismayed silence. It seemed to sweep from them the very foundations of stability to have their mother unable to be, in the future, at the helm of their domestic bark.

Out of the silence Theodora said: "The Maulsbys

want me to take charge of their shop. They will give me better pay, but it won't be enough for us to live on."

Sandra, listening, let her sister plan. She felt she ought to tell Doady she was going to marry Rufus Fiske and that it would make a difference. But somehow she couldn't bring herself to do it. Since Rufus' message over the telephone, she had been oppressed by a sense of impending tragedy. Why should he write instead of coming? And why should he want her prayers?

She tried to tell herself that she was unnerved because of her mother's illness. But she could not sleep, and at last she got up and went out on the balcony. Below her and across the way the balcony on which she had first seen Rufus was blank and empty. Once more there was a late moon, and the world was spectral under it. To Sandra the night seemed sinister. In the room back of her, her mother slept a drugged sleep and in the house among the pines Rufus was heavy-hearted.

She felt very small, very insignificant, in this moon-lighted world. As for her prayers, how far would they carry in that vast overarched space? Yet she sent them forth, little messengers of faith:

"Help Rufus. And don't let me be hurt. And make mother well."

Such a child, this little Sandra, on her balcony!

The next morning, Mrs. Claybourne was out of pain but weak. When the doctor came, he talked for a long time, then told Mrs. Claybourne the truth.

"You'd better give up work for a month or two. Perhaps longer. Can't you get leave?"

" I might."

" It would be best if you could go away somewhere. You've been used to country air."

Madge said eagerly, " There's my old place in Virginia — Windytop."

" If it is as cool as it sounds, it ought to do the trick."

When the doctor had gone, Sandra sat on the edge of her mother's bed and told what the Maulsbys wanted Theodora to do.

" She could stay in Washington, and you and I could go to Windytop, Mumsie. And when Rufus and I are married, it can be in the old garden."

There were tears in Madge's eyes. " My darling, it would be wonderful. If you could know how I've longed for the old house! "

Hand in hand, they talked about it, these dreamers of dreams. The rest of July and a part of August and then — the wedding.

" And by that time I would be well enough to come back here, and Doady and I could have a maid, and you could keep house for Rufus."

How simple it sounded! Sandra, as she went out to make a lemonade for her mother, wondered how she could have been so silly as to be afraid.

The mail, delivered by a house boy, was always dropped through a slot in the door. This morning it hit the floor with a thud. Sandra snatched it up. Two thick letters.

" One is for you, from Sally Grymes," Sandra told her mother. " Can you see to read it, or shall I turn on the light? "

"I can see," Madge said, "but I don't like the idea of having my bed down in the daytime. Some one might come in, and here I'd be. It doesn't look quite respectable. Sandra, if I go to Windytop, it will be like heaven to have my own big room."

To Sandra it seemed as if her mother's voice came through a thick fog. But she managed to answer, "Don't worry; nobody will be here this morning, Mumsie."

Mrs. Claybourne settled back comfortably on her pillows. "It will be wonderful to see Sally. You got a letter, too, didn't you, dearie?"

"Yes. From Rufus. I'll read mine while you read yours."

Sandra went into her own room and shut the door. Then she tore the letter open! Read it, standing! Page after page!

When she had finished, she felt as if she were frozen . . . as if when she took a step she would stump along on petrified feet . . . as if ice were forming about her heart . . . as if when it got to the middle of her heart she would scream and fall . . . !

But she mustn't fall! The doctor had said they must guard her mother against any sudden shock. . . .

In the next room, Madge, having devoured Sally's letter, lay thinking about it. How good it would be to go back and forth on neighborly visits! To have Sally at Windytop to help with Sandra's wedding things!

But where was Sandra? It was queer she hadn't come back. But then, lovers' letters! Dreams! Madge smiled in her wise way. Dreams! All girls had them!

After a while the door opened, and Sandra entered.

Her cheeks were pink, her eyes bright, her voice cool.

" Did you have a nice letter, Mumsie? "

" Yes.　I'll read it to you."

" Not now.　I must run out and buy some lamb for your broth.　I'll get Ione Morton to stay with you."

" I don't need any one to stay with me."

" Doctor's orders, dearest."

" What did Rufus have to say? "

" Oh, a lot of things.　He's going out of town."　Her hand was on the knob; she spoke over her shoulder. Then she went into the hall.

She stood for a moment, steadying herself; knocked at Ione's door.

Ione welcomed anything that relieved the monotony of her life.　" You needn't hurry," she told Sandra. " I'll take care of her."

But Sandra hurried.　She wanted to be alone . . . in the dim church . . . to find some corner . . . She mustn't cry . . . people would see her eyes . . . but she could gather strength . . . on her knees. . . .

Oh, don't let me be hurt . . . like this . . . !　I can't stand it!　I can't!

She stayed so long in the church that she fairly flew to the market.　When she got there, she told the man she wanted everything for Scotch broth . . . lamb . . . and carrots . . . and celery . . . and barley . . . oh, yes, and an onion . . . and two chops for herself and Doady . . . and something for salad . . . and peaches for dessert.

Reaching home, she put the lamb on at once to boil. Ione watched her with curiosity.

" You're the queerest girl to have your mind on

such things. Most any one as pretty as you would only
think of getting married."

Yes, but Rufus didn't want to marry her.

"We got the recipe for the broth from my grandmother," she told Ione with outward composure.
"Only she used mutton instead of lamb. We think
the lamb more delicate. And of course she made great
quantities."

She was cutting up vegetables — the carrots into
small cubes, and the celery, and the onion into paper-
thin slices. The onion brought tears. They streamed
down her cheeks.

"Let me do that," Ione offered. "Onions don't act
that way with me."

Sandra handed her the knife. "I'll bathe my eyes,"
she said, and fled to her room.

It was not the onion now which made her cry, but her
breaking heart. She flung her hands up to her face
. . .! Let her tears flow and fall. If her mother
asked questions, she could say she was peeling vegetables. . . .

After Ione left, Madge slept, and while she slept
Sandra wrote a letter. The letter was to Rufus, and
she knew he would never see it. He had left no address,
and if he had left one with any one else, she would never
ask for it. Yet the act of writing was a relief from the
thoughts which racked her. She told him that love was
everything. And why should Sherry matter? And
that she couldn't live without him. She couldn't.

Yet all the time she was writing it she knew she
would have to go on living. She knew she would have

to go on taking care of her mother, and doing things for Theodora, and seeing people and talking to them.

Her mother, waking after a while asked, " Are you writing to Rufus? " and Sandra said, " Yes." Then when her mother slept again, she tore the letter into little bits and dropped them in a basket.

When Theodora came home that night, she found Sandra spent and worn.

" You look tired to death," she said. " Why don't you go to bed? "

" I will," Sandra promised. " As soon as I straighten things a bit."

Madge, propped up on her pillows, eating her broth, said: " We'll both have a good rest at Windytop. The doctor wants me to go, Doady, and I'll be glad to, if you can find someone to stay with you."

" Miss Carter will come," said the forehanded Theodora. " I asked her today if she could do it. She's wild about it. She's fed up on boarding houses, and she's old enough to satisfy any of your conventional inhibitions, as Sandra calls them. And when you and Sandra come back in the fall, everything will be just as you left it."

Madge smiled mysteriously. By fall, Sandra would be married. She thought Doady ought to know. It seemed a shame to keep things from her. So when Theodora was out of the room for a moment, she said,

" It would be nice to tell Doady."

" Tell her what? "

" That you are going to marry Rufus."

But she wasn't going to marry Rufus!

Sandra, shaking up the pillows, said with her face

hidden: " Oh, not tonight, Mumsie. She'll want to talk a lot about it, and I'm dead for sleep."

She went away after that and Theodora entertained her mother with an account of the things she had done that day. She had sold a lot of antiques to Mrs. O'Malley, and Gale had come and Stephanie and Ruth, and they had had tea in the garden. But what she did not tell was that Gale had wanted her to keep her promise to go to dinner with him, and that she had not, because she had known she must get back to her mother.

Madge, listening, felt that it was marvellous to have such daughters — Doady so successful, and Sandra with a wedding ahead. She wondered that the child hadn't said more about Rufus' letter. Oh, well, perhaps it was natural. A girl liked to keep something of her romance to herself.

But Sandra, lying wide-eyed in her little bed, staring into the darkness, told herself that there was no romance. Rufus had killed it. He didn't care a fig for it. . . . He had thought love a little thing . . . To be cast off . . . forgotten. . . .

She had eaten no lunch, she had eaten no dinner. She would never, she was sure, sleep again . . . She would only go on and on, forever . . . wanting Rufus!

Chapter XXII

A SNUFFED–OUT CANDLE

THEY had been at Windytop a week when Sandra told her mother what had happened. Rufus had gone. And he was not coming back. Madge had known something was wrong. The child had been like a snuffed-out candle. At first, she had thought her own illness the cause, but as she grew better, she guessed that Sandra was hiding some deeper hurt.

The story finished, Sandra said, " If you don't mind, Mumsie, I'd rather not talk about it."

So they didn't talk about it. Yet as time went on, Sandra was aware of the subtle spiritual influence of her mother's sympathy. Though unexpressed, it comforted her. It was something strong to cling to. A rock which hid her.

There came a night when she cried in her mother's arms. " I ought not, Mumsie . . . you're not well . . . but I can't help it."

When she had worried herself almost into a relapse, Madge spoke to Sally Grymes. " Of course, you've noticed the change in Sandra? "

" A love-affair? "

" How did you know? "

" Dearest, when a girl of Sandra's age doesn't eat — doesn't sleep — ! "

" I'm not sure I ought to tell you."

" Nonsense! Isn't Sandra half mine? I held her in my arms before you did, and I told you then that since the Lord had brought no child to me and had brought you twins, one of them belonged to me."

The two women were in the library — a shabby room with shelves of ancient books. Set against the dingy background were garden flowers in bowls, and the open window showed today the rich green of a rain-drenched landscape with the foothills of the Blue Ridge against a blurred and distant skyline. Sally knitted while Madge talked, and when she had heard it all, she said,

" Of course, you realize it's your own fault? "

" Mine? "

" Yes. For bringing the twins up on moonshine and magic. How could they know that men swear by inconstant moons as well as constant ones? "

" I can't think of Rufus Fiske as inconstant."

" It's a queer story. And you've only his word for it. Those ivories — perhaps they weren't his after all, and he didn't want Sandra to discover it."

" Oh, Sally, he's a gentleman! "

Sally shrugged her shoulders. " Let us hope you are as discerning as you think you are. You're such a baby when it comes to worldly-wiseness. Sandra had no doubts, of course."

" Only of his love for her. She feels if he had really cared, he couldn't have left her."

" Oh, the youth of it! Settling things that belong to the gods. If Rufus Fiske is intended for Sandra, he'll be brought back to her. Things work themselves out, Madge. You and I know that. What seems frustration is often only preparation. If Romeo and Juliet had had an ounce of commonsense, they wouldn't have furnished a classic example for hot-headed lovers."

" I wish I dared let you talk to Sandra, Sally. You're so sensible."

" Well, why not? "

" I hate to seem to probe."

" She can't feel that, Madge. She knows we both love her."

So it happened that a half-hour later Sally, driving a small and mud-splashed car over a squashy road, saw ahead of her a figure in a green slicker, straining against the wet wind and looking for all the world as if one of the blown-about bushes had become suddenly peripatetic.

" Sandra," she called.

The green figure whirled. " Aunt Sally, what made you leave so early? I thought you were staying for supper."

" I am. But I want to talk to you. Get in, and we'll drive on a bit."

Sandra, with sudden premonition, demanded, " What do you want to talk about? "

" Dear child, your mother has told me."

" About Rufus? "

" Yes."

" Oh, she shouldn't."

" I think she should. It was much on her mind. She felt I might advise."

" I don't want advice, Aunt Sally. I've got to go on — by myself." Such a stern little face with the rain driving down upon it!

Sally Grymes spoke sharply. "Don't stand there getting your death. If you don't want to talk about it, we won't. But I think you're very silly."

Fire and flame in Sandra's cheeks. "You don't expect me to wear my heart on my sleeve, do you?"

"No. But you're hurt and needing help. Would you think me kind to pass a kitten on the road if I could ease its pain?"

Sandra laid her hand impulsively on the older woman's arm. "Aunt Sally, you're a darling. But he's gone away, and that's the end of it."

"Nothing is the end. Life unrolls."

Sandra got into the car.

"Some day he'll be coming back," Sally said, as they drove on.

"I don't want him back."

"Ah, but you do, my dear."

Silence. And out of it Sally Grymes asking, "Have you written to him?"

"No."

"Why not?"

"He didn't ask me to, and I have too much pride."

"Pride has nothing to do with it. I want you to write, Sandra. Tell him that you'll have faith in him for a year. But if he doesn't come then, he can never come."

"Why should I say a year?"

"Because you must set a limit to his imagination. He has gone off madly at the urge of an old grievance. He thinks he is doing the chivalrous thing not to drag you into it. He'll stand on that till the end of time if you don't shock him out of it."

" You mean that the letter will shock him? "

" It will wake him up to the fact that if he doesn't claim you while he can, he will lose you — forever."

But Sandra wouldn't promise to write. The best she would do was to promise to think of it.

" She is in the grip of disillusionment," Sally said to Madge on her return. " Love isn't what she had thought it. The world well lost and all that. She will learn as life goes on that love is long patience."

Upstairs in her own room Sandra was dressing for dinner and telling herself that silence was the only self-respecting thing. When a man left you and said he was never coming back, there was nothing to be done about it.

She was conscious, suddenly, of a restlessness which confused and confounded her. She hated to go down and eat supper with the two women. She hated to think of tomorrow, when she would work in the garden or walk in the woods. She hated to think of the evenings in the library when she would read to her mother, and Sally Grymes would come and knit. And all these things she hated, she had once loved.

" Oh, I'm like Doady," she said. " She always thought Windytop was deadly, and I never did."

When she was dressed and ready, she looked in the glass. Any one could see she had been crying. She had wept more tears in these few weeks than in all the years before. She hadn't thought of herself like that — a Mariana of the Moated Grange, "*I am a-weary, weary — I would that I were dead.*" She had believed herself able to weather any storm. And here

she was, a little ship floundering in dark seas, with no
light ahead.

The only thing ahead was having supper with her
mother and Sally Grymes. She must go down and play
her part as gallantly as she could. Help Aunt Louisa to
put things on the table, carve the ham, talk and smile,
and seem at her ease.

Aunt Louisa was the third of the solicitous group of
adults who gave an anxious eye to the change in Sandra.
She was a mulatto of uncertain age who had nursed
Madge's babies, and who now lived in a cabin up the
hill back of Windytop, and came to cook and clean and
refresh her lonely soul with the company of her beloved
mistress.

And to her mistress Aunt Louisa had said that very
afternoon when Sally drove to met Sandra:

"I shore is glad Miss Sally is stayin'! I likes to
have somebody that knows how to flatter my cookin'!
You and Miss Sandra ain't done nothin' but pick and
peck since you came."

"I'm worried about Sandra," Madge said.

"Doan you worrit, honey," Aunt Louisa advised.
"Now she's weepin' in the valley, but some day she'll
climb the hill and look off and see the sun shinin' and
a young man comin' along high-steppin' and handsome."
Madge laughed and let the subject drop. She wondered how much the old woman guessed. Aunt Louisa's
intuitions were sometimes clairvoyant.

Supper in the huge dining-room showed a bare
stretch of mahogany table with three places set at the
end. "Sandra wanted to have a little table put in the
bay window," Madge explained to Sally, "but I don't

ever want anything little again. Not after our efficiency
apartment. I simply gloat over the big things at Windytop. This table and the big sideboard and the big
chairs, and over the thought that nothing revolves or
shuts up or looks like something that it isn't. I even
had Aunt Louisa boil this big ham yesterday, though
goodness knows how Sandra and I are going to eat it."

Sandra carved. She stood to do it, and her keen knife
slid through the brown crust and across the pink and
white expanse with an expertness born of years of prac-
tice. Like everything else she did, she made an art of
it. The slices curled down upon the bone, pink as the
petals of a flower. A quick slash severed them, and
they showed luscious half-moons of rose and white
on the gold-banded plates which had been a part of
Madge's wedding china.

While she carved, Sandra talked with seeming tranquillity of a thousand things — of the news in the morning paper, of the way the melons were coming on in the
garden, of the opening of the county horse-show, of a
letter from Theodora which she had found in the box.

" I'll read it after dinner," she said. " It's such a
big one, I thought Aunt Sally could enjoy it with us."

She did not say that Theodora's letter had been forgotten in the rush of emotions which had followed her
talk with Mrs. Grymes. It seemed dreadful that she
should have forgotten Doady for one minute. They
had always been so close, and now no one seemed close,
not even her mother. The world seemed a vast space,
empty except for Rufus and herself. Other people
simply revolved on the edges, calling to her from afar.

Sally Grymes was stopping over night. She was a

widow and had no family ties. " Many's the time," she said, as the three of them returned to the library after supper, " that I've stayed at Windytop. It was a gay old place then. With a lot of young people."

It was not gay tonight. Just Aunt Sally with her knitting, and Madge lying back in her deep chair, and Sandra on a low seat with Griselda on her lap.

The transferring of the white cat from one habitation to another had been a triumphant progress. There had been, to be sure, a dreadful day in the express car when she had nearly yowled her pretty head off; but after that had been her introduction to the great barn, piled with sweet hay, and with dark nooks and corners where the mice flickered in and out; to the cow which was milked by Aunt Louisa, who set saucers of warm foam on the dairy floor and watched Griselda while she drank; to the garden with its bed of catnip, which Griselda visited every morning and came back smelling like a bunch of herbs.

To Sandra, Griselda was the one link between herself and Rufus. Out of the deadening silence which followed his departure had come this little creature. Griselda was Sandra's shadow, pattering up and down and in and out in pursuit of her. She slept in Sandra's room, walked with her in the garden, was her constant attendant, her adored companion.

Sally Grymes, guessing something of the emotion which stirred Sandra when she held her pet, wished that the wandering lover might see them now — Sandra in her dull green, with the bright flame of her hair, the pale oval of her face, and the white cat like a great muff against her.

"Read Doady's letter," she said briskly, "and I'll hold your pussy-cat."

But Griselda stayed with Sandra. She liked Sally Grymes, but she would not desert the heart that loved her.

"My Dears and my Darlings," said Theodora, "I am leading a double life. One here at the shop with my lovely things about me, and the one at the apartment with Susan Croker and Ione Morton. For Ione and Susan have become great friends. It is frightfully funny, because they are so different. But Susan has conceived an idea of herself as a missionary to the proletariat, or whatever you call 'em! She believes that etiquette and the ten commandments would save the world for democracy! She feels that in Ione's case etiquette is more important than the ten commandments. Ione, she contends, is honest at heart and straight-thinking when it comes to the *big moralities!* That's the way Susan puts it! But that she might as well be a South Sea Islander for all she knows of the small amenities. So that the best of her is hidden, and she gives the effect of boldness and rudeness, when really she is only consumed with a great loneliness and a desire to be like people above her. Susan says that Ione is worried about her husband and hints he is a bootlegger, and Susan is working on that. She says that bootleggers are modern buccaneers, and that there's a sort of romance about the business, and men follow it not because of wickedness but from a sense of adventure. She thinks Ione's husband can be reformed if some occupation can be substituted which will satisfy

his sense of romance. She and Ione talk a lot about it.
And every night they have a lesson in etiquette. Ione
is learning how to meet people, and when to shake
hands, and when not to fold your napkin, and a lot of
other things. She loves to set our table, and knows
where to put the forks and spoons. She says her husband has noticed his own forks and spoons and likes
the change, and Susan says that's a great step and may
lead to his wanting moral beauty and orderliness in
his own life!

"I didn't mean to say so much about Susan and Ione,
but it will explain in a way why I stay so much at the
shop. I can't stop Susan from trying to make Ione over,
and I wouldn't if I could, for Ione is so grateful that
it is like a lonely little dog wagging its tail. And then,
there isn't a moment in the apartment that I don't miss
the two of you, so I've got in a way of coming down here
and going on with my cataloguing of the Sheffield collection, which Mr. Maulsby asked me to do, and for
which I can't find time during the day. There's a
nice old watchman who sits in the hall by the elevator
shaft, so I am not afraid, and sometimes on the hot
evenings I go into the garden where it's cool and quiet.

"Everybody is out of town. Washington is dead in
August, except for the few men who don't quite know
what to do with themselves, and who make one feel
tremendously popular, because there isn't any one else
to pay attention to, and they hang around as if you
were really the One Woman.

"I am speaking particularly of Gale. He seems to
enjoy being with me. We go around quite a bit to-

gether, and Mrs. Markham has asked me up several times, and one night I had a few people here in the garden and served fruit punch and little cakes and had a party.

" But the great news is that I am taking dancing lessons. And who do you think is giving them to me? — Susan! Would you think that any one who wore horn spectacles and took life so seriously could dance? But Susan can, and she can teach it, too, because when she learns anything, she does it thoroughly. Every evening, before I leave for the shop, she gives lessons to Ione and me, and oh, my darlings, it's a scream to see us. We are all so different . . . but I won't try to describe it — I leave it to your vivid imaginations!

" But to go back to Gale. Please, don't build up a romance, Mumsie. His particular star is Stephanie. It is a pity to have him wasted on her. She is such a dog in the manger. She doesn't want to marry him, and she doesn't want any one else to have him. If he had money, I'd do my best to cut her out. But I am not going to marry at all if I can't marry some one who will let me dine at eight and have breakfast in bed. Of course, this will shock Mumsie, but she mustn't feel that way about it. She has one romantic child, and that's enough for any family. I intend to put us all in the way of having money, and if I can't marry it, I'll make it.

" Well, take care of yourselves, and stay as long as you can. I am really enjoying life, although I miss you loads. People should never be born twins; it's hampering to the affections, and so are mothers. I could live alone perfectly if I didn't love you both so much. But I do. Although I try to be cold-blooded and calculating to balance the two of you.

" By the way, everybody here is talking about Rufus Fiske's article, which has just appeared in a current magazine. Gale says it is a smashing indictment of both the sentimental internationalists and the complacent nationalists. In a business letter that Mr. Maulsby wrote yesterday, he enclosed a copy of one he had sent to Mr. Fiske, urging him to return to Washington. He says that a lot of interesting people want to meet him. And that this is his moment. If he will stay right on in Maryland, he'll have a chance for political prominence. People are tired of platitudes, and he has a new message.

" It was queer, his going away so suddenly, wasn't it? Has Sandra heard from him? They seemed frightfully friendly before he left. It began to look like the real thing. But romance doesn't come to Cinderellas easily in these days. They have to work for it. And Sandra wouldn't lift her little finger. But I shall lift mine if I meet the prince with a coach and four. He can't escape me.

" Oh, I must stop. Write and tell me everything. And here's a wave of my hand to the garden. The flower garden, I mean. If it were Sandra, she'd wave to the vegetables and have all the tomatoes and peppers blushing. With love to both of you and to darling Sally Grymes,

" Ever your own,

THEODORA."

As Sandra folded up the letter, she wondered how she had kept her voice steady when she read that reference to Rufus Fiske. Her heart had jumped at the sight of his name, and the beat of the words was still with her,

" *Mr. Maulsby says . . . that this . . . is his moment.*"

Madge was complaining " That letter doesn't sound like one from a child of mine — all that sophistication."

" It's only surface sophistication," Sally declared, " and nothing to be disturbed about. Doady has a level head, and she'll keep her balance. Her work is an outlet for her energies. She is making a success, and for the moment it intoxicates her."

Sandra had a wild feeling that she wanted to be up there with Doady, doing things — and with men " hanging around." With Gale, comfortable Gale, with his little limp and his pleasant manner. Not a figure for romance, but such a good friend. It would be something to take her mind from this aching loneliness.

The three women went upstairs early.

" It is such a joy," Madge remarked, " to know there is an upstairs."

Sandra, going in after a while to kiss her mother, said, " Aunt Sally wants me to write to Rufus."

" Well, why not, dearie? "

" Oh, how can I? How can I? " passionately. " I love him too much to want anything but big things from him. I thought his love was wine poured into the cup of my heart. I don't want to beg for a drop — to ease my thirst."

The poet in her was speaking, and the woman.

Madge agreed with her. Love was a man's free bounty. It must not be coerced.

" I can't advise," Mrs. Claybourne said helplessly. " I only want you to be — happy."

Sandra, going back to her room, felt there was no help anywhere. Even God had failed her. The God to whom she used to say her little prayers and get therefrom a secure sense of peace, gave nothing now to ease her pain.

Griselda came in, and Sandra shut the door. Enclosed now in the four walls of the room where she had spent her childhood, she felt she could face her thoughts, unafraid of the effect of a tell-tale countenance. She undressed slowly, pouring cool water for her ablutions from the big pitcher into the big basin which stood on the old-fashioned washstand.

All the furniture in the room was old-fashioned. And there was no modern lighting. On Sandra's dresser were two red candles in cheap glass holders; there were red cushions on the chairs. The bed was a massive affair of carved walnut, towering toward the ceiling and heavy at the top with wooden fruit. The fruit carvings were repeated on the dresser, the washstand, and a clumsy old desk in a corner. Windytop had been furnished in the mid-Victorian period when there was nothing light and lovely for a young girl's room, and Sandra and her sister had had adjoining chambers, cavernous at night, but flooded with sunshine during the day. In these rooms the twins had acted out the gay and gorgeous drama of their youth. They were sixteen when their father died, and the knowledge came that he had left his family little but a heritage of honorable dealing and of romantic ideals which matched their mother's.

It seemed to Sandra tonight that the ghost of the little girl who had been herself came out from the shadows and looked at her. The little girl with the zest for life. And now the zest was gone.

She put on the white kimono she had so often worn in Washington, turned down the bed, said her prayers, hung up this and that, and did it all with stiff and mechanical motions as if her mind were not upon it.

The thing her mind was on was the desk back there in the shadowy corner. In the daytime light was shed upon it by the window near which it stood. At night in order to write one needed a candle.

The wind flapped a curtain. Sandra went to fix it. Found herself beside the desk. Started away as if it had stung her.

No, she was not going to write to Rufus!

She crossed to an open window which faced the south. The rain had stopped, and the moon sailed high through streaming clouds. The sound of the wind in the trees and certain minor noises of night insects, of owl and whippoorwill, seemed only to intensify the blessed tranquillity of the countryside. Madge, in her room across the hall, was thanking her stars she was not in the cramped apartment, where from the court came the raucous monotonies of radio and phonograph, and from beyond the archway the roar of motor cars and the voices of the passing crowd. Madge was glad to be away from it. Glad to be again under this old roof. What matter if it leaked? It had sheltered her as a bride. It had sheltered her babies, and under it she and her husband had lived in happiness.

But to Sandra the night seemed sinister. The moaning wind, the haunting cry of the whippoorwill, the note of the screech owl shuddering among the shadows, filled her with a sense of depression and disaster. Oh, what she wanted was John McCormack singing — Rufus on his balcony — herself leaning down — " *her beauty hangs upon the cheek of night like a rich jewel . . .*"

She turned back into her room. Took a candle from the dresser and walked toward the corner where the desk stood. The light flowed over her whiteness, intensifying it. She carried the tall, red candle stiffly as one might who walked in sleep.

She opened the desk. Set the candle on the broad leaf. Drew toward her a sheet of paper. Her pen traveled swiftly. The letter finished, she signed and sealed it, then sat with her hand upon it, gazing out toward the hills which billowed in purple waves against the golden sky.

The white cat leaped to the sill, curled her tail about her feet, and, immovable as a statue, gazed, too, upon the hills. In her eyes, limpid as little moons, was a mysterious light. Perhaps she saw more than her mistress saw. Perhaps, in some occult way, she pursued the fortunes of a lonely figure amid higher hills in a rocky land — a figure with its face upraised to a midnight sky as it had been raised when first Sandra had looked upon it.

Chapter XXIII

A BARGAIN WITH OMNIPOTENCE

IT was strange, the way that Rufus thought of Sandra when he was separated from her. Not as he had seen her on the balcony — although he had written it would be that — but rather as once when he had walked with her in broad daylight up Connecticut Avenue.

He had been saying things to her — tumultuous, tender things of their future together — and she had turned toward him with a swing of her slender figure.

"I can't feel that it's true," she had said.

"What?"

"Our happiness."

"Why not?"

"It's too perfect, Rufus."

Well, it had been too perfect. And she had known it could not last. His wise little Sandra, swinging along beside him in her cheap green hat.

She was always beside him now in spirit, although physically they were separated by the breadth of the continent. Since Sherry was in the East, Rufus had gone back to the familiar hills near his old home. There was a ranch house where he could get board, a horse, and quiet in which to write. He had finished a second article in a series which had been asked for by the editor of a magazine of commanding position in the literary world. The first article had been published, and he had already had echoes of it.

Maulsby had wired: " Congratulations. You have struck a new note in the jangle of international dissonance."

And Williamson had written: " People are talking about you. They want to meet you. Come back and let them make a lion of you. Why stay in that God-forsaken country? "

It was not a God-forsaken country. But why try to tell Williamson of the beauty of these bare hills, brown and purple against the shimmer of the sky; of the glimmering loveliness of the sea under the still heat; of the starry nights when he rode for miles on his little mare amid amazing solitudes?

At this time of the year there was no one at the ranch but the owner, Tom Wicks, and his wife, and the people who worked for them. In the winter there were boarders, people who came from crowded cities for a season of contrasting activities out-of-doors.

Wicks and his wife had known Rufus' father. They knew Sherry. They knew the terms of the will, which had made interesting reading when the newspapers got hold of it. They were sorry for Rufus. Tied up to a proposition like that. A wife and no money. Or the money and no wife.

Molly Wicks had a healthy curiosity. She wondered why Rufus was there.

" He's changed," she told her husband. " I'll bet there's a girl in it."

" What makes you think that? "

" Well, why shouldn't there be? When a man knows

he can't have a thing he always wants it. He is probably trying to decide whether if he chooses poverty,
love will fly out the window."

Molly was kind to Rufus, but then women always
were kind to him. There was something in his dark
good looks which appealed to their imagination and set
him apart from the commonplace.

The mail came every morning to Molly Wicks' desk,
dumped there by a cowboy who rode down each morning to the box. Now and then Rufus had a letter.

"But no woman ever writes to him," Molly said to
Tom.

"Well, it isn't your business if they don't."

She made a little face at him. She was buxom and
blooming, a happy wife. But in the summer the ranch
had few excitements. And Rufus furnished her with
something to think about.

"It may not be my business, Tom," she admitted,
"but it's queer. A man like that. So good-looking."

Then one morning came a letter.

"My soul! " said Molly, when she saw it.

It had a Virginia postmark and was addressed in a
feminine hand. The penmanship was firm, clear, and
had a certain grace. It was a thin little letter. Molly
reflected that if it had been a love-letter, it would have
been fat. Women were like that, writing everything
that came into their minds. Not knowing that what
they left unsaid was more important than what they
said.

When Rufus came in for the midday meal, Molly
was at her desk. She saw him before he entered the
house, framed by the open doorway, tall, picturesque

in his khaki riding clothes, and her eyes approved him.

She handed him his letters, two in business envelopes, the thin one with the Virginia postmark.

He shuffled them over, stared for a long moment at the one with the Virginia postmark, then put the three of them in his pocket.

Molly was disappointed. She had hoped he would open the thin letter. She had a feeling that it was, somehow, significant.

Rufus went straight to the dining-room, and Molly followed him. There were just three of them at the table, with Tom coming in at the last moment, and an old Chinaman to serve them. The food was appetizing, chicken with noodles and a lot of fresh vegetables. Rufus ate with seeming appetite.

Yet he could not have told what he was eating. He was going through certain motions because they were expected of him. He used his knife and fork automatically. He talked to Molly and her husband, laughed in the right places, gave a surface effect of being interested.

But he was not interested. What did he care for the light things they were all saying? In his pocket was a letter from Sandra. *Sandra!* He had not dared open it. Would she blame him, or beg him to come back? Either way — it would tear his heart.

He was amazed at the rush of emotion the sight of her graceful script had brought. He had been hungry for a word from her. Yet now that she had written, he thought it might have been less difficult to endure her silence. He had chosen his way; he did not mean to depart from it.

He asked Molly Wicks, "Can John Lee put up a lunch for me?"

"Supper?"

"Yes. I'm off for another ride. I'm not sure how soon I shall be getting back."

Molly went to the kitchen herself to see that John Lee spared no pains. When, a little later, she handed Rufus the packet, she said,

"I put in the things you like."

He smiled at her. "You're too good to me."

She smiled back. "You're the kind people are good to."

So he went away, riding high up into the hills.

After an hour or two he rode down again on the other side of the mountain, toward the sea which from that height seemed like a great, gray carpet spread from the horizon to the shore.

And halfway between the sea and the height from which he looked was the house in which he had lived as a child — with its square towers, its red-tiled roofs, like some old Moorish palace.

He could not have told why he had come here to read his letter. Perhaps some sense of homelessness had driven him to gaze upon the place which had once been home. Perhaps because here where he sat his mother had once sat beside him, having ridden with him up to the heights that she might lose for a moment the sense of oppression in the house which held no happiness.

Rufus dismounted, let his horse graze, and sat down with his back to a rock. He took Sandra's letter from his pocket. Tore it open with hands that trembled.

He read the first words and found his eyes blurred. For Sandra had written not out of the worldly-wiseness of Sally Grymes, but out of the memory of those nights on the balcony. She had written with honesty and sincerity, and with a certain dignity.

" Rufus, Dear:

" I had thought I would not write. You left no ad-dress, and that seemed to settle it. I have been hurt and unhappy, and have blamed you a lot. I felt that if you loved me, you could never have chosen a path which led away from me. But you have chosen it, and tonight, for the first time, I find that I can talk about it.

" I am here in my room at Windytop. Mother has been very ill, and so she and I came down together. Doady is staying in Washington, but it is not likely we shall go back, for mother cannot go to work again, and we must have more income to live in the city. So that's that and disposes of me for the present.

" But it doesn't dispose of you, Rufus. Today a letter from Doady says that every one is talking about your article, and Mr. Maulsby wants you to come to Washington. He thinks you have a great future, and that this is your moment.

" So I am writing to beg you not to let anything interfere with that future. Not the thought of me, or of what I have been to you. My dear, here in this old house at Windytop lovers have lived and died, and now their passions are dust, and as I have sat here to-night, it has seemed to me that their living would have been in vain if something big and fine in them had not been immortal. And the big thing for you and me will be that our love shall have its consummation not, perhaps, in the romance of our dreams, but in some growth of spirit which shall bring us together, even when there are miles between . . .

" So, though I may never ask anything of you again, I do ask this, that you go to Washington. I shall know if success comes to you, and I pray that it may, Rufus. Remember that always, won't you? That my prayers are yours, and my heart.

" Please don't answer this . . . it will be easier not to have you. Not that I don't want to hear. But I mustn't. SANDRA."

The pride of her! In every line. Not ashamed of her love. But refusing to ask anything of him.

He sat for a long time looking down at the stretch of sea, crinkling now under the breeze and shot with rose and amethyst as the sun went down. A last ray touched the towers of the red-roofed palace below and made them blaze. Sherry's house! How she had schemed to get it! And what a mistress Sandra would have made for it! Driving away its gloom. Bringing her gay and wholesome youth to balance the effect of its baleful history.

And Sandra's children . . . ! Not afraid, as he had been, of a sword which hung above him. Not weighted with secrets hardly understood. But with faces lighted and laughing . . . like their mother . . . Sandra!

But Sherry had stolen from him his home. His future. He had thought it might be possible to make Sandra happy in the little house among the pines. But not with Sherry triumphant! Mocking!

He mounted his horse. In the deepening twilight he rode down toward the red-roofed palace.

It was dark when he came to the garden which overhung the sea. He went at once to the stables. The men who were there knew him. English, both of them; the red-faced, stout fellow had taught Rufus to ride.

"Glad to see you back, sir," he said, his voice respectful, his eyes, under the stable-yard light, bright with welcome.

"I'm not back," Rufus said, "not to stay. I'm putting up for a time at Tom Wicks'. So I rode over."

"The Madam's not at home," Bartlett said.

"I know. I saw her in Washington. She was on her way to the North Shore."

"She's got Ito with her," Bartlett vouchsafed, "and a maid. She's buying two new cars. Likely that means she'll sell some of the mounts, an' that me and Bob will be out."

"Let me know when that happens. I'll try to get some of my friends to take you on. You'd be a valuable man anywhere, Bartlett."

"It's just as one 'appens to think, sir. Now, the Madam wasn't born to the saddle. She wants a motor to show off in. An' us stablemen is out of it with 'er, as you might say."

Rufus did not discuss it. Whatever Sherry's shortcomings, they were not to be talked over with servants. So he said,

"I can't think of these stables without you, Bartlett, — and Bob."

"No more can I think of the 'ouse without you, sir. An it's a sin and a shame you ain't in it."

Rufus gave a short laugh. " Possession is nine-tenths of the law, Bartlett."

He went on, and Bartlett, looking after him, said to the sympathetic Bob:

" He's the cream of the dish. And she's cheated 'im out of things. Cheated 'im. And she's as common as skim-milk."

Rufus did not enter the house, but he stood for a long time looking up at it, seeing its beauty, its spaciousness, seeing it as it might be if it were his, with Sandra in it.

There were no lights in the windows, except at the back where the housekeeper slept, and two maids. A Japanese houseman and cook had their quarters in the garage. With Sherry away, there was still a retinue of servants to be fed and housed. And the time had been when Sherry had cooked her morning bacon over a gas jet and had dined sumptuously at a cafeteria.

Oh, well, why be a snob about it? Better women than Sherry had had to scrimp and save. There was Sandra, counting her pennies. " Melons are too expensive, Rufus, so we are having grapes . . . Lovely baskets of Concords selling for a song." So she had telephoned in those halcyon days when she had invited him to dinner.

But the difference was this, between Sandra's thrift and Sherry's, that Sandra did not scrimp and save to spend on gorgeous raiment. Sandra's poverty was no bleached skeleton with a glittering cloak to cover it. It was, rather, a Spartan figure, wearing homespun with an air.

At the end of the terrace was a little pavilion where

his mother had served tea.   From it he looked out now into the vast abyss of night.   The moon had not come up, and the lights of the stars overhead were matched by the lights on the shore road far below, and on the boats which rode at anchor in a sheltered cove.

There was no furniture at this season in the tea-house, but Rufus remembered it in his mother's time. The low table, the chairs of lacquered cane.   And he and she alone together.   Lilo would bring cocoa for him and thin bread and butter, and tea and rice cakes for his mother.   How good it had tasted, and how he had loved it!   But it was not only the bread and butter he remembered.   There had been roses in dull blue bowls, and a pink porcelain teapot that matched the roses, and his mother in sheer white with her beads of lapis lazuli, and himself in clean white linen.

Long after that, Sherry had come to the pavilion with the people who made up her parties.   People who thought tea stupid and ordered something stronger; and who yawned at the view, and asked about the swimming pool, and spent riotous hours splashing about in it.

Rufus, his eyes on the brooding darkness, saw the pavilion as it might be if Sandra came to it . . . like his mother in her cool white . . . with a child happy beside her with his bread and butter . . .

He was aware of a step on the stones outside, and turned his head to see a dark figure coming towards him.

" It's Bartlett, sir."

" Yes? "

" Mr. Rufus I came to tell you somethin' I couldn't speak of before the other fellow.   It's about that will.

If you'll let us, us fellows 'ull help you break it."

" *Break it.*"

" Yes. We could say the old gentleman was out of 'is 'ead. An' he was . . . An' she put 'im up to it. We're willing to swear, sir. Us boys and the 'ouse-maids."

" But, Bartlett — "

" If you'd break it, she'd get her widow's share, and the rest 'ud be yours with no strings tied. D'you see ? You could have your wife and your money. An' no thanks to the Madam, either."

Rufus laughed, a short laugh of incredulity. " Do you think she'd give it up, Bartlett? She'd fight to the finish."

" Fight 'er back, sir."

But Rufus knew what fighting back would mean. He had tried it years ago, and always she had found some way to hurt him. Yet to wrest from her that for which she had schemed! The thing was worth think-ing of.

" Do you mean," he asked Bartlett, " that my father really didn't know what he was doing? "

" 'E did not, sir. Any of the men will tell you. He 'ad a shock, and after that 'e wasn't right. An' she 'ad no doctor for 'im. Not till the last. An' we'll swear to that."

" We'd have to be very sure."

" Well, you let us try, sir, and we'll swear with all our 'earts. We all 'ate 'er."

" It's a wonder she keeps you on."

" Oh, well, sir, we has civil enough tongues w'en it comes to that."

Rufus stood up. "Don't hope too much, Bartlett. I'll have to think about it. Sherry's a little cat, all claws out, when it comes to taking things away from her. And she'd get the best lawyers in the state."

"Lawyers or no lawyers, you'd win, sir."

Long after Bartlett had left, his words rang in Rufus' ears, "You'd win, sir," as if the thing could be done, and there was no doubt about it.

As he rode away on his little horse, he looked back at the house. The moon, rising back of it, gave it a weird, unearthly grandeur. A palace for a Princess! What were the lines that Sandra had loved to say to him? About the happy princess? *"Beyond the night, into the day . . . through all the world . . . she followed him . . ."*

He could hear her laugh, lilting and lovely. "You don't mind my dropping into poetry, do you? I've always done it."

It was late when he got back to the ranch. But Molly Wicks was at her desk.

"Did you like your lunch?" she asked.

He confessed with some confusion, "I didn't eat it."

"Oh! After John Lee and I had taken so much pains with it!"

"I forgot it."

"And you haven't had any supper?"

"No."

She stood up and said with decision, "You're going to have some."

"I'm not hungry."

But she persisted. "I'll have coffee in a minute,

and you can eat your sandwiches."

Rufus followed her into the dining-room with its great stone fireplace, its festoons of pepper-berries. Under Molly's direction he drew a small table in front of the fire, and she set a tray upon it. Presently she was sitting opposite him with a plate of sandwiches between them.

"I'm hungry, too," she said, "and the coffee will taste good."

But what she wanted was not the coffee, but a chance to talk to him.

"It's that letter," she told herself. "He's had it on his mind, and lost his appetite."

Except for the lamp on their little table, there was no light in the big room. Instinctively they lowered their voices to avoid the echoes. And after a while Rufus said,

"Molly, did you see my father before he died?"

She nodded. "A week before."

"How did he seem to you."

"Much broken. He should have been in bed."

"Was — Sherry with him?"

"Yes. She never left him. Not for a moment."

"Do you think he was in a condition to make a will?"

She gave him a sharp glance. "What do you mean?"

"He dictated that last will two days before he died."

She leaned forward. "You think she made him do it?"

"Yes."

She caught her breath. "Oh!"

" I have been advised to break the will."

She was eager. " Do it. Tom and I will help. We've both talked about it — his health, I mean, and how his mind had weakened."

"Sherry will fight back."

"Let her! "

He flung up his head. " Molly, it means more to me than just the money."

" A girl? "

"Yes. I want to marry, but I won't turn everything over to Sherry. It's what she's waiting for. And she shan't have it."

He was sitting back in his chair, his hand beating the table. Molly's eyes feasted on him. Not many men were that way — handsome without vanity. Red-blooded yet remote.

"She's not to be talked about, Molly — too lovely. But I can say this — that if the house up there were mine, she'd be the one woman I could see in my mother's place."

Molly was Irish. Romantic. " Then see her there," she cried.

He stood up, a new light in his eyes. " By Jove, I'll do it! "

" And good luck to you! " said Molly.

Rufus' room was on the first floor. When at last he went to it, he could not sleep. He resolved to walk off his restlessness, and crept quietly out of doors. The world was in the hush of the hours which come before the morning. He made his way past the corral to a place where the sheep were folded for the night. A collie came to meet him, wagging a welcoming tail. A dim lamp burned in the shepherd's hut.

Rufus stopped by the open door. "Still up, McIvor?"

An aged man with a beard was reading a book. He laid it down and took off his spectacles. "The old cannot sleep," he said, "but the young should be in bed."

Rufus sat down on the step. "How many times you've said that to me, McIvor, when I was a boy!"

"It is still good advice, Mr. Rufus."

"And you told me to say my prayers."

"And I hope you do it."

Rufus' hand beat the doorstill. "I stopped praying when the Lord took my mother away."

"It was not the time to stop."

"If he'll give me the wife I want, I'll worship him forever."

"It is not for us to make bargains with Omnipotence."

Rufus did not argue. He sat there looking up at the stars. After all, if men could make bargains with the powers of evil, why not with the powers of good? If the Lord would give him Sandra, he would burn altar fires forever.

Chapter XXIV

BURNING BEAUTY

OCTOBER at Windytop was a season of burning beauty — red flame of Virginia creeper on dead tree trunks, a hot blaze of goldenrod sweeping up the hills, fierce glow of sumac in the fence corners — a conflagration of color in the midst of the snapping coldness of the first frosts.

Lovely out-of-doors, but shivery inside. No modern heating. Bedrooms icy in the morning. A fire in the library, with your back freezing. Aunt Louisa's kitchen the only toasty place in the whole house.

The thing worried Sandra. How were they going to winter in the barnlike structure? They had done it before, but Madge had been strong then, and well. She had put hot-water bags in the beds, helped bring in the wood, and made a game of it all, while she piled on blankets when the wind howled and the snow flew.

But such hardihood was not for these days. Madge must be comfortable.

"I'll buy a little stove," Sandra thought desperately, "for mother's room, and move my bed in there."

She was taking her daily walk to the mailbox. She wore a sweater and cap of a red that matched the flame of the Virginia creeper. The sky above her was like blue smoke. The air like wine. And everywhere was that burning beauty.

It was not a morning in which to worry about stoves, it was a morning to be glad in, a morning to sing in, shout in, to laugh and be gay. Yet Sandra was not gay, and it was better to think of stoves than of Rufus.

She had not heard from him. She had told him not to write. Yet there had been, perhaps, a faint hope that some word might come. So every morning, when she reached the mailbox, her heart would stop beating while she unlocked it, and her hand would tremble as she shuffled the envelopes. Then would come the shock of disappointment, the despair. She was always glad of the long walk back, which made it possible for her to conquer the wild feeling of desperation, and to meet her mother with composure.

And so this morning. Five letters. None of them from Rufus . . . One from Theodora.

Sandra read Theodora's as she went along.

" DARLING:

I've such marvelous news for you. Mr. Maulsby wants me to go to London. *To London!* There's a house full of old things to be sold. And he knows the owner. And he says I'm the only person he can trust to buy what he wants. Oh, I'm flattered to tears, Sandra. And he will pay all of my expenses, and my salary, and I'm to travel first-class, 'n'everything!

" And he wants you to come up and take my place in the shop. He has to have some one, and it will give you the extra money, and while you haven't the experience, you've a lot of tact, and Mr. Maulsby thinks you'll handle the customers in the same way I do. Of

course, you won't, because you'll have a darling way
of your own!

" You must come. You can stay with Miss Carter
in the apartment, and leave mother with Sally Grymes.
You know how many times Sally has asked her, and
you'll be saved from the arctic fastnesses of Windytop.

" Of course, it will last only until Christmas, as Mr.
Maulsby wants me to be back by the first of the year,
and perhaps by that time he'll be able to give you a
permanent place in the shop, and we can bring mother
on and get some one to look after her. But that's too
far to look forward. We'll just gather our rosebuds
while time flies, and leave the rest to fate.

" Wire if you'll come. At Mr. Maulsby's expense.
I must sail on Monday, so you'd better come Saturday,
so that I can see you.

" Ever your own,

DOADY."

Sandra ran the rest of the way home. She burst in
on Madge and found Sally Grymes there. She told
the news breathlessly. Read Doady's letter.

Sally said: " It's the thing for you to do. And
Madge will keep me from being bored by my own
company. And my new furnace is simply burning its
head off. She'll have a tropic climate."

Madge had hold of Sandra's hand. " Do you want
to go, my darling? "

Sandra told her honestly: " I don't want to leave
you. But the work will be a good thing for me. And
you'll be more comfortable at Aunt Sally's."

She went to the telephone and wired Theodora. She

would reach Washington, she said, on Saturday morning, taking the night train up.

This was Thursday. Sally stayed and helped them pack, and before lunch the next day took Madge off with her. Sandra was to go over later and dine with them. She would need the afternoon to get things settled in the house and give final directions to Aunt Louisa.

For several hours she was very busy, and came finally about four o'clock to her own room and a short rest on the bed, with a big blanket over her. The golden glow of the late afternoon flooded the big chamber and touched its shabbiness with a sort of splendor. As she lay looking at it, it came to her that once life had seemed to her rather splendid in spite of all its poverty and privations.

Half-asleep, she was aware of Aunt Louisa's voice.

"There's a gentleman to see you, Miss Sandra."

Sandra sat up. "Did he give his name?"

He had not. He was nice-looking, Aunt Louisa stated, and might be a book agent. She had put some big sticks of wood on the fire, and there was a fine blaze. Sandra yawned, got off the bed, drew a comb through her short locks, put on her red sweater, and went down . . .

And straight and tall in front of the roaring fire that Aunt Louisa had built was Rufus Fiske . . . !

For a moment, Sandra, in her red sweater, with her shining hair, stood on the threshold looking at him . . .

Then he caught her up. Sweeping her off her feet into his arms.

"Sandra, Sandra . . ."

After a while, she whispered, " Why did you come? "

" Why did I ever go away? "

She clung to him. " And you have come back . . . because you . . . love me? "

" Yes."

He bent his head. She gave him the quick response that he demanded . . . met his kisses! Her world was whirling . . . he was back again . . . and he was hers!

At last she released herself.

" It's too good — to be true — Rufus." Her laugh was shaky.

" But it is true."

"And nothing else counts? "

" Nothing."

They sat down opposite each other in front of the fire. " I've so much to tell you," Rufus said. " But I can't, with you so far away from me."

So she drew up a little stool and sat with her head against his knee, and his fingers touched her flushed cheek as he talked to her.

At first, Sandra hardly heard what he was saying. The mere fact of his presence brought a sense of rapturous content. The feeling of nervous strain was gone. The light from the fire seemed to lap over her in waves of lovely warmth. The touch of Rufus' hand set her pulses throbbing.

He was talking about his visit to his old home — about a red-roofed palace — about a garden that overlooked the sea — about a tea-house on a terrace — and of his mother in a white dress — of blue bowls and pink roses — of pink porcelain — of thin bread and butter — of Sherry and her awful friends — of his thought of Sandra in his mother's place — of Sandra's children.

It seemed to Sandra utterly unreal that she should be sitting there, listening to that enchanting voice, seeing the softened light in the dark eyes that had once held that sardonic gleam, knowing that the strength of him, the grace and charm, were hers, and that love had at last brought him back to her.

Then she heard him saying:

" I started to write it. Then the thought came that I might tell you, and I couldn't get here fast enough."

She smiled up at him lazily. " Tell me what? "

" I am going to break my father's will."

She was still smiling, " Oh, why, Rufus? "

" To get the money. But most of all to be free from Sherry."

Sandra's smile faded. In her eyes was a puzzled look. " How will you be free? "

" If I can prove my father was coerced into making such a will, you and I will have the money, and Sherry will get only her widow's share."

" You and I? " She sat up on her little stool and faced him. " You and I, Rufus? But what if you aren't able to break the will? "

" There aren't any ' ifs.' I'm going to do it."

She drew her hand across her eyes as if to clear away some mist that obscured her vision. " But there's a chance you won't win. And what then? Do you mean if you shouldn't, that things will go back to where they were? That you won't marry me . . . unless you get the money? "

"Dearest heart, why worry? I shall win."

She clasped her hands tightly together. She had the look of a frightened child. "Rufus, do you still hate Sherry more than you love me?"

"I love you more than I hate anything."

"Yet . . . you will leave me . . . if . . . if things don't turn out your way?"

He had no answer for that. He knew what she wanted him to say. That no matter what happened, she was his forever? But he could not say it. Not if his life depended on it.

She began to cry, hopelessly, helplessly. He took her in his arms, and she clung to him, but when he tried to kiss her, she turned away.

"My dear," he said, "my dear . . . you know I love you . . ."

She released herself and stood up. "I don't call it — love. Oh, I suppose I've been a romantic little . . . idiot . . . but I thought love was like all the wonderful stories I had read. That nothing could ever come between two people who cared. But you've let Sherry come between. And I won't take love on such terms. I can't. I shouldn't be happy. If I can't know that you're mine without doubt or question, I'd rather go on alone — forever!"

She flung it out. Such a little thing. Demanding of him the best. Willing to cast everything to the winds; but not willing to take anything less than love, no matter what she lost by it.

He, too, had risen. "Then you're sending me away?"

Her face was white. "I must . . ."

He turned and started for the door, turned back, caught her up in his arms . . . and spoke in a husky voice.

"You're right," he said. "You are wholly and entirely right. It is I who am wrong. No man should ask of a woman like you anything, unless he gives her everything. Remember that, my dearest. That you are right. And that I shall never blame you. I shall only blame fate for having let me pass your way."

He kissed her gently and set her down. She put out a hand gropingly as she saw him go. Then she crouched beside the chair in which he had sat, her face hidden. She heard his step in the echoing hall, the door open and shut. Silence.

Chapter XXV

DREADFUL LAUGHTER

GALE MARKHAM, coming into Maulsby's shop on a gray December afternoon, found Sandra arranging a set of Staffordshire on a display table.

" I haven't Doady's courage," she told him. " I am simply scared stiff for fear I shall break some of these darling old dishes. Doady handles them as if she had always done it."

"Where's everybody? "

" Susan Carter is at home with a cold, and Mr. Maulsby is in New York. I am having things to myself."

She put one of the nice old cups carefully in its nice old saucer. " Can you stay till I shut up the shop? If you can, I'll make some tea."

" Nothing would suit me better — provided you'll dine with me later. Mother is having dinner with some old friends, and I came over to ask you to take pity on me."

" Well, it's providential, I'll say," Sandra informed him. " Susan's doctor won't let her have anything but broth, so Ione's going to give her that, and I planned to stay down town tonight and work. There are so many things I don't know, and with everybody away my sense of responsibility is tremendous."

She smiled at him and went on setting the Staffordshire in place. Gale sat and watched her. She was dressed charmingly in a belted frock of Chinese red. Velveteen. He liked the plainness of it, the long sleeves with narrow embroidered cuffs which matched the collar. It was snowing outside, and within only one low lamp was lighted, so that Sandra stood out richly among the shadows like a figure in an old painting.

In the weeks since she had come back to Washington, Gale had been aware of a great change in Doady's twin. She was no longer the gay little girl he had known in the summer. She was thinner and paler. Yet she was no less lovely. There was, indeed, a wistfulness which drew him. What an appealing pair they made, these two! He remembered Doady's tears that afternoon of his mother's tea, when she had slipped and fallen. He had soothed her as if she had been a child, and now here was this other child also needing sympathy.

When they sat together a little later in the room where the prints were hung, he looked up at the Vigée LeBrun which had taken the place of the one Rufus bought. "You're not so much like that as you used to be," he said. "You've lost your color. What's happened?"

She was pouring the tea. She set the pot down and looked at him. Her voice was calm, but there was a strained look in her eyes.

"My heart is broken," she said, "like the heroines in old books."

"My dear . . ."

"It sounds — silly — doesn't it? But it's true." She

picked up the teapot with a hand that trembled. "I fell in love . . . all in a minute . . . and now I've got to fall out again."

The cup overflowed. Gale took the teapot from her. "I'll do it," he said, "and you're to have yours first — hot with lemon and two lumps?"

He gave her time to regain her composure, then he said, "Tell me about it."

"I can't. I shouldn't have spoken of it. Such things are better kept to oneself."

"I think not. It's a relief to confide in some one. I know a bit about heartbreaks myself. That isn't a masculine confession, is it? Perhaps I'd better put it this way, that I've killed a few — dreams."

She hesitated, then brought it out, "You mean — Stephanie?"

"Yes."

Silence for a moment. Then, "Gale, how did you manage to go on?"

"I played the surgeon. Took a sharp knife and — amputated."

"You don't love her any more?"

"That part of my life is — gone."

"But that's the dreadfulness of it. To lose a thing that means so much."

"Better to lose it than to suffer."

Both of them had forgotten their tea. The front of the shop was dark, and the heavy curtains that hung from the archway shut the two young people into a world of their own. Gale had a feeling that one might speak here as in a confessional, with a sense of inviolate secrecy.

He found himself saying: "I wish I might tell you about it. I've always wanted you to know. It may help with your own problem."

"Will you? I'd love it." She leaned back in her chair, relaxed a little. The strained look went out of her eyes.

Gale began with his boyhood. "You see, we grew up together. She was a lovely little creature with long curls and a gentle manner. It took me years to realize that the gentle manner was not all it seemed. As I look back, I realize that Stephanie usually had her own way. She is still having it.

"Well, I adored her. I spent all of my pocket money on her and counted no task too great if she imposed it. After I went away to school, she became the romantic lady of my dreams. No one measured up to her. She had no faults.

"I was still at her feet when I finished college. Then came the war, and when I went overseas, I begged her to marry me. But she wouldn't. She agreed to an engagement, however, and the thought of her as my promised wife helped a lot when things were hard. I felt that if I died she would mourn me, forever. That if I lived, she would give me happiness.

"Well, I didn't die. But I came back lame. Stephanie made a bit of a hero of me. She was very sweet, and I — well, I worshipped her —" He stopped abruptly.

"We were to be married in October," he went on presently, "and in June Stephanie went to Paris to buy her wedding clothes. I planned to go over later in the summer. My father was not well, and he needed me to look after the affairs of his office. It was then I learned the state of his financial affairs, but even then I did not grasp the full extent of the disaster.

"In August my father died. In September I lost — Stephanie. As soon as I found that everything except the house must go to our creditors, I wrote to tell her that we should have to delay the wedding. I did not offer to break the engagement. I thought nothing could part us — that at most it would be only a matter of waiting. But Stephanie wrote a sensible letter. She said she wasn't made to be a poor man's wife, and that what she had would not keep the two of us in the style to which she had been accustomed. She loved me, but she knew what was best for both of us. Perhaps she was right. I don't know how far dreams fit one for life. I only know that if she had cared, nothing else would have mattered."

It was the echo of Sandra's own words to her mother at Windytop.

"Oh," she said now, impetuously, "nothing else matters if one really loves."

"I thought that. But Stephanie didn't. I can't tell you what I suffered. It was as if a part of me had been torn away. I released her at once from her engagement and felt it was the end of everything. But when she came back from France, I found she didn't consider it the end. Stephanie wouldn't marry me, but she wanted to keep me dangling — a scalp at her belt — that sort of thing. She wanted me to go on, expecting nothing, giving everything. And for a time I was weak enough to do it."

He rose and stood looking down at Sandra.

" I wonder if I dare tell you what helped me finally to — amputate? "

" Please."

" My friendship with you and your sister. Since that night at Stephanie's party things have been different. I'm not at Stephanie's beck and call, and she doesn't like it. She wanted me to go up to her place on the North Shore last summer, but I wouldn't. I had a much better time here in town. I played around with Doady and kept my self-respect. Doady's a good little pal."

" Doady's a darling," Sandra agreed.

" Both of you are darlings," Gale was smiling. " If I were a Turk or a Mormon, I'd ask you both to marry me, and we'd live happy ever after."

Sandra's answering smile was wistful. " Does anybody live happy ever after? "

" Your mother did, and mine."

" Oh — women of their generation."

" You mustn't lose faith in life," he said, " just because you've lost faith in one man."

" I'm not sure I've lost faith in him, Gale. He isn't like Stephanie. He isn't afraid of poverty for himself. He's afraid of it for me. As if I minded being poor! Why, I'd tramp the roads with him, sleep under the stars, make a home anywhere between four poor walls if only we could be — together."

She brought out the last words with a passionate force which made Gale stare at her in wonder. Here was no child to be kissed and comforted; here was an awakened woman, ready to fling everything to the winds for the sake of her lover, ripe for romantic adventure — a dauntless creature afraid of nothing except disillusionment.

Dimly he was aware that here was what he had sought in Stephanie — a constancy which would match his own, a courage which would flaunt itself in the face of disaster. He, too, would have tramped the roads, slept under the stars . . .

He wrenched himself back from the vision. " I don't know the man, of course," he said gently, " but he is fortunate."

" No . . . he suffers, too."

He laid his hand on hers. " I hate to see you hurt. Will you let me know if ever there is anything I can do to help? "

She began to cry quietly, turning away from him a little, her face hidden. For a moment to Gale the air about them seemed filled with the beating of wings, with the roaring of waves, with all those pulsing sounds which come when the blood flows fast in one's veins. He wanted to take her in his arms. Soothe her. Say to her, " May we not comfort each other? "

He put the temptation from him. Her grief was sacred. She was not the sort of woman to turn from the arms of one man to those of another. So he sat silent, tightening the grip on her hand, waiting until she was herself again.

She drew her hand away presently and wiped her eyes. " Please forgive me. When I cry, I never know when to stop. And we've got to go to dinner."

It was snowing hard when at last they came into the street, and there was about them the silence of the storm. The lights along the way were blurred, and the

lamps were topped with white cones like nightcaps.
The wind blew strongly, and Gale took hold of Sandra's
arm to steady her.

" Some storm! " he said.

" I love it. Don't you? "

He dared not tell her he loved being out in it with her.
To feel her nearness, to know she was glad he was there,
and less lonely because he was her friend.

They came at last to a quiet place where the prices
suited Gale's pocketbook, and where there was a satisfying *table d'hôte*. Sandra found herself eating with an
appetite until, as the salad came on, Gale remarked,

" By the way, have you seen Rufus Fiske? "

A startled moment. Then, " Seen him? "

" Yes. He's back again. Living like a hermit out
there in his cottage, and writing like mad. Williamson
told me. I thought he might have come into the shop."

" No . . ." Sandra could not manage any more
than the monosyllable. She felt frozen. As if the shock
of knowing Rufus' nearness had in some way devital-
ized her. She could hardly hold her fork. As she laid
it down, it made a little clatter on her plate. Gale,
glancing up, saw the whiteness of her cheeks.

In a flash the truth came to him. " Sandra," he
asked, " is it Rufus? "

She nodded. " You might have guessed . . . we
went around a lot together."

" I know. But I thought he looked upon you and
Doady as I did — as charming children."

" I should think by this time we'd seem grown up,"
she said with a touch of weariness.

" I hope you will never grow up," he said earnestly;

" and as for Rufus, the gods made the two of you for each other. I can't believe he would hurt you willingly."

She lighted a little at that. " It is good to have you defend him, Gale, though I can't do it myself. I can only blame him because he won't trust life for the best that's in it."

He wished she would tell him more, but she did not, and he would not force her confidence. But while they talked of other things, the thought of Rufus was with him. No wonder the child suffered. There was an enchantment about Fiske which was felt by men as well as women. Gale, lacking in himself the picturesque qualities, admired them whole-heartedly in others. Sandra and Rufus. A perfect pair. With healthy sanity Gale forced from his mind the envy which assailed him.

When later he took Sandra back to the shop, he said, " Do you want me to stay? "

" I want you. But I mustn't let you. I've got to be very busy."

" Sure you aren't afraid? "

" Not with the janitor in the hall and everything locked up."

" How will you get home? "

" In a taxi. Mr. Maulsby pays for it, and I have one ordered for ten-thirty."

He left reluctantly, and when she was alone, Sandra washed the teacups and set them in place. Then she busied herself once more with the Staffordshire. Gradually the excitement which had stirred her when she heard of Rufus' return subsided. Shut away in this quiet place, she could find absorbing occupation for hands and brain. Since she had come to take Theodora's place, she had been too busy to let her mind dwell constantly on her tragedy as it had done at Windytop. Mr. Maulsby had been very kind, and tomorrow she was to go to Marcia's for dinner. It was to be, she understood, a somewhat formal affair.

"I want you to meet some of the nice people who like your sister," Mrs. Maulsby had told her.

Having arranged the china to her satisfaction, she returned to the room where the prints hung, carrying with her some pieces of fine old Sheffield in flannel cases. In this room she was conscious always of a ghostly presence, of a shadowy Rufus striding in beautiful tallness through the archway, stopping in front of the Vigée Le-Brun, speaking in his crisp voice,

"Do you like him?"

And her own voice: "I didn't, at first."

"Why not?"

"I hoped I was better-looking."

And then his teasing laughter . . .

Oh, she must not think of him. She must think of her work. A customer was coming in the morning to look at the Sheffield — a man Doady had met on the other side. She had written a letter about him and had made some suggestions as to the best methods of display. Sandra hunted now for the letter among the papers in her bag, found it, sat down, read it over, and came finally to this:

"He has loads of money, Sandra. And his name is Stephen Leeds. We went over in the same boat, and he said at first that he found me 'amusing'; a little

later he condescended to call me 'charming'; and by
the time we reached Southampton, he told me he was
'mad about me.' He didn't propose, however, until we
had been a week in London. And since then he has
proposed three times. And now he has to go back to
New York and will come to Washington. I want you
to look him over and tell me what you think of him.
Would you like him as a brother-in-law? I haven't
given him the least encouragement, but of course if I
could make up my mind to marry him it would be quite
thrilling for us all. He belongs to a nice Baltimore
family, and knows the O'Malleys and the Difficult Customer to whom I tried to sell the milk-pot. At first, he
didn't see anything very funny in my trying to sell it
to her. I think he was disturbed a bit because I didn't
recognize her right to be rude. 'Such people,' he said,
'don't have to think about their manners. She was a
Duval of Duval.'

"'Well,' I told him, 'I'm a Claybourne of Virginia.
If she had a right to be snippy, so had I.'

"It rather took his breath away, but he saw my point,
and I'll say for him that while he has a certain conceit,
he's not snobbish. He never thinks of his money. Not
half so much as I do, so that I am really the vulgarian,
aren't I, as they say in London?

"Of course, darling, you will think me dead to romance. But I can't have my cake and eat it, too. If
I were out simply for a love affair, I'd choose Gale
Markham. But he hasn't any money, and he thinks
he's in love with Stephanie. Which makes it rather
final, doesn't it? But I shouldn't consider it final if
he were rolling in wealth. I have a feeling that getting

a husband is like achieving a career — you can arrive
if you know the way to do it.

" But anyhow it is Stephen Leeds we have to consider. Aside from his matrimonial inhibitions, he is
interested in old Sheffield, and I want you to sell him
some. I wish I were there to arrange it, but if you'll
put it on the Sheraton sideboard and hang a square of
tapestry back of it — the one with the birds and fruit
— you'll get the best effect. Oh, Sandra, I am crazy
about my work. I'd hate to marry and give it up. So
that's that, and there's a lot to think about . . .

" The amazing part of it all is that Mr. Leeds fell
in love with me when he first saw me dancing the
Charleston. Do you remember Stephanie's party?
And how we felt? With all the men running away from
us? And now, thanks to Susan Carter, I can top any
of the others. At least, Stephen Leeds says I can . . ."

Sandra, setting out on the rich old sideboard the shimmering collection — the porringers and orange cups, the
candlesticks and salts and peppers, the big tray with
its grapevine border, reflected that if Doady had ever
been in love, she couldn't talk that way about it. But
Doady's heart was untouched. Perhaps people were
happier who went through life with untouched hearts.
At least, they did not suffer.

She finished the arrangement of the Sheffield, then
searched some time for the piece of tapestry of which
her sister had spoken. At last she remembered she
had seen it in the front room, and went to get it. She
had to turn on the lights to find it, and as the shades
were not down at the great window, or at the small one

which made the upper half of the door, she was vividly revealed, in her glowing gown, to such passers-by as braved the night. But there were few pedestrians. The wind boomed with dull detonations; the snow swished against the glass with gentle sibilance.

As she switched off the light and returned to the other room, another sound besides the wind and the swishing of the snow broke the stillness. Some one was rattling the knob of the front door.

Sandra raised her head and listened. She was not afraid. The watchman was in the hall, which was reached by the main door of the building and by a side door which led from the room in which Sandra stood. The chances were that some drunken wayfarer had mistaken the house and would presently go on.

As the rattling persisted, however, and was supplemented by a sharp tapping on the glass, Sandra went swiftly through the archway and, standing in the dark, looked toward the door. Outlined against the square of glass which made the upper half of it, she saw in the glimmer of the street lamps the outline of a woman's head, without a hat, and with neck muffled in a fur collar. The vestibule canopy formed a protection from the snow, and beyond the woman and through the wider space of the big window, Sandra was aware of the blurred bulk of an imposing car.

Well, a woman in evening dress ought not to prove formidable. Sandra opened the door, leaving the chain up.

" What do you want? " she demanded.

" May I come in? "

Sandra hesitated. " The shop is closed for the night."

" I know that," impatiently, " but as I was driving by, the lights flared and my eye was caught by your red dress. I am always doing impetuous things, and I decided to come in. I know the Maulsbys. I am dining with them tomorrow night. And I want to ask about some antiques."

Sandra took off the chain. " If there's anything I can do for you," she said, " I'll be delighted."

She led the way to the middle room where the lights showed the visitor in a great wrap of pink velvet, silver-embroidered and lined with ermine, and with an ermine collar. As she laid the wrap aside, a gown of the same pink velvet, supple as satin, showed deep-pointed areas of bareness at back and front, and her arms were bare. Her head was faultlessly shingled, with a distinctive and rather severe cut. There were pearls in her ears, and ropes of them about her neck.

A beautiful woman, one would have said at first glance. But to Sandra she was not beautiful. There was a hardness in the lines of the round little face, a mocking coldness in the eyes, an impudence in the wide, red-lipped mouth, which was like that of a gamin of the streets.

" I adore this shop," the woman said, her eyes roving about it.

" You've been here before? "

" Once in the spring — to see Felix Maulsby. I met his wife afterward at her summer place on the North Shore."

She began to prowl restlessly around the room, picking up this thing and that. " I don't care for Sheffield," she said, coming to it at last; " it's too dingy for my taste. But I suppose it is expensive."

" Some of it. These orange cups are very rare," Sandra turned them over to show the marks.

The lady in pink was, however, unimpressed. " The thing I am interested in is ivories."

It seemed to Sandra that her heart stopped beating. " Ivories? "

" Yes. A set of figurines — the Five Senses — were taken from my house last spring and brought here and sold. Felix Maulsby bought them."

The room was rocking. The Sheraton sideboard jiggled itself somewhere up near the ceiling, with the Sheffield slanted so that only a miracle kept it from falling down like silver rain. Sandra had to wait until things righted themselves before she could speak. " Are you sure they are the same? "

" Absolutely. My step-son sold them, Rufus Fiske."

So this was Sherry! Dressed like a queen, with her ruthless eyes and gamin's mouth contradicting her right to royalty.

" So far, Mr. Maulsby has refused to sell them back to me," Sherry was saying fretfully. " He insists it's a family affair and that Rufus may have a right to them. Which is absurd."

Without waiting for an answer, she again went prowling about the room. " I've seen that picture before," she remarked, coming to a stop beneath the print of " The Boy in Red."

Her eyes dwelt on it for a moment, then she smiled a secret smile as if she remembered but did not mean to tell about it.

Turning away at last from her survey of the print, she said, abruptly: " Are they here?   In the shop? "

" The ivories? "

" Yes."

" Mr. Maulsby keeps them locked in the safe."

" Do you know the combination? "

" Yes."

" Could you show them to me? "

" I'm sorry. I should have to have Mr. Maulsby's permission."

" Nonsense." Sherry's restless fingers beat a tattoo on the polished surface of the sideboard. " I have set my heart on seeing them. If you could manage it, I'd make it worth while."

" What do you mean by — worth while? "

" Oh, well," significantly, " girls like — pretty things."

Sandra, slim and scarlet, surveyed the other with level glance. So this cheap little Sherry, who had sold herself for money, was offering her, Sandra Claybourne, a bribe. It would have been funny if it had not been — outrageous.

" It would be impossible for me to — break the rules," she said.

Sherry's voice was sharp. " Do you think I want to steal them? "

She had so nearly struck the truth that Sandra found her sense of humor stirred by it. Her eyes were lighted suddenly by a mischievous, sidelong glance. " Mr. Maulsby says all collectors are — pickpockets."

Sherry did not answer. She was staring at Sandra with a widening gaze.

" What's your name? " she demanded.

" Sandra Claybourne."

" Do you know my step-son — Rufus Fiske? "

" Yes."

Sherry began to laugh. It was dreadful laughter, a derisive, hateful, fleering sound — the sound that had come years ago to the ears of a little boy and had shattered his world. Sandra began to understand what Rufus had suffered. Her own flesh was creeping. Her cheeks white.

After a while Sherry stopped laughing. " So he's going to marry you and lose the money? "

It was Sandra's turn to stare. " How did you know? "

" I recognized you from that." She pointed to the print. " Rufus showed me one like it. He said he had it there because it reminded him of the girl he loved . . ." She broke off to say, " My dear child, I have a lot to thank you for."

" You have nothing to thank me for."

" Why not? "

" He is not going to marry me."

Sherry's face changed. " What do you mean? "

" Just what I have said. He is not going to marry me." Sandra's voice was as brittle as ice.

" Do you mean he has broken it off? "

" Yes."

" But why? "

" Because he hates you more than he loves me."

As the words fell from Sandra's lips, she would have given anything to recall them. There was a kind of treachery to Rufus in thus stripping bare his tragedy.

Yet she had said it, and Sherry had pounced on it:

" You mean he loves the money more than he loves you."

" He hasn't taken a penny," Sandra told her hotly.

" Ah, but my dear, it is always there for the taking. If he marries, that will be the end of it."

" You don't understand him. You have never understood him."

" Better than you."

Sandra did not answer. Sherry's words had recalled a nursery rhyme: " *Oh, grandmother . . . What big eyes you have . . . The better to see you, my dear . . . Oh, grandmother . . . What big ears you have . . . The better to hear you, my dear . . . Oh, grandmother, what a big mouth you have . . .* THE BETTER TO EAT YOU, MY DEAR . . . ! "

Sherry was that way — a wolf masquerading as a woman . . . !

The Wolf-woman was wrapping herself in her cloak, all rose and snow, with her hard little face above it. " I won't waste any more time in asking you to let me see the ivories. You won't, of course. But you know they are mine."

" Saying it doesn't make them so."

" You take his side," Sherry asked with some curiosity, " after the way he has acted? "

" I shall always take his side."

There was something lovely about Sandra as she said it, something innocent, appealing, exalted. Sherry recognized the loveliness as some dark angel faced by a creature of light discerns a beauty beyond its own compassing.

She tried to carry it off with an air, however. " You're a bit upstage, aren't you? But you'll get over it."

Drawing the cloak around her, she went through the archway. Sandra followed her. Heard Sherry's receding voice in the dark.

" Of course, you know this isn't the end of it."

Sandra did not answer, and as Sherry opened the front door, the chauffeur jumped from the big car and hurried forward.

The snow was whirling in a wild dance, the pavement was covered. " I shall ruin my slippers," Sherry said irritably, as the man reached her. " You'll have to carry me, Ito."

The Japanese, imperturbable, strong as an ox, lifted her lightly. And so, all rose and white, she was borne away to be lost in a moment in the blurring storm.

Sandra shut the door, locked it, and looked out the window. The car had driven on. Sherry was gone. The whole thing was like a dream.

CHAPTER XXVI

GHOSTS

THE taxi came at ten-thirty, and Sandra went home in it. The storm was subsiding, and as she paid the driver, he said,

" It will be clearing before morning."

As she approached the door of her apartment, Sandra wished her mother were there to greet her. To no one else could she unburden her soul, tell of the happenings of the night — those strange happenings which seemed more like melodrama than real life, yet were real and had to be reckoned with.

She had taken the living-room for her own and slept in the bed which had been her mother's. Susan Carter had the room which had been Sandra's and Doady's. She opened her door as Sandra entered. She wore a gay kimono which seemed a bit out of key with the horn glasses.

" Ione Morton has some oysters for you," she said. " She's going to bring them in."

" I do nothing but eat," Sandra told her. " Gale Markham had tea with me, and I dined with him, and here I am doing it again."

Susan gave her a shrewd glance. " The chances are you didn't eat enough either time to keep you alive. I've been watching you lately. No appetite. That's why I had Ione get the oysters. She's always crazy to do something for you, and you are going beyond your strength."

"No, I'm not. I'm strong as a horse. But it was dear of you to think about me."

Susan flung that off with an air of not deserving it. "I wanted some myself. I am seldom altruistic. I have lived alone long enough to be consistently selfish."

"All of which," said Sandra, as she got out of her coat, "is utterly untrue. Look at the way you spend your time on Ione."

"She's an interesting experiment," Susan stated. "It's like seeing a locust come out of its shell."

She opened the door into the hall. "I'll tell Ione you're here. She set the table herself, and arranged that dish of fruit in the center, would you believe it?"

Sandra, getting herself into a warm dressing-gown, was rather glad of the diversion planned by these two strangely consorted friends. She dreaded to be alone, to face the tumultuous thoughts that were clamoring for consideration.

Ione, coming in presently with Susan Carter, and with the oysters hot in a china pitcher, was almost miraculously changed from the untidy creature of the preceding summer. She wore a crisp blue smock, and her hair with its boyish cut gave an air of refinement to her highly-colored features.

"I feel as if I was coming to a party," she announced genially.

"Were," Susan corrected.

"Were," said Ione, "only I shan't remember it."

"You've got to remember it," Susan said calmly, "if you're going to get anywhere."

"Well, if you can do as much with my tongue as you've done with my looks, I'd be glad. But it's harder."

There were two places set at the little table. "I'm not eating anything," Ione said. "I don't want to break in on my diet. My husband noticed tonight that I was getting thinner, and he thinks it's becoming."

Susan, eating oysters with the zest of a recovering invalid, asked, "Is he out again?"

"He's always out."

"There is nothing in my book of etiquette," Susan remarked, "that pertains to keeping husbands at home."

"He's taking more notice of me than he did," said Ione with some wistfulness, "and he thought my dinner was swell."

"Delicious," said Susan.

"Delicious," said Ione.

When the little feast was over, Susan went back to bed. Ione stayed to wash up the dishes, and Sandra, feeling rested and refreshed, got out a dress she was to wear the following night and which needed a few stitches.

It was a charming thing of flame chiffon with a gold rose on the shoulder. Ione, surveying it enviously, said: "I've never had a dinner gown. Of course, I've worn light things to public dances. But I've never had invitations. Girls like you have a good time."

"We have our troubles, too, Ione."

"Yes. But not like mine. Ignorance. If I'd 'a' known anything, I'd of been different, and I might of kept my husband from doing the things he's doing."

There was a note of anxiety in her voice which made Sandra ask, " What is he doing, Ione? "

" Boot-legging, Miss Claybourne. I haven't told Miss Carter. I haven't told anybody but you. But I'm worried all the time."

" You're afraid something will happen? "

" That and the way it's workin' on him. It's making him sneaky, being underhand about things. And he's getting a good living out of it. That's the worst. He can't make so much money any other way."

She talked for a long time about it. It was a revelation to Sandra to find, under all the surface crudeness, Ione's real force of character and common sense.

It was late when at last the dress was ready and Ione returned to her apartment. Sandra was not sleepy. She wrapped herself in her coat and, opening the long window, went out on the balcony. The storm had been succeeded by a crystalline clearness. The moon was sailing high. The wind blew freezingly through the court. On the other side of it, and one floor below, was that other balcony, deserted. Haunted by ghosts — the ghosts of a tall man and of a little white cat . . . *Her beauty hangs upon the cheek of night . . . like a rich jewel . . .*

Sandra caught her breath! Oh, to have it all again! The summer warmth. Rufus in the lighted window . . . the wave of his hand . . . herself leaning down . . . the thrilling ecstasy . . . !

She turned back into the room. She was shivering with cold and excitement. She went toward the telephone. Stopped. Laid her hand on the receiver, but did not take it from the hook.

Out there in the cottage among the snow-powdered trees, Rufus would be writing. He did not know she was near. He would be thinking of her as still at Windytop.

And now, if she spoke to him, she would hear his voice, " *Sandra!* "

" Rufus, I am here, in Washington. I want you to come."

" When? "

" Tomorrow morning."

She took her hand from the receiver. No, she would not call him. Things were just as they had been in spite of Sherry — cheap little Sherry with her dreadful laughter.

CHAPTER XXVII

THE SPIDER SPINS A WEB

STEPHEN LEEDS, arriving the next morning, gave Sandra a dismayed sense that she didn't want Doady to marry him. "He's nice enough, but he'd never make her care." She couldn't have told on what she based this conclusion. He was a clean-cut, stocky chap, good-looking, well-dressed, and bore himself with apparent modesty.

"But he's dominant," Sandra guessed shrewdly, "and Doady's nerves wouldn't stand for it."

She was nice to him, however, and his eyes followed her as she moved about the shop in her velveteen frock.

"New idea, isn't it? " he asked, "wearing things like that to work? "

"Mr. Maulsby likes it. He and Doady talked it over when she came. He doesn't want anything in these rooms that is incongruous. And dull clothes would be, with all this richness around us."

Leeds was handling the orange cups. "These are choice," he said. "Where did they come from? "

"From some people we know in Virginia. We told Mr. Maulsby about them, and we promised to try to find some one who would appreciate how fine they are."

He smiled. "That's subtle flattery."

"It's not flattery."

"How do you know I'd appreciate them? "

" Doady told me.   In her letter."

" Did she tell you that I want to marry her? "

" Yes."

" Well, what do you think of me? "

" Give me time."   She slanted her eyes at him mischievously.

He laughed with her. " I usually get what I want."

" I don't want you to get Doady unless she loves you."

" I can love enough for the pair of us."

She shook her head. " That's what men think. But it's not safe. Love comes. You can't compel it."

He looked down at her. " You speak as if you knew something about it."

" Perhaps I do."

" Better not care too much. Let the man do that. He'll like it better in the end."

Would he? Would Rufus?

She flung a challenge. " What about Romeo? "

" Old stuff."

She went back to the orange cups. " You see, they have the same pattern as the salts and peppers."

" I'll take the lot of them.   And you can let me know when others come your way."

" Really?   How nice!   Where shall I send them? "

He gave an address in Carroll County. " I've a lot of things you'll like to look at. You and your sister. I've asked her and told her to make up her own party. So I'll see you, I hope."

" I'll come if Doady does."

" She will," he said securely, " and some day she'll come to stay."

Sandra longed to tell him that he must not be too sure about it — Doady was, as it were, here today and there tomorrow — but she had no opportunity, for Felix Maulsby arrived from New York at that moment and was at once introduced to Mr. Leeds.

" Doady sent him. And he's bought the Sheffield."

Felix glanced at the display. " You showed taste in the arrangement."

" It is Doady's taste, not mine. She wanted Mr. Leeds to like it. She wrote out her idea, and I followed it."

" She has a great head." Maulsby remarked. " I don't know what I'd do without her."

He left them for a moment, and Leeds said:

" He may have to do without her before he knows it. And now — can't you and I play around a bit together? Have dinner and the theater? Tonight? I want to talk about your sister. It won't bore you, will it? "

" It won't bore me, but I have an engagement. I am dining at the Maulsbys'."

" Tomorrow, then? I'll stay over and get tickets. May I? "

She agreed, and in a little while he went away. Later she remarked to Felix,

" He wants to marry Doady."

" Who does? "

" Mr. Leeds."

" Nonsense. She can't get married. She belongs to the shop."

" I wouldn't say that exactly. I don't think she's in love with him. But he has loads of money."

" She's not mercenary."

"She thinks she is."

"She thinks too much. When she gets a real love-affair, she'll know it."

Sandra agreed with him. But then the question was whether Doady really wanted a romance. She wanted so many other things. And perhaps her way was best.

At lunch time Sandra spoke to Felix Maulsby of her experiences of the night before.

"I thought I ought to tell you. Rufus Fiske's step-mother was here." She made a dramatic recital of it.

When she had finished, Felix swung his eyeglass with a nervous air. "I'm glad you didn't show the ivories," he said. "I don't trust her. Ever since she got that letter from me last spring, she has been trying to get me to sell them. And I won't. I said that I had prom-ised Rufus that I wouldn't. If she could prove they were her property, it would be a different matter. But until she has proved it, I must stick to my promise."

"She says she knows your wife and that she's dining with you."

"Tonight. Yes. She met Marcia in the summer, and she hung about the place until they got to be rather good friends. She's amusing, and Marcia will take up with anybody who keeps her from being bored. Be-sides, she says the whole thing is exciting. I'm afraid she's rather getting Mrs. Fiske's point of view, that the ivories don't belong to Rufus."

"Oh, but they do."

"Of course, we have only his word for it." Felix's glasses were whirling wildly on their black ribbon. "But I'm inclined to trust him."

" I should think anybody with two eyes could see that he's honest and that she's tricky," Sandra told him.

Felix, noting her flaming cheeks, said shrewdly, " He's a great friend of yours? "

" He's enough of a friend, so that I — trust him."

Felix nodded. " I agree with you. Young Fiske is our best bet when it comes to having confidence in either of them. But his stepmother has fed Marcia up on the story of his shortcomings. He told me enough, however, in the beginning to make me doubt the truth of her side of it. And anyhow a promise is a promise, and I shall keep it."

With that Sandra had to be content.

The thing came up again that very afternoon. Mrs. Maulsby got her husband on the telephone, and Sandra, busy with a customer, caught a word now and then of the one-sided conversation. It had, she was sure, something to do with the figurines, and when Felix joined her after the customer was gone, his first words confirmed her belief.

" Marcia wants the ivories sent up to complete her dinner decorations. I told her I thought we had done them to death, and that as Mrs. Fiske would be there it might lead to unpleasant revelations. She's the kind that would tell the world if she thought she could make a good story of it. But Marcia insists — so that's the end of it."

But Sandra knew it was not the end. Sherry would never let it be the end. Riding that night in a taxi to her dinner-party, she told herself with an attempt at lightness that Red Ridinghood was going forth to meet the Wolf, and that the Wolf might be surprised at the encounter.

If Sherry was surprised, however, she made no sign. It was a large party, and there were no introductions. Red Ridinghood sat at one end of the long Italian table with the Wolf at the other. Most of the people seemed to know each other and to know Sherry. Some of them had homes near Marcia's on the North Shore. It was there Sherry had met them.

She was a sparkling figure in her favorite pink, this time of chiffon heavy with silver. She wore a diamond circlet about her small head; diamonds dripped from her throat and ears and banded her bare arms. So metallic did she seem with all her glitter, that Sandra had a fantastic feeling that she was like Midas' daughter, after the fatal enchantment, and that everything she touched must be as hard and shining as herself.

The table was covered with a cloth of heavy, hand-made lace, and the ivories were associated tonight with candlesticks of pale amber crystal with violets in tall holders of the same pale glass. The little figures had an ineffable look to Sandra, who had seen them hitherto only in their case. She heard people talking about them. She expected every moment to hear Sherry say, "They are mine." But she did not. She seemed content to talk a great deal and to have all eyes upon her.

Young Mark Beveridge, who sat at Sandra's right, said,

" Who is she? "

" A Mrs. Rufus Fiske. Of California."

" Likes herself a lot, doesn't she? "

" She seems to."

" Where do you suppose Marcia Maulsby picked her up? "

" Met her on the North Shore and thinks she is amusing."

" So's a clown. But one doesn't invite him to one's dinner parties."

Sandra, agreeing with him absolutely, hid her satisfaction under a cool, " Aren't you a bit high-hat? "

All through dinner, as she talked to Mark and to the young man on the other side of her, Sandra watched to see if Sherry recognized her. If she knew, there was not the flicker of an eyelash to betray it. Nor did Sherry seem to have any interest in the decorations. For all the notice she took of them, they might have been lead soldiers or any other cheap or trivial thing.

At the end of dinner they went into the drawing-room for coffee. And then for the first time Sherry spoke to Sandra.

" Aren't the Maulsbys being rather good to you," she said with a touch of insolence as they stood together, " to have you here tonight? "

Sandra's light laugh, the mischievous slant of her eyes, showed no hint of the smoldering passions within her. " Perhaps I am being good to them," she said with an effect of casualness, and went on to meet some of Doady's friends, who, Marcia had said, were looking for her.

" You young people will want to dance presently," her hostess told them, " when I round up the older ones for the bridge tables."

Swept gaily into the group, Sandra was aware of the place Doady had made for herself. Theodora Claybourne had, it seemed, become in a small way the fashion. As she had once dreamed, people now turned their heads, " *There goes Theodora Claybourne,*" and looked after her. She had the dramatic art of making the most of her personality. Sandra would never have it. But she would always make friends, as she made them now, by the force of her simplicity and charm.

It was while she sat among them that she saw Sherry speak to the man who was serving the coffee. He went away, presently, and brought back to her a large silk reticule. It was a gorgeous affair of pink brocade with insets of *petit point* and much silver embroidery. It swung from long pink cords, and when it was opened, it overflowed with something silken and pink with knitting-needles stabbed into it.

Sandra heard Mrs. Maulsby's voice. " Sherry, you're not going to knit tonight? "

" Why not? I don't play bridge."

" But there's dancing."

" Later? I can do this until then."

Some one asked to see what she was knitting.

" A shawl," said Sherry. " My Christmas present to — myself."

She held it up, and exclamations of admiration came from the crowd. The rosy delicate thing unrolled in lengths of incredible fineness. It was like a cobweb with the light of dawn upon it — silvery, shining, sheathing Sherry from head to foot as she wrapped it around her.

Mark Beveridge, leaning over Sandra's chair, said, " Another spot-light pose."

Sandra nodded. " She seems to know how to do it."

When the young people went away at last to dance, they left Sherry spinning her pink web. A glittering spider, Sandra told herself. She was not sure which rôle suited Sherry better, that of wolf or spider, but one thing was evident, no one else in that company was aware of her as a sinister influence. She was undoubtedly, to all of them at this moment, as innocent as Miss Muffett on her tuffett, or the nice gray brute of modernized fairy lore who carries Red Ridinghood's basket politely and dines on bread and butter instead of grandmothers.

Sandra, dancing with Mark Beveridge, said, " I don't do it as well as Doady," and when he tried to protest, she assured him: " You can't hurt my feelings if you say I don't. Doady thinks nothing is worth doing if it isn't worth doing well."

Mark laughed. " I remember the two of you at Stephanie's party. I was Doady's partner, and I ran away afterward — left her high and dry during supper. And she's remembered it and made me smart for it."

Sandra opened her eyes at him. " Really? "

He nodded. " She never gives me but one dance and not always that. Now, you wouldn't hold a thing up against a fellow forever, would you? "

" Doady says I'm too good-natured."

" Well, you're pleasant balm after the bruises she inflicts." He smiled at her and guided her down the wide hall in which they were dancing so that they might get beyond the other couples and have a clear space to themselves.

It was thus that, dancing, they passed the door of the dining-room. And as she passed, Sandra, glancing into it, saw that the tables were cleared. A dim light burned, and in that dim light Sandra was sure she glimpsed in the shadows of a far corner the flutter of a silver flounce.

As she danced on with Mark, her heart was beating wildly. Was Sherry in the dining-room? And if so, what was she doing?

Chapter XXVIII

THE PINK BAG

IT was Sherry who had asked Marcia to have the ivories on the table.

" Are you so under the thumb of that husband of yours that you don't dare let me see them? "

" I'm not under his thumb. But he says we have done them to death as table decorations."

" You haven't had them for me. And I think you might."

In the end she won. Marcia called Felix up. Sherry, she insisted, would be hurt by their lack of confidence in her.

" You misjudge her, Felix. You act as if she were an arch-schemer when she's nothing but an amusing little climber."

But Felix was not convinced, and that night before dinner he had said to his butler, " Keep an eye on the ivories, Mattock, and after dinner lock them in the cabinet and take care of the key."

Yet Sherry had seemed innocent enough when she arrived, all prinked up in pink like a Paris doll. Felix's eyes noted approvingly the contrast of Sandra's simplicity.

" She has distinction. She doesn't need diamonds."

All through dinner Sherry ignored the figurines. She

mentioned them, indeed, only once, at the very beginning, as she and Felix entered the dining-room.

"It was adorable of you to let me see them." Then,
with a rising inflection, "Some day you are going to
sell them to me?"

There was a sort of childish impertinence in her
manner, which, in spite of his prejudice, won his
laughter.

"If that's a wager, I'm afraid you'll lose your bet,"
he told her as they sat down.

She was on his right, the guest of honor, though why
under the heavens Marcia should have thought her important enough was beyond his understanding.

He found himself rather enjoying her. She had a
fund of inconsequential chatter, a crude kind of wit,
and her sharp tongue spared no one. Felix didn't in
the least approve of her, but as a table companion she
was piquant.

In this less critical mood he told himself that no one
could blame her for wanting the little figures. Heavens,
how beautiful they were — pure and palpitating under
the pale light! Yet Sherry couldn't possibly appreciate
them. She wasn't that kind. He had a feeling that she
wouldn't know Chelsea from a Cheshire cat!

As she rose from the table, Sherry blew a kiss to the
five Small Senses, "Good-by, lovely things!" Then
she laughed up into Felix's face. "You see, nothing
happened," she said. "I am really most — harmless."

It was when Marcia made up her tables for bridge
that Felix lost track of the guest of honor. The last
he remembered seeing of her was posed under a lamp,
weaving her rosy web. She had refused to play.

" When I get tired of knitting, I'll join the dancers," she told Marcia. " I have five partners to choose from. And it's nice to keep them waiting."

As the players grew more absorbed in the game, Sherry's sharp eyes surveyed them. At last she rose in leisurely fashion, rolled up the delicate shawl, stuck it in the pink bag, and with the bag on her arm left the room, unnoticed.

She stopped for a moment in the hall, looking down toward the dancers swaying to the measure of a dinner program broadcast on the radio; then she went on, slipping at last stealthily through the great door of the dining-room.

The table had been cleared, and there was nothing now upon it but a tall epergne set on a strip of Spanish leather. The only light came from two wall-lamps, shaded and serving only to intensify the rich gloom. The candlesticks of amber crystal and the violets in their holders had been placed on the sideboard. But the figurines were not there, nor, as Sherry's eyes swept the room, could she discover them.

She wanted to be sure, however, and prowled about in the dimness, her silver gown glinting among the shadows.

While she prowled, Sandra saw her!

Beyond the dining-room was the library, with a high, carved screen between, and rounding this screen, Sherry gave a little leap, as a cat leaps towards long-pursued quarry. For in this room were many of the treasures of Felix's private collection. And in a cabinet in a far corner were the figurines. They were set by themselves on one of the shelves and showed frail and remote through the glass door.

Sherry, grasping the knob of the door, said impolite things under her breath. It was locked. Mattock had obeyed his instructions. She picked at the lock with one of her knitting needles. But it held fast. She looked about the room, and suddenly her eyes were lighted. On the library table was a heavy paper knife of bronze. Near it were roses in an opalescent bowl. Sherry reached for the knife, ran to the dining-room door, and glanced around. Everything was quiet. She peeped into the hall — there was the shuffle of feet, the crash of a jazz band.

One crash more in the midst of it, and who would hear? She ran back to the cabinet and with a quick lift of the knife shattered the glass, then whirling about, in the same fraction of a second she shattered the opalescent vase. After that she listened . . . listened . . . The water ran down the length of the long table and dripped to the floor; the roses were scattered. . . . If any one came in, she could say she had knocked over the vase in passing, and who would look beyond it to that shattered door?

But no one came. The music crashed on. Still Sherry stood there, bent a little forward, her eyes watching, her figure tense, the pink bag on her arm wide open. Suddenly she straightened, went to the cabinet, reached through the hole she had made in the glass, grasped the ivory figures, and dropped them one by one into the yawning bag.

Then, with a quick breath of triumph, she turned. And stopped in her tracks. For beside the tall screen stood a silent figure. In a dress of flame! With scorn in her eyes! Sandra Claybourne! The girl whom Rufus wouldn't marry!

Sherry, with the pink bag hugged close, stood perfectly still for a breathless moment. Then she flung out a hand toward the scattered roses. " I'm afraid I've made a dreadful mess of things."

" What happened? "

" I broke a — vase."

Sandra's quick glance went toward the cabinet. " You broke something else."

Sherry, cornered, braved it out. "Well, what if I did? "

" Do you think you can get away with it? "

"Why shouldn't I? "

" Because I sha'n't let you."

" How can you help it? "

" I saw you take the ivories. I shall have to ask you to — put them back."

" And if I won't? "

" I shall tell Mr. Maulsby."

Sherry's eyes were shining like a cat's. " Tell him, then. He's in the card-room."

It was lightly said, but back of the lightness Sandra divined a deeper motive. Sherry wanted to get her out of the room. By the time she came back with Felix Maulsby, the ivories would be gone.

She took a step forward. " I think you'd better let me have your bag."

Sherry laughed: " Don't be ridiculous. I am only taking what is mine."

Another step brought Sandra close to the lamp on the

table. Its light swept over the scarlet of her gown like a flame.

Sherry spoke violently and unexpectedly: " Oh, why do you wear that atrocious color? I hate to have you near me."

" Only for that? " There was a gleam of mischief in Sandra's slanted eyes.

" I suppose you wear it because of that picture on Rufus' wall," Sherry taunted.

But Sandra simply shrugged her shoulders and stood there, smiling.

" What are you waiting for? " Sherry demanded.

" For the — bag."

" You'll wait forever."

" Or till somebody comes? "

" Oh," Sherry's voice was full of venom, " so you are playing Rufus' game for him? Why not let him play his own? And as for the ivories, I shall send Maulsby a check for them. That's fair enough, isn't it? And Rufus is getting half of his father's fortune. That ought to satisfy him."

" Why should it? When the terms of the will make him lose his happiness at your hands? "

Sherry fluttered her fingers in a gesture that showed all the glitter of her rings. " Why not at my hands? They are pretty enough."

The utter heartlessness of it, the impudence, were like tinder to Sandra's temper. " Rufus will not have to lose his happiness at your hands. There are other ways."

" What ways? " tensely.

" He may break the will."

" Break it? "

" Yes. Why not? People are saying there was undue influence."

" What people? "

But Sandra had gone as far as she would. Already she was frightened. What did she know of Rufus' plans? And what right had she to reveal him to Sherry?

" Does he think — " the spots of rouge on Sherry's cheeks showed up against her pallor like those of a painted clown, " does he think he can get away with a thing like that? " She began to laugh again, then with a sudden rapid movement, she started for the door.

But Sandra was too quick for her. They met and wrestled silently amid the shadows. Suddenly, out from the library and up the hall, sped a scarlet figure, a pink bag clutched tight and making a clash of color . . . Sandra's young strength had been too much for the older woman. The spider had lost her web. The adventure with the ivories was over.

CHAPTER XXIX

"WHETHER I WIN OR LOSE!"

O F course, I knew she'd get away at once," Sandra told Felix and Marcia after the other guests were gone, " but I had the ivories, and I was sure you'd rather not have a scene."

Marcia, convinced at last, cried, " The little cat! "

The three of them were in the library with all the wreckage about them of shattered cabinet and shattered vase.

" How she dared," Felix wondered.

" She'd dare anything," Sandra stated. " If you had seen her! She fought like a tiger — but I was too strong for her."

Marcia's gold-slippered foot tapped the floor. " The impertinence of her! She even sent a maid to me to say she was not well and was leaving early. I rushed out to see if there was anything I could do. But she was gone."

" Serves you right, old lady," her husband reminded her. " Of course, she'll never come back, and she'll trust us not to make the matter public."

" Oh," Marcia raged, " I'd like to shout it from the housetops."

" If we have any sense, we will keep it quiet. We're in the somewhat uncomfortable position of having tried to foist a rather crude sort of criminal on society."

Felix touched a bell, and when the butler arrived, he said:

"There's been an accident, Mattock. You'd better clean up all this without saying anything to the other servants. Some one tried to get the ivories, but Miss Claybourne was too quick for him. I'll keep them in my room tonight and take them down to the shop the first thing in the morning."

"Very good, sir." Mattock did not wink an eyelash.

On the way to the drawing-room, Felix remarked: "Mattock knows more than you'd think. I'll bet he saw through Sherry's maneuvers. But he'll keep his mouth shut."

In the drawing-room the ivories stood on a small table where Sandra had put them when she first showed them to Felix and his wife. The pink bag, flung on a chair, overflowed with the silken rosiness of the knitted shawl.

Felix, lifting the bag, said, "What will you do with it, Marcia?"

"Send it back to her with my compliments and with regret that I am forced to keep a part of the contents."

Her husband laughed. "She'll hate you."

His wife retorted, "Well, I may have been fooled, but I am not going to take it lying down."

Felix gathered up the ivories. "You'd better stay here tonight, Sandra. I'll send you a glass of wine, and you can rest after your excitement."

"I don't want wine," said Sandra sensibly, "I want sleep. And I must get home. I have to be at the shop early in the morning, and I can't go in dinner clothes."

" We might let you off from the shop for one morning."

But Sandra shook her head. " Doady would never forgive me. I am on honor to keep things going till she comes back."

But it was more than Sandra's sense of responsibility to the shop which sent her home that night. Since that blazing exchange of words with Sherry she had known that in some way she must reach Rufus. She had put a weapon in the hands of his enemy. At this very moment Sherry might be talking at long distance with her lawyers in California.

All the way home her mind was on it. It was snowing again, a blustery night. She was comfortable in the Maulsbys' big car, but when she reached the apartment and crossed the pavement to the entrance, the wind almost swept her off her feet. She hoped Susan was asleep and would not ask questions. Susan had a way of being at times somewhat insistently curious about the affairs of others.

As she passed Ione Morton's door, she hesitated a moment, then tapped. She had seen a light as she drove up, and knew that late vigils were now a part of Ione's program. Her husband's hours were more and more irregular. There were nights, indeed, when he did not get home at all.

Ione opened the door. " Come in," she said at once. Sandra stepped inside. " Ione," she said, " may I use your telephone? "

Afterward, when Sandra thought of it, she wondered why she had chosen Ione rather than Susan to share her confidence. It was, perhaps, her knowledge of some quality of strength and fortitude which had been developed in this simple creature by her fears for her husband. And by her striving for something better than she knew.

Sandra went to the telephone and gave Rufus' number. Waited. Found herself shivering, but not with cold. Found herself, too, half afraid to hear his voice, though wanting to hear it more than anything in the whole wide world.

But she was not to hear it. The operator answered presently, " Service had been discontinued."

" No telephone — " Sandra hung up the receiver. She had a dazed feeling — and stood undecided.

Ione's keen eyes saw her agitation. " Look here," she said, " you're shaking all over. I'm going to make you a cup of tea. Run along and get in bed with the hot-water bag, and I'll bring it up to you."

" I'm not cold." Then, unexpectedly, Sandra poured the whole story into Ione's ears.

" I don't know what to do. I've got to reach Mr. Fiske — Rufus Fiske, you remember? It's important. A business matter that may mean a lot. I just learned it tonight. And now his telephone is cut off."

" Where is he? "

" In his country cottage — near Rockville."

" Why don't you go out? "

" But how, Ione? "

" Take a taxi. We'll go together."

" Oh, but I couldn't! " all the protest of generations of conventional Claybournes was in Sandra's voice. " Not at this hour of the night! "

"Well, I don't see why not," Ione persisted. " You'd

have me and the taxi driver. There's a friend of my husband drives one of the cabs, and he's as safe as safe."

The friend of a bootlegger! and Ione for chaperone! High comedy, if one looked at it from one angle. Yet, after all, why not? Rufus would be writing — he always wrote late. Sandra could see him standing tall and splendid in the door as he opened it . . .

She wrenched herself back from the vision. " It would be better to go early in the morning. Can you? And if he isn't up, we can leave a letter."

So it was settled. Ione was to make the arrangement with the trustworthy driver, and they were to leave at seven. " We can have breakfast downtown when we get back," Sandra decided.

As she crept quietly into her own room, Sandra heard a sleepy question from Susan,

" Didn't I hear you and Ione talking? "

" Yes." Sandra shifted the topic. " I'm nearly frozen. I'm going to take a hot bath and go to bed. I have to be up early in the morning. I'll get breakfast down town. How's your cold? "

" Rotten," said the precise Susan inelegantly, and went to sleep again.

But Sandra lay awake, staring into the darkness. Her brain was busy with the exciting events of the evening. She saw Sherry weaving her pink web; she saw among the shadows of the dining-room that gleam of silver; she saw herself standing by the screen; she heard herself saying, " He may break the will . . ."

Oh, why had she said it, and what did she know about

it? Since that day in the library at Windytop, there had been utter silence between herself and Rufus. She had not even known he was in Washington until Gale told her.

She was up and ready at the time appointed, and found Ione waiting for her.

" He hasn't came back," the young wife told her, " but I've set out his breakfast and left a note."

It had stopped snowing, but the city was white with the storm, and under the lamps the streets looked bleak and deserted. As they reached the countryside, however, the dark sky was cut by bars of shining silver, and presently the stark trees and the sleepy, silent houses stood out against the clear light in sharp relief.

" How lovely it is! " Sandra said.

Ione nodded. She spoke presently with some hesitation: " It seems queer to be riding like this with you. Do you remember the first time on the balcony when we got acquainted? I thought you were stuck up. I never dreamed you could be so nice and friendly. And I said things about Rufus Fiske. And I oughtn't to have done it. I didn't know anything — really."

" It didn't make any difference. We got to be — friends — afterward."

" Well, I used to think it was smart to talk about people. But when your mother was here, she was such a lady . . . and you and your sister . . ." Ione floundered hopelessly. " I don't know how to say it . . . only I'd never met — your kind."

Sandra, helping her out, said: " Mother's a darling. I hardly hope that Doady and I can ever live up to her."

The silver light had given way to pale primrose as the taxi whirled along the road to the foot of the path which led to Rufus' cottage. They were facing the east, and as the sun came up, they seemed to look through a shimmering curtain of golden gauze. A redbird flew down, a grackle, and a blue-jay to some seed which had been scattered for them on the cleared path. Their color was superb against the whiteness. The whole scene had the effect of a stage setting before the actors enter.

Sandra had a letter ready. " If Rufus isn't up, the man can take it in."

But Rufus was up. And as the taxi stopped, they saw him on his own doorstep in short leather coat and leggings and a fur cap, tall and splendid, behind that curtain of golden gauze, with the red and blue and raven-black birds flying about him.

As his ear caught the throb of the engine, he looked up and came striding down the path. Sandra spoke to Ione breathlessly,

" I'll go and meet him."

She got out of the cab and went toward him. Facing his tall splendor, her strength seemed to leave her. She stopped and stood waiting for him.

His voice rang out incredulously, " Sandra! "

Then he swept her into his arms.

She gasped, " Rufus, put me down."

He carried her, protesting, into the house, drew a chair to the fire.

" Take off your hat and let me have a look at you."

" Rufus — I mustn't . . ."

" Nonsense."

He lifted the little hat from her bright hair, unfastened her coat, and when at last she was revealed straight and slim in her red velveteen, he gazed at her with burning eyes.

"You're lovelier than ever."

He sat down opposite her. "Where did you come from — Virginia?"

"No. I've been in Washington for weeks."

"And you didn't let me know?"

"How could I? I came today only because something happened. Rufus, I've seen Sherry."

"Sherry?"

"Yes. Twice. I tried to reach you last night by telephone. But I couldn't. So I came out this morning with Ione Morton. She's in the cab."

He rose. "She'll freeze. I'll bring her in here and take you into my den where we can talk."

He opened a door and Sandra saw another fire blazing, and above the mantel the picture of "The Boy in Red." There was a big desk, an Indian blanket on the floor, and books on open shelves.

When Rufus came back with Ione, he said:

"You and Mrs. Morton are to have breakfast with me. She tells me you both came off without yours, and my coffee is in the pot. We can have toast and bacon and eggs in a second."

"Rufus, I haven't time — really."

Ione interposed. "Look here, you and Mr. Fiske talk while I do the cooking. I'd love it. And if I were you, I'd call that taxi man and let him sit by the kitchen stove. It's cold enough outside to freeze a furnace."

So it was settled, and the taxi man came in with

alacrity, with his meter ticking up a huge tariff outside, and the prospect of good cheer within, while Rufus carried Sandra off to his little room and shut the door behind them.

" Now, tell me about Sherry," he said.

Sitting opposite him by the fire, she began with the night when Sherry came to the shop. She told it dramatically, and he saw the two of them, Sandra at bay, Sherry in her pink, sneering, laughing; disappearing at last in the snowy night, held high in Ito's arms.

When Sandra came to that, Rufus said:

" That's the way she always does things. Like an actress on a stage. That's why she held my father. It was a perpetual puppet show."

" Rufus, she was dreadful. She made everything seem evil. When she laughed, I understood for the first time why you hate her more than you love — me."

Dead silence. Then, " I deserve that, I suppose."

" I don't blame you. Not since I've seen her."

She went on to speak of the night at the Maulsbys'. The theft of the ivories. " We fought like tigers, Rufus. And when I got the bag, I ran and ran until I reached the drawing-room, then I went in as if nothing had happened and watched the card players. I knew she wouldn't follow me."

His face darkened. " To think that she dared! "

" She'd dare anything to get her own way."

He agreed. " Yes, she would. Oh, I've seen it a thousand times. There was once with my father. She wanted some pearls, and my father wouldn't give them to her. The price was out of all reason, he said, and she had enough. So one day she went to San Francisco and had the dealer send the pearls down, and that night at dinner there was plenty of champagne, and when she had my father in a melting mood, she went upstairs and said she'd come back. My father sat in the court with his coffee and cigarettes. He was very comfortable. I had my book by the fountain. There were tropical plants all about, and some macaws and cockatoos whistling and screeching. At last Sherry danced in, singing a little song. It had a queer Eastern sound with a beat like a tom-tom. She had put on a fantastic Oriental dress of sheer gauze, and she wore the pearls — ropes of them around her throat and in loops from her headdress. She sang her little song and kept time with her dancing feet. And when she came finally to my father, he saw the pearls. Well, it might have made him furious. But it didn't. Just the very cheek of her doing such a thing delighted him — flaunting them in his face.

"'They aren't paid for, Rufus,' she said. 'I'll send them back if you say so.'

"But he didn't say so. He roared with laughter and told her she was a gold-digger, but he didn't blame her . . ."

Rufus caught himself up. "Here I am, dragging in old memories and not letting you tell the rest of your story."

"I haven't come to the worst. I'm afraid I made an awful mess of things. But Sherry was so maddening — and I lost my temper and at last I told her — you were going to contest the will."

He could see the frightened throb of her throat, and reassured her quietly. "There's no harm done. I'm not going to fight the will."

"Oh, but you must, Rufus. She deserves to lose everything. People like that ought to be punished."

"I'm not so sure of that." He rose, restlessly prowled around the room, and returned to the hearth. Then, leaning his arms on the top of a high-backed chair, he spoke with a sort of tense composure. "I'm not so certain as I used to be, Sandra. Since I have been alone out here, I have thought a lot about myself. About my life as I have been living it since my father's death. I've shut myself up and blamed Sherry for all my — unhappiness. Yet my life is my own. Sherry can't take away or give me anything but money. Why should I let all my days be darkened by the shadows she has cast?"

He answered his own questions, thinking it out as he went along. "In a way, working here, I have forgotten Sherry. The things I have written have given me a sense of power. People listen, Sandra. They believe what I say. They want me to say more of it. It has been an amazing revelation — as if I had what we used to call a message . . . And why not call it that? It is not a material thing — but it is my own — and the world wants it."

He had been looking down, but now he raised his head and gazed straight into her eyes. "I wanted to tell you all this — but I waited. I had to find if I were really free. I was afraid that some day I would let Sherry ride my soul again — like a witch. I had to wait."

Sandra rose and stood, facing him. "She will never ride your soul again. But she must be punished. You must break the will. It is the right thing to do, Rufus."

He said with some sternness, " Yet it was because of the will that you sent me away."

She flung out her hands in an appealing gesture. " But I hadn't seen her. She's a thief, Rufus. She's everything that is wicked. I can't bear to have her flourish like a green baytree."

They were both of them so much in earnest that they had no smile for her florid scriptural phrase. Rufus began to speak with deep emotion. " I must tell you this. That side by side with my work has been the thought of you. It is because of you that I have been able to write what I have written. My love for you has worked some change in me. You said a moment ago that I must contest this will. Well, there's only one thing on God's earth that will make me do it, and that's your promise to marry me! Whether I win or lose! You said a while ago that I hated Sherry more than I loved you. It isn't true. It has never been true. I've loved you more than I could hate the — devil. I've only been afraid of my own darkness . . . But this morning, when I saw you coming up the path, I knew myself for a fool. You were like a torch lighting my world. I knew you would always light it."

He held out his arms to her. With a little cry she came to him. In the silence the pine logs snapped and sputtered. " The Boy in Red " looked down with slanted eyes. Tall and splendid, Rufus bent his head to his lady's lips. Sandra, vivid as a flame, shut her eyes and saw — a balcony . . . *her beauty hangs upon the cheek of night . . . like a rich jewel.*

Chapter XXX

LOVE AND LIFE

THE next night, when Sandra dined with Stephen Leeds, he was aware of some exquisite and ineffable quality in her which had not been there at their earlier meeting.

"By Jove," he told her, leaning across the table, "you and your sister have something about you like violets in the spring — or little brooks on mountain sides — or nymphs dancing under evening stars — as if all the world were young with you . . . unspoiled. I don't know how to express it."

"Doady would hate to have you say that. She thinks herself very worldly-minded."

"Yet she lives on tiptoe. Both of you do — getting a lot out of life."

"I had a letter from her this morning. She's coming back for Christmas."

"Good. And now you must tell me what to get her. For a gift, I mean."

"Flowers, books, candy," chanted Sandra. "Mother's frightfully old fashioned."

"It must be something more than that. A bracelet? I saw one today — diamond and emerald links."

"Heavens, no! Mother would die of suppressed conventionalities. And anyhow Doady wouldn't take it."

" Why not? I am going to marry her."

Sandra smiled. " Are you? "

" I have said it." He leaned back in his chair and flashed a laughing glance at her. " There's every reason why she should have me."

" You are modest! "

" Oh, I'm not as bad as they make 'em. And I love her a lot." A flush came up in his cheeks. " Sounds silly to put it that way, doesn't it? But you know what I mean."

She liked him a little better for that touch of boyishness. But she didn't like him well enough for a husband for Doady. Oh, Doady must know real happiness, that thrilling ecstasy which had been Sandra's since early morning. Doady must not miss it, and she would never have it with Stephen Leeds.

Perhaps because the thought of Rufus was beating with every pulse, she found herself enjoying the dinner, the play, and the dancing afterward. Stephen was charmed with her.

" If I had met you first, your sister would have had to look to her laurels. But I fancy that's the twin complex, that you're alike."

" Oh, but we're not."

" More than you know, perhaps," he judged shrewdly. " The differences are on the surface."

They had gone back to the big hotel on Connecticut Avenue to have their dance in the supper room, and it was while Sandra in her flame-colored chiffon swayed to a perfect measure that she saw Gale Markham smiling at her from a table in the corner. Stephanie was with him, cool as ice in silver and green, and not so well pleased when Gale brought her over later to see Sandra.

Sandra presented Leeds. " He has a lot of news of Doady. They sailed on the same boat. And they saw each other in London. She's coming home for Christmas, and we're going down to Windytop to be with mother."

Gale was eager. " Really? "

Stephanie glanced at him. Then she said lightly:

" Gale and I are to spend the holidays at Ruth O'Malley's. She's having a houseparty at her place on the Chesapeake."

Gale said nothing. He had made no promises. He was a bit restless at the way Stephanie of late made plans for him, as if she had the right. She had called him up tonight:

" Let's be gay and go down town. I'm bored with myself."

She had come in her big car and had been very charming. There had been a pensiveness about her which was appealing. " I have been thinking of old times," she said, out of the soft, warm darkness of the limousine, " and of how happy we were . . . and of how I wish things had never been — different."

He wondered what she had meant by it. Was she simply playing the game? Or was she in earnest? And if she were in earnest, how was he going to meet it?

Leeds danced with Stephanie, Sandra sitting with Gale and watching the others.

" He wants to marry Doady," Sandra confided.

" Leeds? "

" Yes."

" The nerve of him! "

" He's got lots of money. But I don't want her to
do it."

" She won't, of course."

" It's hard to tell with Doady. If she'd ever been
really in love, she wouldn't. But she hasn't, and she
won't know what she's missing."

He was aware, as Leeds had been, of the change in
her, of the light in her eyes, the laughter in her voice.
And in a moment she told him the reason.

" Gale, I'm going to marry Rufus . . . I'm going to
marry Rufus . . ." It rang like a chime of bells.

" My dear girl! "

" I saw him this morning." Then, as the music
stopped, " I'll tell you some other time," she promised.

She went home soon after that, and Gale went with
Stephanie. There was a moon, and the world was white
and still under it.

" It's a wonderful night," Stephanie said. " Let's
ride for a bit, shall we? "

He acquiesced with a show of enthusiasm, but he was
not sure he wanted to meet Stephanie's mood. As she
sat back in her luxurious corner, the moonlight glimmered on the whiteness of her furs and on the pearls in
her ears and hair. She was like a snow woman. He
contrasted her pale beauty with Sandra's bloom.

They came to Rock Creek Park — deserted at this
late hour except for a few cars making short-cuts home
from evening entertainments. The trees were heavy
with snow, the shadows sable; the creek itself, as they

went through it at the ford, showed plumes of white foam as it rushed along.

"If we could ride like this forever!" Stephanie murmured.

Gale felt the light touch of her finger-tips on the back of his bare hand. He remembered when her touch had thrilled him.

He found himself saying, "You'd be bored stiff to ride forever."

"I shouldn't . . . Oh, what makes you say that, Gale? Just because I tried to be sensible, you think I'm lost to romance."

"Well, aren't you?"

"Do you really think I am?"

He wondered what she wanted him to say? What he would have said a year ago?

He turned it off with a gay, "So we're going to Ruth O'Malley's for Christmas, are we?"

"Yes. Perhaps I shouldn't have made the engagement without asking you. But Ruth wants you awfully. And so do I."

"But, my dear girl, I shall have only Christmas day. I can't possibly spend the week."

"Haven't you any leave you can take?"

He had two days. But how dared he tell her that since Sandra had spoken of Windytop, he had had a wild idea of going down to celebrate with the Claybournes?

He hesitated, then capitulated weakly, "Well, I suppose I might stretch the time a bit."

"You aren't very enthusiastic."

"Tell me what to say, and I'll say it."

She turned toward him, leaning forward. " Do you really want me to tell you what to say? "

He had an uncomfortable sense that a crisis was imminent. But there was no way out. " Yes."

" Say — ' Stephanie, I forgive you.' "

There was a queer break in her voice as if a sob were back of it. He had never known Stephanie to speak like that. Her composure had always been perfect. For a moment he found himself swept by a sense of the old tenderness. He recovered himself, however, and spoke without enthusiasm.

" My dear girl, what is there to forgive? "

" Don't say it that way, Gale, as if you didn't care. I can't bear not to have you care."

His voice was stern. " And if I cared, what then? What good would it do? Things are just as they were when you broke our engagement, Stephanie. No different. No better."

" We might make them better."

Gale had a moment of panic. Surely it hadn't come to this? That Stephanie was asking something of him which he couldn't grant? Couldn't. After all these years. Yet Stephanie would never have wanted him if she hadn't seen him slipping away. If it hadn't been for his friendship for Doady and Sandra!

" Dear girl," he told her, going back to that gay note, " it's the moonlight. You know you won't feel this way in the morning."

" I shall. I shall feel this way — always."

" I don't believe you. If I met your mood at this moment, you'd call me up before you'd had your breakfast chocolate and tell me you'd made a sad mistake."

" Gale — I wouldn't."

But he refused to listen. He refused to consider it a sentimental situation. Moonlight always went to people's heads, he assured her. The thing to do was to go home before either of them went mad with it.

Yet that night he could not sleep for thinking of it. It seemed incredible that such a scene should have taken place between him and Stephanie. For so many years he had hung on her words. Had been happy or miserable as she smiled or frowned. And now she could not move him by her frowns or smiles. He would rather have the friendship of Sandra Claybourne than all the love that Stephanie could give him.

And of Doady?

Oh, surely the child wouldn't marry Stephen Leeds! She must not. The man was apparently decent enough, but not the kind for Doady. What she should have was — love . . .

He lay there, thinking about it. Little Doady — a darling child. Too good for Leeds. Made for love . . . and loving . . .

In the meantime Sandra reaching home found Susan Carter up and in a great state of excitement.

" Ione Morton's husband has been shot and is in the hospital? "

" Shot? "

" Yes. He's a bootlegger. Would you believe it? And I've been teaching his wife the etiquette book. It would be farcical if it weren't tragic."

" Where is Ione? "

" In her room. She is just back from the hospital.

She's broken-hearted. If he gets well, he'll be up for trial, and there's every chance of a hard sentence."

Sandra went to Ione's door and knocked. "My dear," she said, as she went in, and took the white-faced, stricken creature in her arms.

It crossed her mind, as she did it, how little she could have foreseen this moment of deep feeling. How she had hated the crude creature in the pink bungalow apron who had talked about Rufus Fiske! And now Ione was clinging to her for consolation, sobbing out her grief.

"And while I was cooking breakfast for you, Miss Sandra, he was bleeding to death. And I was just thinking about the eggs and bacon and carrying the tray in to you and Mr. Fiske, and sitting with my feet up on the shelf of the kitchen stove and making toast for myself and the taxi man. And now — in the morning they're operating on him. And it's his only chance. But if they save him, it won't be much better. They'll shut him up. And if he dies, he'll die in his guilt! "

Life and Ione! Stern justice and a pink bungalow apron. Sandra wondered what there was to say to her.

She began hesitatingly: " Ione — if my mother were here, she'd tell you perhaps your husband was like a little child. He didn't know the harm he was doing . . . Perhaps he was sorry, but didn't know how to break away. But the evil couldn't go on. Evil mustn't. It has to be stopped . . . This was a hard way to stop it, but perhaps it was — the only way."

She was holding both of Ione's hands, trying to soothe her by her own quiet.

"When you go to the hospital, I'll go with you.

Susan can look after the shop. And before we go, we will spend a few minutes in a little church where I go every morning . . . it's a great help, Ione. I couldn't have lived in the past weeks without the little church — and the prayers I've said there."

"Oh, prayers," sobbed Ione. "Will God listen? Will He cure my husband? Will He keep him out of the penitentiary?" Her voice was rising on a hysterical note.

"He will give us strength," said the quiet voice, "to bear what we have to bear. And He will find a way out for you . . . Oh, I don't know how to say it like my mother would. I wish she were here."

Ione, fighting for self-control, gasped: "You're like an angel . . . I — I think I can get along if I have you near me."

"I shan't leave you. And tonight you're to come in and have Doady's bed, and Susan and I will look after you."

But Ione wouldn't. "I'll call you if I need anything. But if you don't mind, I'd rather cry all to myself and not disturb anybody. Oh, Miss Sandra, I keep thinking and thinking of this morning when we were riding along and having a good time afterward, and he out in the cold and dying."

Sandra went back to Susan Carter and talked it over.

Susan, worldly-wise, said: "She'll be better off without him. She'll have a chance to rise in the world."

Sandra winced. "Perhaps," she said, "but oh, what a price to pay for her future."

When Susan was in bed, Sandra wrapped herself up warmly and went out and stood on the balcony. Snow was everywhere, and the world was white under the moon. Six months ago young Juliet had leaned from her balcony, and her pulses had beat to the mad rhythm of romantic verse. She had dreamed, and now her dreams had all come true. Rufus' kisses of the morning were still warm on her lips. Love and life! She stretched out her arms to the moon as if begging its benediction on her happiness.

Love and death! The moon shone, too, through that hospital window where Ione's young husband lay dying. It was all so hard to understand. Happiness and unhappiness! Good and evil! Through all the centuries the moon had looked down on the rhapsodies of young lovers! Through all the ages, when Rufus and she were dust, it would still look down on other lovers!

Chapter XXXI

KEEPING STEP WITH DOADY

IT was three days before Christmas. Doady was home again, and Rufus was in California. Ione's husband had died under the operation, and Ione had gone ahead of the twins to Windytop. Mrs. Claybourne had written that she must come.

"Sally and I will be so glad to have her, and in helping us get the house ready for our Christmas party she will find solace."

Ione had been almost pathetically grateful. "Do you mean that she really wants me?" she had asked.

"Really, Ione. And you'll adore Sally, and see Griselda — and there'll be your talks with mother. She's so wonderful."

Mrs. Claybourne had written also of Rufus:

"It will be splendid to have him for a son, Sandra. And now that Doady is back in the shop, you can do all your sewing here. Or won't you have any sewing? Sally says that a few scraps of pink crêpe are enough, in these days, for any bride. But I'd like to see you have the old honeymoon chest full, as it has been for every other Claybourne. If you're married in the spring why not spend the summer at Windytop? There's room enough for a dozen of us, and Rufus can write, and Doady can come down, and we'll all be together. I hope he isn't planning to take you off too far, dearest. You and Doady and I are knit so closely."

298

Sandra had laid the letter down to think about that. If Rufus won his case against Sherry, he would take his wife to California to the red-roofed palace, with the terrace that overlooked the sea, where he once sat with his mother.

Oh, mothers, mothers — how one clung to them! Even in the midst of her happiness, Sandra's heart was torn! Love and life!

She wrote back to her mother:

" We have as yet no plans. Rufus writes that his lawyers think he has a case. They may, if they have strong enough evidence of coercion, get Sherry to compromise. Rufus would like it better that way. He wants justice and not revenge. Oh, he is so big, Mother. So much bigger than I. I want to make Sherry suffer. But Rufus says that with me and the recognition that is coming through his writing, he has no room for anything else. He's wonderful, Mumsie — wonderful."

Doady, having been told all about it, was stricken with astonishment. " And to think I never dreamed of it, and it all happened while I was away! Well, he's a heavenly sort of person, Sandra. And with more swank than I ever hope to marry. Stephen Leeds will look like a penny's worth of popcorn beside him."

Sandra laughed. " Doady! "

" Well, he will. In spite of his money. Rufus has a sort of prince-in-a-castle manner. And he'd have it if he didn't have thirty cents. Stephen is a gentleman, but not one of royal blood, if you know what I mean."

The two girls were in the shop. It was early morning. Doady had brought back marvelous things — old brocades, a Jacobean chest, potteries and porcelains, prints and etchings, mirrors and miniatures, paper-weights and snuff-boxes.

" These snow-storm things," Doady broke off to say to Sandra, " are for a collector who always wanted one he saw as a child and wasn't allowed to have. And now he'll pay fabulous prices for things like this." She shook the glass globe, and the snow went flying about the austere figure of a monk kneeling before a shrine. " It always freezes me to look at him," Doady said. " And here's another — a Columbine without a cloak. It seems a shame to shake the snow down on her."

She set the paper weights on a shelf and returned to the subject of Rufus. " Heavens, if he wins that case you'll be millionaires. And if I marry Stephen Leeds, we'll be a pair of plutocrats. The thing doesn't sound real to me, Sandra, not when you think of six months ago."

" And if Rufus doesn't win his case, and you don't marry Stephen Leeds — " Sandra reminded her.

" I've got to marry him," Doady said. " I've acquired a lot of new tastes along with my new clothes. Aren't I the last word, Sandra? "

She was bubbling with wild spirits. She could see herself in an antique mirror slanted above the sideboard, and she knew herself to be perfect. Her hair was adorably shingled, with a wave or two set in by the most sought-after coiffeur in Paris. She wore a queer little frock of dull purple with a fichu caught at the front by the huge bunch of violets Stephen Leeds had sent her that morning. Her stockings matched her dress, her shoes were little shining pumps, low-heeled like a child's slippers. With everybody else tipping about awkwardly on high heels, Theodora danced along lightly with a charming boyish effect of freedom.

" I've acquired a lot of new tastes with my new clothes," she reflected, " or rather they are old tastes revived. I want a background and atmosphere, and Stephen can give it to me."

" Marriage," Sandra told her, " is something more than an atmosphere."

" Of course. But I shouldn't dare let myself in for a *grande passion* like yours. I'd get the worst of it." She sat down, crossed her knees, and swung one of her feet back and forth in her childish slipper. " It will be a lot easier to let Stephen love me, and have a nice affection for him, than be wondering everlastingly if he loves me."

" But why wonder, if you know? " said the secure Sandra.

Theodora shrugged her shoulders. " How can you know? " she asked. " People fall out of love as well as into it."

" Rufus and I will love each other for a thousand years," Sandra assured her.

Doady sighed. " My darling, I'm glad you feel that way about it. I wish I could. I haven't any idea that Stephen and I will love for a thousand years. But I rather fancy we'll jog along nicely for a few decades."

" Have you accepted him, Doady? "

" Not — exactly."

" What do you mean by that? "

" Well, he met me at the boat — and took everything for granted. And he's sent violets every day, and called me up by long distance, and telegraphed night letters. I simply wouldn't let him come on with me. I told him I had to get my things in the shop and have my mind on it. So he's going to wait until New Year's to have it out with me."

"He wanted to give you a link bracelet," Sandra informed her, "but I told him mother would die of disapproval."

Doady agreed. "Everybody gives everybody anything in these days. Mother's standards won't admit the truth. She'd feel that I'd sold my soul."

There was silence for a moment while they unwrapped more paperweights, then Sandra said, as she set one with a ship in an arctic sea among its fellows:

"Gale's coming over to have tea with us when the shop closes. He wanted to meet you last night at the station. But he had an engagement with Stephanie."

Doady stopped shaking up snow flurries on paperweights to say, with a shrug, "So she's still playing tag with him?"

"I'm afraid it's more than that."

Doady sat down again and swung her slipper. "What do you mean?"

"Oh, I don't know. Only — he's going down to the O'Malleys' with her for Christmas. He goes everywhere with her. I don't know whether it's because he wants to go or because she asks him. But everybody is talking about it. They think she's going to marry him. The Maulsbys do, and a lot of people."

"But why? She wouldn't do it a few years ago, and things haven't changed. He hasn't any more money, and she hasn't."

Sandra unwrapped another paperweight. " I wonder where they got their weird ideas? " She held up a glass globe in which a shepherdess shivered in a pink pannier while her equally lightly-clad lover held over her an in-effectual pink parasol. " Your collector will certainly be repaid for the one he wanted and couldn't have," she remarked.

She went back to Gale.

" If you want to know why Stephanie's trying to get him back, I think it's because of you and me — Doady."

The purple-clad figure in the big chair had an effect of rigid attention. " You and me? " in a puzzled voice.

" Yes. He told me this, that since he had had our friendship, he didn't care so much for Stephanie's love."

Doady stared at her. " He said that? "

" Yes. And that if he'd been a Turk he'd have liked to marry both of us."

The color came up in Theodora's cheeks. " The conceit of him! "

" Doady, he didn't mean it that way. He hasn't an ounce of egotism. What he meant was that he liked us so much that he wanted to be with us."

" Well," said Doady, whiffing the fragrance of her violets, " if you want to know, I don't consider it much of a compliment to bunch us."

" But, Doady — "

" When he comes tonight, I shall tell him what I think of him." Theodora got up and looked at herself in the glass. " I'm going to put my violets in water," she said with some irrelevance. " This room is too hot for them."

When Gale arrived, late in the afternoon, however, the violets were again beautifying Theodora. Gale, catching up both her hands, was enveloped by the fragrance of them.

" May I kiss you? " he asked.

" No . . ." she backed away, " but you may look at me. Aren't I spiffy? "

The three of them shouted.

" You're the same Doady," Gale told her.

" I'm the same and not the same," she assured him. " Gale, look at my paperweights."

She set them all snow-storming for him, the old monk and the Columbine, and the pink shepherdess and the ship at sea.

" Won't they be wonderful in summer when the thermometer is ninety? "

While Sandra poured tea for them, Gale asked,

" What do you mean by saying you are not the same? "

" Well, I am trying to decide whether to marry Stephen Leeds. It isn't good taste to talk about it. But Sandra says you know it. The thing that holds me back is that I'll have to give up some of my personality. People won't say any more, ' There goes Theodora Claybourne! ' They'll say, ' There goes the wife of Stephen Leeds! '

" Surely you don't mean all that — seriously? "

" Why shouldn't I? "

" You're not in the least in love with him."

" He's in love with me. And nobody else is at the moment."

She lifted her cup and drank, looking at Gale over

the rim of it. She was like an exquisite imp, he reflected. He couldn't imagine any one else doing that trick with her teacup and being adorable.

She set down the cup. "And anyhow, it is better than being bunched with Sandra in a sort of job-lot and being told if you were a Turk you'd marry us."

He reproached Sandra. "Did you give me away like that?"

"I said it before I had time to think," she apologized.

"I'm glad she told me," Doady said. "I can count it as a half-proposal, and with Stephen Leeds it makes one and a half. Which is not so bad at my age."

"Do you mean," he demanded, "that nobody else has ever asked you?"

"They haven't. Yet I think they would if they could see me in this frock, and the violets, 'n'everything."

"Doady, be serious," Sandra advised.

"Oh, I can't, I can't." Doady's voice had a singing note. "I'm so glad to be here with you and Gale, drinking tea and unpacking my snowstorms."

The three of them collapsed with laughter. They were so young — and such darlings, Gale told himself. Doady was such a — darling.

"Where did you get your violets?" he ventured a little later.

"Stephen Leeds. They come every morning like the daily paper and orange juice for breakfast."

"Don't they mean more to you than that?"

"I'm not sure."

She jumped up and began to rummage through one of the packing cases. "Gale, I've got something for you — a Christmas present. But I'm going to give it to you now."

She brought it out at last — a music-box, a gaudy little affair with full-blown roses painted on it. She wound it up and set it on the table. It tinkled uncertainly for a moment, then played a waltz.

" It's the *Blue Danube,* Gale. Don't you love it? "

Doady stood on tiptoe in her childish slippers. Her arms waved in a beckoning gesture. And suddenly Gale found himself dancing with her — he who had not danced since he came back from the war . . . keeping step with her . . . keeping step with Doady . . . keeping step . . . !

When the tinkling music stopped, he said in a sort of daze: " It was magic. How did you make me do it? "

" I knew you could. Only you were afraid."

" Perhaps you're right. I hated to bore anybody with my awkwardness."

He looked at the clock and rose. " I wish I could stay, we'd all go somewhere for dinner."

" Why can't you? "

" I have an engagement with Stephanie. She's asked four of us out to the Country Club with bridge afterward."

" How stupid! When we three could have a gorgeous time at some nice little *table d'hôte,* and come back here and go through the rest of the boxes." Again she glowed with enthusiasm. " Oh, Gale, you'd go mad over the most perfect Kien-Lung group in pink coral! "

When he had gone, Doady surveyed herself once more in the glass. Violets and pink coral! Stephanie and bridge! Weighed in the balance!

Thinking it over, she said after a time to Sandra, " Stephanie knows I'm back, but she hasn't called me up."

" She's asked us there for supper Sunday night."

" Tomorrow? "

" Yes. I forgot to tell you — there's been so much else to talk about."

" Who is she having? "

" Ruth O'Malley. And somewhere after supper there's a big radio program broadcasting. She thought we'd like to hear it."

" Bromidic."

" Doady! "

" Well, it is. Here I'm just back from London, with a lot to say, and I'll have to sit and listen."

Since the death of her mother, Stephanie's apartment in the big hotel had been presided over by an aunt who eliminated herself as far as possible from the scheme of living of her somewhat dominant niece. She presided at a supper party on Sunday night which seemed to her simple soul fantastic as to food and sophisticated as to decorations. In the days of her own girlhood, there would have been pink roses as a centerpiece, chicken salad at one end of the table, a platter of sliced pink ham at the other, hot biscuits passed in relays, ice-cream meringues at the end. And here was Stephanie's table with purple candles in gold holders with a purple bowl of scarlet fruit. And for food there were anchovies topping a slice of tomato, a strange, hot dish of crab with caviar, toast in crisp curls as tasteless as brown paper, romaine with paprika and a touch of garlic.

And at the very last fresh peaches blazing in a bath of hot brandy!

Fantastic! Nobody ate as they used to do; everything was changed. And the way they dressed! Aunt Agatha felt that Stephanie's gown of gold tissue should have been superimposed for respectability's sake on a structure of stout underwear.

In her opinion the little Claybourne girls were the only ones who were properly clothed. She wondered how they had escaped the blight of modern fashions. For how could gentle Aunt Agatha know that Doady's busy brain had worked to create a contrast, and that the result was a triumph.

She and Sandra were dressed alike.

" They are doing it in Paris," Doady had assured her, " and that's why I bought the two of them."

The gowns were *costumes de style* as the *couturiére* called them. They had rather long and *bouffant* skirts, bodices with puffed sleeves and round necks, and were made of white taffeta, crisp and creamy as the petals of magnolias. Only their flowers were different. Doady wore Stephen Leeds' violets, while Sandra had a tight bunch of scarlet buds. As they entered the room, everybody gasped.

" They are like something out of the moving pictures," one woman whispered, " those girls in ' The Two Orphans ' — you know the sort of thing — quaint and simple."

All the evening Doady lived up to that phrase — " quaint and simple." She had little to say. She just sat, composed and quiet, with a smile on her lips — a pensive smile, Gale told himself. A Mona Lisa smirk, was Stephanie's different interpretation. The rest of the company thought her smile that of a charming child. They spoke of her in that way to Stephanie — as a child — and charming.

It was that effect of youth which maddened Stephanie. The sisters seemed the youngest things, yet there was actually little difference in their years and Stephanie's. She was forced into a maturity which did not belong to her. She felt herself put definitely on the shelf. Everybody was looking at the twins; everybody was talking of them. Yet only a few months ago at her own party they had been wallflowers.

She found herself saying spitefully to Gale:

" I think they've overdone it a bit. They can't afford to be conspicuous."

" Conspicuous? My dear girl, they are utterly unaffected and delicious."

But Stephanie knew Doady's tricks and manners! She felt that the whole effect was premeditated. Not by Sandra. She absolved her from all tendency to upstaginess. But Theodora Claybourne had her eye always on an audience.

Oh, well, the evening would soon be over, and at Christmas she would have Gale to herself. Stephanie leaned back and listened to the announcer. The feature number of the evening was at hand; a voice was to be heard which had never before been broadcast.

Then happened one of those coincidences which seem too amazing for credence. The great singer gave first an aria which showed her range. Following, there came through the ether the strains of a waltz which was

caught up in a moment by the lilting, lovely voice.
Gale's eyes went to Doady's, and into her own flashed
an answering gleam. Her right hand was lifted in a
gesture of salute. The song that the great singer sang
was the one played the day before by the tinkling music-
box. " The Blue Danube," if you please, ladies and
gentlemen, as old as our grandmothers, as new as the
latest love-affair!

Stephanie saw the exchange of glances and was stung
by it, but outwardly she gave no sign. She said no
more to Gale about the " charming children." Why
worry when she knew he loved her? He had always
loved her. She had only to say the word to bring him
back. She was silly to think that his fancy could be
caught by one of these bobbed-haired babies.

But that night, when the guests had gone, and Aunt
Agatha said, " Those little Claybourne girls — they reminded me of the days when your mother and I were
young — " Stephanie answered with a certain bitter
emphasis:

" Doady Claybourne is an inveterate *poseuse.*
Sandra isn't so bad. But Doady has a modern mind.
You must remember that, Aunt Agatha, when you com-
pare her with yourself and mother."

Doady and Sandra, having been sent home in Stephanie's car, talked about their evening.

" We were marvelous," Doady said dreamily.

Sandra was wistful. " Darling," she asked, " are
you getting — spoiled? "

For a moment Doady sat very still, then she clutched
Sandra's hand. " No, I'm not. Inside of me, sometimes, I'm afraid of — Theodora Claybourne."

They clung together. "If I marry Stephen Leeds," Doady whispered, "I shall go on being — Theodora Claybourne. But if I wait — Sandra. If I wait — I think I could be myself for somebody who made me — care — ! "

Chapter XXXII

UNDER THE CHRISTMAS STARS

TO Ione Morton Christmas at Windytop seemed
like something out of a dream. For her —
straight from her small quarters — the activities which took place in Aunt Louisa's huge kitchen
had a sort of story-book quality, as did the great old
range with its mammoth pots and pans, the stout oak
table that would have blocked all entrance to her kitch-
enette, the dresser which stretched to the ceiling, and
which bore on its wide shelves the china platters and
covered dishes of silver plate which had belonged to the
days of prodigious hospitalities.

Her eyes grew round as she looked upon Aunt Louisa,
kneading huge loaves out of a puffy mass of dough,
sliding pies in relays into the yawning oven, stuffing
turkeys and boiling hams, bringing up out of the cellar
jars of pickled peaches and of strawberry jam, and
bringing down from the attic the rich damask napery
which had been packed away when the Claybournes
went north.

For the amazing thing was this, that Ione had never
lived over a cellar or under an attic. She had spent
her childhood in two rooms in a tenement, and her
married life within the limitations of an " efficiency."
The amount of space at Windytop impressed her as
almost criminally wasteful. The height of everything,

the width and length. The closets were incredibly spacious, the stairways and halls were like nothing she had seen except in moving pictures.

In her black dress, with Griselda at her heels, she wandered up and down, observing everything with eager curiosity.

" You don't mind? " she said to Mrs. Claybourne on the day before Christmas. " I've been up in the attic for an hour."

" Weren't you half-frozen? "

" I was wrapped up. It's a queer place. But I like it — all those old dresses and bonnets, and spinning wheels and — cradles. We never had any place to keep things. We threw them away. Somehow it makes me feel lonesome. As if there isn't any one back of me. Now you can just go up and look at those old dresses and read some of those old letters, and there's your mother and your grandmother and your great-grandmother."

" That's what I tell the children," Madge said. " If we sell Windytop, there'll be nothing left to link us with the past."

Ione sat down to consider it. Griselda jumped on her lap. The little cat had displayed an almost uncanny perception of Ione's need of comforting. In the short time the two had been together, they had established a kind of occult relationship. Griselda did not, apparently, squander on this newcomer the adoration she had given Rufus and Sandra, but she exchanged, as it were, loneliness for loneliness, and lent herself freely as companion and friend.

Ione, smoothing the snowy fur, said: " I never even

had a kitten. Nothing alive to play with. And all the out-of-doors I knew was the tenement courtyard."

She stopped there. She didn't want to bore Mrs. Claybourne with her own tragic memories. But there was one thing she had to say.

"If I had lived in a place like this — when I was little — I might have been more like — your girls." She sat staring into the fire.

"What we did not have ourselves may come to our — children," Mrs. Claybourne told her gently, "and as long as we keep Windytop, I should like to have you with me."

"It would be wonderful . . ."— Ione's breath was quick —"it would be wonderful . . . if a child of mine . . . could play . . . in a garden . . ."

The two of them stared in the fire. They shared a secret.

The twins were coming down late that afternoon. Old Marcus Brooks had cut the tree for them. Old Marcus was black and wrinkled and gnarled with rheumatism. He had eaten Christmas dinner in the Windytop kitchen for seven decades. His grandmother had been a slave and cook at the great house, and his mother, a free negro, had followed her. In those days feasting had been feasting, relatives and neighbors had come from round about, and the gaiety had lasted until the New Year.

The tree that old Marcus brought now into the hall was aromatic with forest fragrances, and plumed with branches which spread out at the bottom to a great circumference like a flounced skirt and narrowed toward the feathery tip which almost touched the ceiling.

" I had to git Henry's boy to he'p me," he told Mrs. Claybourne.

As a matter of fact Henry's boy had cut the tree and brought it home, but old Marcus was loath to admit it. In the days of his youth he had been proud of his strength.

" That boy of Henry's," he told Aunt Louisa in the kitchen, " kain't do with two hands whut I could do with one."

" I believe you," said Aunt Louisa, mincing giblets for tomorrow's gravy. " All of um's lazy in dese days."

" An' they has to have the bes'." Old Marcus held out his hands to the glowing range. " My ole Granny used to give my Mammy the neck an' feet fo' soup, and after the w'ite folks ate the tukkey, we had the skeletums en all the pickings . . . um . . . um," he moaned ecstatically at the memory.

" You won' have jes' pickin's this time," Aunt Louisa remarked impressively. " Miss Madge done said to give you a drumstick effen nobody else gits one."

" I ain't worryin', honey, effen I don' git no drumstick. I kin eat my fill of backs an' gizzards."

Aunt Louisa wasted no time in argument. " You set down an' eat," she ordered. " I reckon you-all's hongry, wukkin in the cole."

She set his lunch before him, bacon and cabbage and cornbread.

" Fat meat terday and a feast termorrer. And glad of bofe of 'em," she exulted emotionally.

" Bless Gord! " said old Marcus in a brief grace.

With the tree set up in the library, Madge and Ione ascended to the attic to get the Christmas trimmings.

" The girls wouldn't be satisfied with new ones,"
Madge said, as she opened boxes. " They know every
ball and bit of tinsel. Many of the ornaments they
made themselves, and we've saved them from year to
year."

Some of the decorations seemed to Ione shabby. Yet
with the gorgeous baubles Doady had sent down, the
tree was resplendent when they finished it.

" I am so glad Doady got back in time to be here,"
Madge said, as she hung the last sparkling star.

Ione, sitting back on her heels, asked, " Which is
your favorite? "

" Of the twins? "

" Yes."

" How could I choose between them? "

" Miss Sandra's mine," said Ione. " Nobody can
ever be like her. Nobody! " She began to sob, " That
morning when she took me to church."

" Yes — Sandra is like that."

She was like that, and more than that, Madge told
herself proudly. Such a daughter! And soon she was
to lose her.

For Sandra's plans had changed. Rufus had written
that he was coming to Washington as soon as he could
get away. And they must be married. Why wait for
a happiness which was at their hands?

Sandra and Doady on the train were talking about
it. " It will be dreadful to have you go so far."

" We may stay right in Washington," but in the
back of Sandra's mind ran the lines about the happy
princess . . . *through all the world . . . she followed
him.*

She spoke out of her thoughts: " I could live on a desert island with Rufus."

" You couldn't, of course," said the worldly-wise one, " but it's nice of you to think it."

When they arrived late at Windytop, the tree was lighted for them. Sally Grymes was there and a lot of others, and the twins were caught in a whirlwind of welcome. They escaped to run upstairs and change, and when they came down Sandra wore her red velveteen and Doady her purple crêpe.

Old Marcus, having brought in more logs for the fire, went back to Aunt Louisa.

" My soul and my soul," he moaned with that note of ecstasy, " they's puttier than Miss Betty Claybourne, and she were a belle and a beauty."

The presents were distributed that night. Most of them simple ones, although Felix Maulsby and Marcia had sent Mandarin coats for the twins and a hand-tooled book of verse for Madge.

" She'd rather read poetry than eat," Sandra had told Felix. " You couldn't please her better."

There was a box for Doady into which she peeped, then set it aside without showing it. There was a box for Sandra over which she blushed, then displayed it proudly — a string of pearls from Rufus.

" They were my mother's," he wrote. " She would want you to have them."

It was late when the company left, and Madge and her daughters went upstairs. There were open fires in all the chambers and the effect was cheerful.

" Come in my room," Doady said to Sandra, " and I'll show you something."

What she showed was a bracelet from Stephen Leeds. "Oh," said Sandra, "I told him not to."

Doady held it up so that it caught the light, a sparkling, flexible thing of emerald and diamond links. "He thinks he can buy — me."

"But you won't let him, Doady?"

"How do you know I won't?"

"Because you're too fine for it."

Doady, hugging her knees, said: "How do you know I am fine? He might make me happy."

"You wouldn't be happy. Not if you didn't love him."

"I'm not romantic."

"Oh, you are. Only you will never let yourself think it. You've always felt that mother and I were not practical and that you had to act as a balance wheel. And you've done so much for both of us. I don't know what would have happened when mother was sick, if you hadn't made good with Mr. Maulsby. You're marvelous, Doady. But you mustn't marry Stephen Leeds unless you love him."

Doady chose to be obstinate. "I might be as happy with my Stephen as you are with your Rufus."

"Do you really think that, Doady?"

Doady poked the fire with the tongs. "Well, I'm not looking for ecstasies."

Madge appeared just then at the door and asked, "Aren't you ever going to bed?"

"Come in, Mumsie, and tell Doady what you think of her."

Madge sat down in a chair cushioned with turkey-red and surveyed her daughters fondly. "I know what I think. That there never were two such children."

Doady, gay in her Chinese coat, produced the brace-let. "Stephen Leeds sent it." She swung it from her finger, and it gave out opulent gleams.

"Doady! You aren't going to keep it?"

"Why not?"

"It isn't done."

"But it is, Mumsie. In your day flowers and candy were everything that was allowed. But now there's more than that."

"If you were engaged to him, it would be different."

"Well, I may be in a minute."

"But, Doady, you haven't given him your heart . . ."
Still swinging the bracelet; "Perhaps I haven't any."

"You mustn't talk that way."

Doady, a bit tense, demanded, "What way?"

"Not meaning a word of it."

"Perhaps I do mean it." She began to roam the room. "I'm not like Sandra. She'll probably make Rufus live up to things. But my head isn't in the clouds. I want something I can get hold of — like Stephen Leeds' money."

Madge caught at her hand as she passed. "My dear, think what you are saying!"

"I don't want to think." She dropped on her knees in front of her mother. "Mumsie, I haven't told you the thing I am afraid of. If I loved anybody very much . . . and he didn't care . . . I could be dreadfully hurt . . ."

Madge's arms tightened about this temperamental little daughter. The two were alone. Sandra, recog-nizing one of Doady's moods, had gone into her own room and was writing a letter to Rufus. She had had one from him that morning with amazing news in it. He had been asked to come to Washington in February to present his views to the distinguished members of an organization in convention there at that time.

" Of course I shall accept. And by that time you will be Mrs. Rufus Fiske. How simple it sounds, yet what a stupendous thing it really is, that you are going to be my wife . . . that I shall have you . . . always! "

Sandra was just finishing her letter when her mother came in and stood beside her.

" I've put Doady to bed. She was over-excited, and cried. We'll let her sleep late in the morning. Her nerves are showing the strain of everything. You are the calm one, Sandra."

" I'm not calm tonight." Sandra's arms were around her mother. " I'm too happy to be calm . . . too happy . . ."

She hid her face against Madge's shoulder and cried a little.

One of them crying for happiness, the other for some hidden hurt. Madge's heart was torn between them. Should she rejoice with Sandra or mourn with Doady?

When she went to bed, she had not settled it. She read late in the new book of verse, finishing off with the Christmas chapter in St. Matthew. She slept, then, resting in the thought that things would work out somehow and she couldn't change them by worry.

In the next room Sandra had put herself to bed with all the appurtenances of romance. She had Rufus' pearls about her neck and Rufus' letter under her pillow.

She lay straight and slim under her covers, with the starlight glimmering on her bright hair and on the pearls about her neck. She looked like a bride and felt like one. She fell asleep wishing Doady might be as happy.

But Doady was not happy. And no one but herself knew the cause. She had had a present from Gale Markham, and so had Sandra and so had Madge. Books. And there was nothing about Doady's book to differentiate it from the others. Not one line or word. And she had thought he might. She didn't know why she had thought it. But she had. And tonight at this very minute he was at Ruth O'Malley's and was probably dancing with Stephanie. And Doady had hoped he wouldn't. The dancing had been a sort of miracle she had worked, and she hated to think that now he was dancing with Stephanie. And Stephanie would be lovely in her ice-maiden way. And for years he had loved her. And he would probably love her again. And that was that!

She got out of bed and put on Stephen Leeds' bracelet. When she was once more among her pillows, she held her wrist so that she might see the shimmer of the gems in the starlight. The links seemed to bind her to something. To a future with Stephen Leeds? Oh, well, why not?

So Sandra with her pearls and Theodora with her bracelet slept at last under the Christmas stars. But there were tears on Doady's cheeks.

Chapter XXXIII

ON A HIGH HILL

RUFUS' Christmas was spent with Molly Wicks and her husband on the ranch. It was a golden day, and the long dining-room, festooned with pink pepper berries on their drooping branches, had blazing logs in the fireplace that seemed a deeper reflection of the sun.

" Gorgeous," said Rufus, " weather like this."

" What are you going to do with yourself? "

" Ride."

" Where? "

" Up in the hills."

" You must be back in time for dinner. Three o'clock."

" Turkey? "

" Yes. And mince pie, 'n' everything. We're doing our best to make your Christmas merry, though goodness knows you don't need it, with those letters coming every day from the East."

" Two this morning." Rufus patted his pocket.

He hadn't read the letters. This was not the moment. He had finished his breakfast and was standing in front of the fire, looking down at Molly. She had never seen him so gay, so gloriously good-looking. The sardonic gleam in his eyes was gone. There was rarely a sound of the bitter laughter.

" It's that girl," she accused him.

" Beg pardon? "

" I've never seen such a change in anybody."

He raised his eyebrows. " Really? "

" You know it! "

" Well, I do," he agreed, light-heartedly.

Of course, he knew. The old Rufus had never had this singing sense of happiness. As if the gold of the morning were a part of himself, an elixir which ran in his veins.

When he rode forth a little later, he stopped to see McIvor. The old man was among his sheep, a patriarchal figure.

" A Merry Christmas," Rufus said to him.

The old man smiled at him. " Your face makes it for me."

Rufus smiled back. " Do I show it like that? Well, why shouldn't I? Do you remember, McIvor, the bargain I made with the Lord — that if he'd give me the girl, I'd worship him forever? "

" I do, sir. And I told you man should not be making bargains with Omnipotence."

" Well, He's given her to me, and it's up to me to keep my word."

" You're in earnest, sir."

" I am."

McIvor waited a moment. " It mustn't be just for that, sir."

" For what? "

" Because he's given you the girl."

Rufus dismounted. " It's for more than the girl, McIvor. Yet it is because of something which came,

I think, through the girl. For years I had had the feeling that life was letting me down — as if nothing really mattered. But now everything matters. And why shouldn't I keep my bargain with a God who has done that for me? "

They talked for a long time. Not to any one else, not even to the woman he loved, could Rufus have so revealed himself. This old shepherd among his sheep was like one of the prophets. He had dignity and understanding. One spoke to him as to a confessor. Of one's soul.

Leaving him at last, Rufus rode up and up, coming finally to the peak from which he could look down on a wide stretch of sea, and the red-roofed palace on the cliff above it. Here, where he had read that other letter of Sandra's, which had revealed her faith in him, he would read these letters with the knowledge that perhaps her faith might be justified. Not that he had proved himself. But he was at least his own man, freed from the fears which had bound him.

Sandra's letters throbbed with the ardor of young romance. There was no silly sentimentality. Her sense of humor saved her from that. But she was deeply in love and was not ashamed to show it.

" I am happier than Juliet," she said, " happier than Nicolette. Happier than anybody should dare to be in a world like this."

He, too, felt that he was afraid to be as happy as he knew himself to be. What if something broke in upon it, shattering it? Yet it must not be shattered — its essence was of the spirit, sustaining him. He could not do without it.

He sat looking off over the illimitable stretch of sea. It was not gray this morning, but a clear, ineffable blue, its low line of breakers falling in silver frills along the sands. The sky which came down to it was of such matching color that there seemed to be no horizon — only a vast distance toward which one might sail to reach at last some shore of eternal loveliness.

The tense ecstasy of the moment brought Rufus to his feet. With bare head lifted, he faced the sky and sea. Why, this was life! Life as he had never known it! It was something which went beyond young love, beyond romance, beyond Sandra in all her beauty. It was something which could never be taken away from him — the knowledge of his power to shape his destiny — his resolute will to do it.

When he got back to the ranch, Molly said, " There's a telegram."

He opened it. It was from the president of a great Western university. It begged him to give, before he went East, an address which would emphasize some of the things he intended to say in Washington. There would be an important audience. As a son of California, it was hoped he would not refuse.

Rufus wired an acceptance. Then he went in to dinner. Molly's guests had assembled. They were, for the most part, ranch-owners from the surrounding country and their wives. They were a healthy-minded, happy lot. Rufus, entering into the spirit of the feast, laughed with them and told his best stories. He had a sense of being radiantly alive; like a sick man healed by a miracle, not knowing how it had happened, but thrillingly aware of the joy that had come to him.

After dinner they all drove to the nearest settlement to see a moving picture. When they came back, they found the supper table set with what would have been a superfluous meal, if it had not been for John Lee's delicate perception of what would whet jaded appetites after a Christmas dinner. The drink was white grape juice, and Rufus proposed a toast to " Virginia." He could not speak Sandra's name in this company, so substituted that of her beloved state.

" To Virginia," he said, and stood up among them, and their admiring eyes saw in him a youth whom the gods cherished.

After supper they danced, and when the company had gone, Rufus, walking out into the night, found John Lee smoking serenely on the porch of his own small cabin. He stopped and spoke to him:

" I don't see what you got out of Christmas day, John," he said, " with all that cooking. You should have had a bit of fun yourself."

John Lee smiled broadly. Chuckled. Then he replied, astonishingly, that he'd rather cook than " dlance." Cooking a Christmas dinner was, Rufus gathered, an achievement. John Lee had put his whole mind to it and to the getting of the supper. He had, consequently, what might be called an elevation of spirit. He felt that the people who had eaten and drunk and gone to the movies and danced had missed his own fine sense of artistic satisfaction. Any one could go to a dance or see a moving picture. But not one among them could have made the mushroom sauce which had accompanied the turkey, nor have compassed the stuffed crabs which were served with the supper.

Rufus, listening to John Lee's attempt to explain all this in rather difficult English, was aware that he had more in common with the old Chinaman than with Molly Wicks' guests. John Lee might not be urged to speak to a great university, but he would always be urged to cook a good dinner. The two things were not so far separated as one might think.

He walked on to where McIvor sat among his sheep. The night was warm, and Rufus dropped down on the ground beside him.

" I've had a long-distance from my lawyers. They say my case is nearly complete. That they have all the evidence they need of my father's condition. They want me to confer with them tomorrow. But now that the thing is almost mine for the asking, I am wondering whether to go on with it. Of course, I'd like the money. I shouldn't be human if I didn't. I want it for Sandra, and I want it for myself. But I don't want to seem to be taking it out on Sherry. And then, of course, there's my father's intention. If I felt he didn't want me to have it . . . I wouldn't touch a penny."

" I think he would want you to have it."

" Have you any reason to think it, McIvor? "

" Well, looking at it from a man's standpoint. Would any of us in his sane senses care to have a fortune wasted by such a woman? Wouldn't we rather it would go to our son's children, his children's children? "

Sandra's children! Her grandchildren!

" Yet, how can I judge my father by myself? "

" All men are alike in wanting that which they have earned to be well spent. And your father was not himself when he made the will."

" You think that? "

" I know it."

" Then you would advise me to go on? "

" I feel it would be what your father wished."

There was a touch of the old bitterness in Rufus' tone. " How could I know his wishes? I was shut out of his life."

" Men like your father," said old McIvor, " have dreams they can never bring to pass. He talked to me often in his later years. He had set his foot on the wrong path and knew it."

" Why didn't he turn back? "

" He had gone too far."

" Did he ever speak of me? "

" Yes. He cared more than you know. Yet he felt he had forfeited his right to your affection. It was very sad toward the last, when he was not himself. He seemed to feel this was the only place where he could get away from the evil forces which surrounded him. He loved the sweep of the sky and land. He loved the sheep. I sometimes wonder if his sad spirit ever comes in the starlight and sits among them."

The picture old McIvor drew seemed to Rufus a strange presentment of the ruthless man he remembered. Yet he was glad it had been shown him. Perhaps there might be more tenderness in his memories if he could think of his father as one who had struggled and lost.

As he walked back to the house, he wished for the first time in his life that his father might walk beside him; that they might be drawn together by some fineness in each that the other had not known . . . that they might speak a language that each would understand.

Oh, if he ever had a son . . . !

On the day before he made his speech at the great university, Rufus had a long letter from Sandra. She was still at Windytop, though Doady had gone back to Washington.

" Ione is with us, and will stay on indefinitely. I believe her coming will solve some of the problems about Mumsie. Ione gets along with Aunt Louisa, and between them they can look after the house and make things comfortable. And with me married and Doady prosperous, much can be done to put the old house in a habitable state. And Griselda can enjoy the fireplaces and the garden until you and I know whether we are to have a house of our own, or go back and be with mother. For my part, I don't care where my fireplace is, or the garden, if only you will put on the logs for me and pick my roses. And why shouldn't I say it?

" Doady doesn't seem to be able to make up her mind about Stephen Leeds. One day she thinks she is going to marry him, and the next she doesn't. She isn't so happy as she ought to be. It is probably her punishment for daring to think of selling her own lovely birthright of romance for the mess of pottage of Stephen Leeds' possessions. And I am not saying anything to you that I haven't told her. I went into her room on Christmas morning and found her wearing a bracelet Stephen had sent her. One of those slave-link things that seem to me so gruesome. Of course, it is gorgeous — emeralds and all that. I begged her to send it back.

But she still wears it, and I am sure that in a way she feels bound to do it. I am really much worried about her — it is the one cloud on my sky that Doady isn't happy.

" There's a rumor that Stephanie and Gale Markham are engaged again. They go around a lot together. They spent Christmas with Ruth O'Malley on the Chesapeake. Perhaps that precipitated things. I didn't believe Gale would do it. But one never can tell. She isn't good enough for him — and she won't make him happy."

Doady's worries and Gale's could not, however, dim to any great extent the glory of Sandra's enchantment. The world at the present moment was made for herself and Rufus. Nothing else really mattered. It might be selfish, but it was the selfishness of enraptured youth, unaware that the radiance of its own drama is not unique in the history of lovers.

She went on to speak of the exquisite joy Rufus' last letter had given her. The one he had written on Christmas night. He had tried to tell her something of the high moment on the mountain peak. And she had understood. As for the invitation to appear at the great university — she was proud of him.

" I shall think of you every moment, my dear, my dear — "

With this letter of Sandra's against his heart Rufus came at last before the great audience gathered to hear him. There were to be many other vast audiences as his fame grew, but none which he wanted more to impress than these people of his native state, his own people. He had no vision now of what he was some day to mean to them; if he had, there would have been no fear in his heart. But he did not know, and only the future would reveal it.

Few of those in the auditorium had ever seen him. Many of them had heard of him only as the son of a rich man who had made an eccentric will. Others had read what he had written and had been stirred by it — but none of them, perhaps, had expected to be confronted by a youth of such splendid presence — the grace and strength of him, the thin and perfect profile, the dark eyes, the swept-back hair.

When he spoke, his voice had a ringing note. He developed his theme with ease, presenting his theories confidently. They were, he insisted, more than theories. They could be worked out practically. America must have no silly sentimentalities in dealing with foreign powers. Why should she be the Mrs. Jellaby of the world? Why should other nations ask her to be? Why not set her own house in order? Keep her own laws? Love the Jew and the Negro within her gates as well as the Turk and the Slav ten thousand miles away?

The trouble, he contended, was in the loss of the old democratic idea that the strength of the nation was in the integrity of the individual. Let each man look to his own sword to save the honor of the regiment. The modern attitude was to let somebody else do it. Yet the measure of every community was in the attitude of each citizen toward the ideals of justice and peace and order. When we achieved these things locally, we could achieve them nationally. When we achieved them nationally, we would achieve them internationally. We were not ready yet for the high estate to which others seemed to be calling us. It was not our arrogance, but our knowledge of present unfitness, which should hold us back.

His logic was not always sound. His conclusions were sometimes crude. But he carried his audience with him.

At least he carried it until the middle of the evening, when a door at the back of the hall opened, and a woman in pink entered.

She was at first unnoticed. But as she made her imposing way along the empty aisle, there was a movement in the crowd, and curious glances were turned upon her. She was in evening dress, her wrap of rose-color with its collar rising about her small and shining head. Some of the people knew her.

" It's his stepmother," went whispering around, and other eyes were turned.

But Sherry, having found a seat, seemed oblivious of everybody but the speaker. She sat with her face up-turned, a little smile on her lips — composed, quiet; like some sibyl who has set herself to weave a spell, devastating, destructive.

Rufus felt the sinister effect of it. He had seen Sherry enter, and his heart had turned over. His voice had not faltered as she came up the aisle and took her seat. But when she smiled, his bones turned to water. Something at once went out of him. The fire. The force. The sense of conviction. The words he said after that seemed to him the babblings of a fool. Why should he think that any one in this assemblage should care to listen?

Gradually those who listened became aware of some letting down of interest, some lack of magnetism. They stirred and yawned. He was saying the right words, but not in the right way. And how could he say anything with Sherry down there smiling; and back of her that sea of faces, growing blank and blanker . . . bored . . . unresponsive?

Subconsciously his imagination caught at that word " sea," and it saved him. There swept over him the vision of a man standing on a high hill . . . the face of the man was lifted . . . himself . . . seeing life as he had never seen it . . . aware of forces which had never swayed him . . . triumphant in his knowledge of power, the strength of his resolute will.

And now the sea of faces was blotted out. Sherry was blotted out. Rufus was looking down from a great height toward a shining distance.

Again his voice rang with that triumphant note. Once more the people hung upon his words. Sherry's smile faded. Was this the boy she had once ruled with dreadful laughter? This inspired young prophet whose eyes no longer saw her? Shrewd, discerning, she knew that she had lost him. She might wrest from him material things. She could never again subdue his spirit. He had gone beyond her. There were elements of leadership in him, and the multitudes would follow.

He finished his speech amid tumultuous applause. After that people surged up to meet him and shake hands with him.

Men, going out, said, " He'll be heard from some day politically. Others: " He's a coming power."

Sherry began to move slowly down the aisle with

the others. When she reached the lobby, she had to wait for Ito, who was taking his turn in the long line of motor cars. So it happened that Rufus, emerging from the hall with a member or two of the faculty who were escorting him, saw her standing alone under the great lamp which illuminated the entrance.

He at once detached himself from the group of men and went to her.

" May I get Ito for you? "

She said, thin-lipped, " He'll be here presently."

He was not to be rebuffed. And as the lights of the big car drew near, he walked down the steps with her.

" I wonder," he said, " what made you come."

" Curiosity."

" Really? And was it satisfied? "

" Yes. You were better than I thought."

" Thank you."

He spoke a word of greeting to Ito and helped her into her car.

She leaned forward from her luxurious cushions and said with a touch of malice: " You'll need all your . . . eloquence to make a living. Of course, you know you're not going to be able to break the will? "

He laughed teasingly. " Shall we bet on it, Sherry? The ivories to be yours if — you lose? "

His foot was on the fender. The light from the lamp overhead shone full upon him and showed his sparkling countenance, his hair ruffled by the wind, the gallant carriage of his tall figure. The few people about them, looked at him, speculating.

Sherry began to feel a raging sense of impotence.

For the first time in her life she couldn't hurt him. She couldn't.

" Oh, I hate you! " she said tensely.

" Why hate anybody? " he demanded. " It's weakening. Sherry, there was a time when I hated you. Think of the years I wasted."

She wanted to scream at him, to pour the vials of her wrath out upon him. But what weapons had she against such insouciance? She allowed herself one last fling.

" Whether I win or lose, I am going to have the ivories."

" And why not? " Rufus conceded pleasantly. " You shall have them as a consolation prize. You ought to get something out of it. I tell you what I'll do, Sherry. I'll give you the ivories for a — wedding present."

" A wedding present! Whose wedding? "

" Mine! "

He took his foot from the fender and let Ito close the door. Then he leaned in through the open window.

" Mine," he said again, and the lilt in his young voice maddened her, " mine and Sandra's. I am leaving tonight for Washington. And just to show you there's no ill will, I'll send you the ivories, Sherry. And when you see them, you can wish us — happiness."

Chapter XXXIV

STEPHANIE TRIES AGAIN

IT was Doady who scolded Rufus. "The idea of sending the ivories to that — cat! "

"Why not? "

"Oh, they're too lovely. Felix says if he hadn't promised you could have them back, he'd refuse to let them go."

"I don't blame him." Rufus was in the shop and was helping Doady pack the figurines for shipment. "I'm afraid I was a bit upstage. But I couldn't resist it. And you should have seen her face — like Griselda's when she flattens her ears." He laughed at the memory.

Doady, wrapping the last of the five little senses in tissue-paper — the loveliest one, with the grapes — mourned over it. "You beauty, you beauty — to think I shan't see you again."

Rufus laughed. "Don't worry. I'll bet that in less than a year, if Sherry loses her case, they will be on the market."

"But I thought she adored them."

"She wanted them because I wanted them, my dear."

"I'm not your dear. Sandra is. I'm nobody's dear," said Doady with a touch of wistfulness.

"Not Stephen Leeds'? "

Her eyes met his. Then her lashes flickered. "I'm

not going to marry him. I told him last night. He didn't take it very well. And he said things."

" You deserved everything you got. You know that, Doady. But I'm no end relieved that you've shipped him. How does it feel to reject a fortune? "

" Well, I'm a bit let-down."

" Naturally. Have you told the world? "

" Only Sandra in a letter this morning. She'll be glad, of course, but she won't grasp it. She doesn't grasp anything these days except the fact that she's going to marry you. And that there's only one like you in the world."

Rufus smiled down at her. " Jealous, little Doady? "

She flamed. " Of course, not! "

" Not of her happiness, perhaps, but of me because I am going to rob you of her."

She melted at that and began to cry. She felt this morning not in the least like Theodora Claybourne, who turned people's heads. She was, rather, a young and much-let-down young person who wanted a strong shoulder on which to weep. And the shoulder was not available. For it was Gale's shoulder that she coveted, and since she had come back from her Christmas holiday, she had scarcely seen him. He had seemed perpetually in Stephanie's train.

And now they were all going down to Windytop on Saturday to see Sandra married. Doady doubted whether Stephanie would have gone if Rufus hadn't asked Gale to be his best man, and she wouldn't risk the danger of letting him go alone. The Maulsbys would be at the wedding, and they had invited Stephen Leeds. But now he wouldn't be there. Doady rather wished that things hadn't come to a climax last night when Stephen had tried to kiss her, and she had told him she would keep her kisses for the man she might some day marry. And she had given him back the bracelet with a sigh, for it set off her purple dress as nothing else did but violets, and there would be no more violets, fresh every morning and filling the air with fragrance.

So, taking it all together, Doady sobbed with a will, and Rufus provided a shoulder, and he patted her back and kept on saying:

" You poor little thing! We've been selfish pigs and let you tire yourself to death."

But Doady knew she was not tired. If she had been happy, her feet would have been winged. She would have felt no fatigue. But she was not happy — she was not — and it was a great help to have Rufus' sympathy.

She wiped her eyes presently. "Well," she said, " you're a comfortable sort of person, if you are my brother-in-law. And I'm glad Sandra is going to marry you. And now, having done your best for me, will you run along while I hunt up Susan Carter and tell her what she will have to do while the rest of us are away? "

So Rufus went, and got Gale Markham to have lunch with him.

Sandra was still at Windytop and marveling at her good fortune. " He is without a fault, Mother," she said to Madge, and that romantic lady came down to earth for a moment to remark.

" He's not any more wonderful than you are, Sandra."

And now this wonderful person was lunching with Gale and saying fatuously, " You ought to get married, too, old man."

" Not I," said Gale, eating his salad.

" Why not? "

" The woman I want doesn't want me."

" You mean that Stephanie — won't? "

" Stephanie? "

" Of course! Who else? "

" I'd rather not talk about it," said Gale, " but if you must have it, Rufus, it isn't Stephanie. The woman I care for is engaged to another man."

So that was that. And nothing more said.

But the truth of the matter was this — there had come to Gale at Ruth O'Malley's Christmas party on the Chesapeake one of those astounding complications which seem to belong to fiction rather than to real life. A dozen young people had gone down on the afternoon train, and it was en route that Gale planned to send a telegram to Doady. He had decided that the thing he had to say could be put in fewer than ten words, " I love you. Letter follows. Gale." He wasn't at all sure that Doady cared for him. But the telegram would prepare her. He'd shoot it along. Mail the letter. And take her decision standing.

Being of a methodical mind, he had thought to send his message to reach her at midnight. Getting it off about ten. It would thus become, as it were, her first Christmas greeting.

But things had moved fast before ten o'clock. As soon as they arrived Ruth had rushed them away to a hunting lodge near the shore, where they were to have an oyster supper, then come back in time to dress for the Christmas party.

Gale, when he heard of it all, had said: " Heavens, Ruth, I'm a working man. And when do I sleep? "

" In the morning, you poor fish. We don't spoil such nights as these by going to bed."

So Gale got into knickerbockers and sweater and wool stockings and leather coat, and came down to find Stephanie looking astonishingly pretty in fur-lined, heather-colored tweed, with a pheasant's feather in her cap.

When they reached the lodge, it was warmed by huge fires, and a fat negro with a blank, taffy-colored countenance was sliding into the oven wide strips of sheet-iron on which were ranged rows of oysters in their shells. The table was drawn close to the fire, and set forth on it were celery, condiments, crisp crackers, and a cabbage salad with chopped red peppers which had been served to generations of O'Malleys on this same shore. A great coffee pot steamed and rocked on the coals.

" This is all you'll get," Ruth told them, " until midnight. So don't be timid about eating your dozens. It may sound big, but it isn't."

The oysters were delicious. Ruffled at the edges, stewing in their own savory juice, they were seasoned with bits of butter and black pepper coarsely ground. No paprika and no salt was the rule with Reuben. The old epicures of the Chesapeake had known that a flavor is a flavor. A squeeze of lemon might be permitted, but paprika was new-fangled, and why add salt to the perfect saltiness of the native bivalve?

Gale had eaten with healthy appetite, and had wished

that Doady were there beside him. How she would enjoy it, and what a child she would seem among them all!
She was so exquisitely young. Not in years, perhaps.
Some of these girls had less than she. But there was a
freshness and springtime delightfulness which none of
them could match. He felt that it would be too much
to hope that her flower-like innocence would ever be
his. But he wanted it.

So the telegram should go to her. As soon as he got
back to the house, he would telephone it to the office.

But he did not telephone. For while they sat at the
supper-table, some one remarked:

" Everybody is talking about Rufus Fiske. And to
think that little Sandra Claybourne is going to marry
him! "

" Good work, I'd call it," said one of the men. " If
he wins his case against his stepmother, he'll have a
fortune."

Stephanie spoke. " And that isn't all of it. The
other twin is going to marry Stephen Leeds."

Gale set down his coffee cup. Of course, it wasn't
true. But why should Stephanie say it?

They all knew Stephen, and there was a chorus of
excited questions.

" How did she meet him? "

" Going over to London on the same ship."

" The luck of her! "

Gale, aflame, wanted to shout: " It wouldn't be luck,
if it were true. She's a thousand times too good for
him."

Another of the men remarked: " I haven't seen her
often. But she's a bit unusual. Modern to the last

degree, but with a subtle personality which makes you think of Romney's women. You know what I mean. You'd turn your head to look at her."

If Doady could have heard him — *There goes Theodora Claybourne . . . There goes Theodora Claybourne . . . !*

Motoring home later, Gale had said to Stephanie, " Who told you that Doady is going to marry Stephen Leeds? "

" He did."

" You mean that it is — settled? "

" Of course. I'm not apt to say a thing, am I, unless I'm sure of it? "

He had wondered, when they reached the house and he had gone upstairs, why he had come with Stephanie. He wanted to be anywhere but here. At home, where he could hide himself, nurse his heartbreak. Yet this was the year that his mother had gone with Trux to a gorgeous houseparty with relatives on Long Island. Trux had begged for it.

" I don't want to miss seeing you, mother, and I don't want to miss the party. Be a good sport and come."

As for heartbreaks, why hadn't Doady told him? And why had he been such a fool as to let himself in for a thing like this? First Stephanie, and now Doady. Or had it ever been love that he had given Stephanie? Hadn't there been, rather, a boy's pride in winning a goddess?

He went downstairs to find the Christmas tree lighted and everybody assembled. There were presents for all the guests, and toward the last a tiny box was put in Gale's hand. It was wrapped in silver paper, and as he stripped it off, he heard Stephanie's voice beside him.

" Don't open it here, Gale. Wait until you get upstairs. Perhaps I shouldn't have given it to you. But
you must try to — understand — "

After that everybody danced except Gale. He
mooned around until supper was over, then made his
way to his room. When he opened the little box, he
found to his dismay that it contained a ring. He stood
staring at it. Years ago, at the time of their engagement, he and Stephanie had exchanged rings. Hers to
him had been a queer twist of pale gold brought from
India by one of her great-uncles. When the engagement was broken, he had sent it back to her, and now
here it was again, freighted with significance. She had
said —

" Try to understand."

There was only one thing to understand, of course;
that she wanted him to wear it, under the old conditions
. . . she wanted him back!

He put the ring from him, went to the window, and
stood looking out into the starry night. Under the same
stars, little Theodora slept with tears on her cheeks and
with Stephen Leeds' bracelet on her arm . . .

But Gale could not know this, and the next morning
he had said to Stephanie: " It will never be the same.
Why should we do it? "

She looked at him with wet eyes. " Don't punish me
any longer."

That was the way she had taken it. That he was
having his revenge. She would not or could not believe that the thing was dead. Oh, well, if it made her

any happier, why not? Doady was going to marry Stephen Leeds. Nothing else mattered.

Yet he had not worn the ring, and there was nothing settled. And as he sat and talked to Rufus, he told himself that it was not fair to Stephanie to let the thing drift. He didn't love her, and he never would, and marriage under the circumstances was unthinkable.

Chapter XXXV

THE HAPPY PRINCESS

THE great hallway at Windytop was flooded with light. The winter sunshine flowing through the high windows on the landing made a luminous cascade down the stairs and gave to the red roses tied to the newel post with gold ribbons a startling, celestial gorgeousness like stained glass.

The red roses were for Sandra's wedding. Intertwined with trailing vines, they were wound up and up the mahogany rail to end at the turn of the stairs in another great nosegay from which fell more golden streamers.

The Maulsbys had supplied the decorations, and the whole thing had been done by a Washington florist. It had been Doady's suggestion to have red roses.

"Why not," she had asked, "when Sandra adores them, and is marrying a man whose name is Rufus?"

And now it was high noon, and every one was at the church, even Ione and Aunt Louisa, and there remained in the house only a few helpers in the kitchen who were busy with the breakfast which was to follow the ceremony.

It was shortly after twelve when there appeared on the upper stair a small, white figure. Very small under the high ceiling. Very white in the cascade of sunshine. The loneliness of the house had driven Griselda to an investigation of the deserted rooms. And now in the emptiness of the hall she mewed plaintively. Getting no answer, she stopped for a moment to add an additional touch to her toilet, then began to descend daintily, dropping from step to step on padded paws. A bit of the trailing vine that was wound about the stair-rail rustled as she passed, and she stopped to strike at it. It sprang back at her, and presently she was having her little game with it, dancing toward it and then away, her eyes like moons, her plume of a tail twitching. At last she drew it out in a long loop, wound herself up in it, and lay luxuriously kicking.

She extricated herself, however, and went padding down the stairs as the front door opened and Doady came rushing in, dressed in her wide-skirted brides-maid's gown of pale blue taffeta. Her arms were filled with red roses, and on her head was a quaint, netted silver cap. Just as she was, she might have stepped from one of the old portraits on the stairs, and she knew it. Her sense of appropriateness had made her dress herself and her sister in a way that suited the old house — Sandra also wide-skirted in white, with strapped slippers and a lace veil.

Doady had rushed home ahead of the others, because she had remembered things left undone in the packing of Sandra's belongings, and she was not only bridesmaid on this important occasion; she was the head and the hoof and the hump of all the wedding arrangements.

Gale had driven her home, but they had had little to say on the way. The silence had been, indeed, almost chokingly oppressive. Once Gale had said,

" Why isn't Stephen Leeds here? "

And Doady had answered, " Why should he be? "

Then a queer sort of silence had gripped them and had lasted until they got home and Doady had rushed up the stairs, leaving Gale to follow.

As she passed Griselda, the white cat struck at her rustling taffeta skirt.

" Pussy cat, pussy cat," Doady said, " did you know that your mistress is married . . . married . . . ? "

Gale in the hall below caught the echo of her words, " Married . . . married . . ." As he looked up at her, ascending through the golden light, she seemed like an angel all in blue, with her silver cap shining.

Griselda approached Gale and begged for his attention. He picked her up, and she ducked her head under his arm in an ecstasy of content.

Presently Doady appeared again on the landing. "Has anybody come? " she demanded.   Then seeing that they had not, she added: " Well, I got the things in — her rose talcum and her bedroom slippers. They popped into my mind just as you were getting out the ring for Rufus."

She was descending the steps as she talked to him, and suddenly he saw her stumble — Her foot had caught in the loop of vine with which Griselda had played her foolish game!

Then down, down, down the stairs . . . a cascade of blue and gold . . . Doady was falling, falling, falling . . .

Gale reached her before she struck the floor, had her in his arms. " Doady, Doady, darling, darling . . . ! "

For one fleeting minute she opened her eyes and tried to smile at him. Then she fainted.

And that was the way the others found them, Sandra and Rufus and Madge and the Maulsbys, and Stephanie . . . and Stephanie entering a little ahead heard Gale's frantic " Darling, darling " . . . and knew that the game was up.

It was Gale who carried Doady to her room. It was Gale who stayed beside her until she opened her eyes, and it was Gale who whispered " I don't care who is going to marry you, I love you," and Doady whispered back, " Why didn't you say it a thousand years ago? "

Then the doctor came, and bound up Doady's head and the silver cap wouldn't hide the bandage, but she was really so beautiful with all her blushes, that nothing else mattered.

Gale, who sat next to Stephanie at the table, with Doady on the other side, spoke under his breath, " You said she was going to marry Stephen Leeds."

" Well, isn't she? "

" No. And you knew it."

He felt that he was being brutal about it. But then Stephanie deserved it.

Perhaps she did. But she was, perhaps, to be pitied. Yet she was one of the women who never acknowledge defeat. Let Gale have his little girl. As for herself, she had been silly to let herself in for a thing like that.

It was not until she got home late that night, however, that Stephanie saw a way out of it for her pride. She was putting away her pearls. From her jewel box, as she opened it, came a faint, exotic perfume. She stood slipping the pearls through her fingers in a shining stream. What was it the young antiquarian had said? " All the odors of Araby are in it! "

She fingered the fragrant relic that had been taken from a queen's tomb. A man like that — ! "I have memories — of amber and myrrh, spices and sandalwood." If she could meet him again! Why not? A year in Egypt. He was over there. And he was subtle — interesting — the kind of man for a woman of her attractions. In a year she would have tired of Gale — with his meager income . . .

She stopped there and stood looking into the mirror, facing the truth. No, she would not have tired of him. But Doady Claybourne had taken him away from her.

Doady and Sandra! Who would have thought it? The shabby little girls who less than a year ago had come to her dance! And she had let herself in for it by a careless invitation. A pair of wallflowers! And now Doady would marry Gale, and Sandra was Mrs. Rufus Fiske!

Mrs. Rufus Fiske was at that moment speaking to her husband.

" How wonderful to have our honeymoon here! "

They were in the cottage in Maryland. They had come straight from the wedding on the afternoon train, and they were to stay near Washington until Rufus' great speech was made and the case settled.

" If we don't get the money," Rufus had said, " we can have our happiness in my little house, and if we do get it, we'll go out and see Molly Wicks and old McIvor and all the rest of them."

" And the red-roofed palace? "

" And stand on my high peak and look off over the Pacific."

It was late. The wind blew, but the logs on the hearth were blazing. Rufus went about locking the doors, barring the shutters. When he had finished, he drew their two chairs close together.

"How often I have seen you here," he said, "on my hearthstone!"

With a swift movement Sandra slipped from her seat and knelt beside him.

"At first, I didn't think of hearthstones, Rufus. I thought of gardens and secret stairs and Romeo and Aucassin . . . but now . . . it is the thought that I'm your wife . . . that I shall sit by your fire . . ."

She could not go on. She heard his tender voice speaking. After that — silence — The logs burned with a deep heart of flame; the wind roared loud and louder. The little house had four walls — yet it set no limit to their great adventure . . . *beyond the night . . . into the day . . . through all the world . . . !*